the Devil
in the
Corner

Also by Patricia Elliot

The Ice Boy
WINNER OF THE FIDLER AWARD 2001
SHORTLISTED FOR THE BRANFORD BOASE AWARD 2003
SHORTLISTED FOR THE WEST SUSSEX AWARD

Murkmere
LONGLISTED FOR THE GUARDIAN AWARD 2004
SHORTLISTED FOR THE CALDERDALE AWARD 2005

Ambergate

The Night Walker

Pimpernelles
The Pale Assassin
The Traitor's Smile

Patricia Elliott

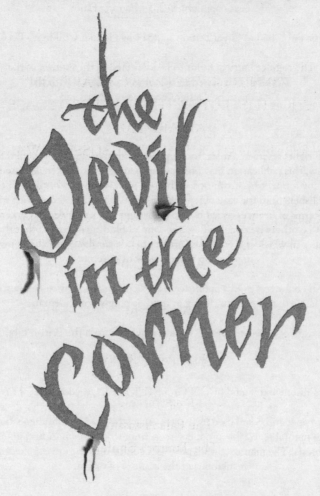

the Devil in the Corner

Hodder Children's Books

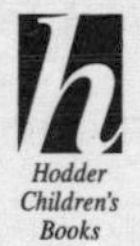

A division of Hachette Children's Books

First published in Great Britain in 2014 by Hodder Children's Books

1

A Catalogue record for this book is available from the British Library

ISBN 978 0 340 95678 6

Printed and bound by CPI Group (UK) Ltd, Croydon, CR0 4YY

The paper and board used in this paperback by Hodder Children's Books are natural recyclable products made from wood grown in sustainable forests. The manufacturing processes conform to the environmental regulations of the country of origin.

Hodder Children's Books
a division of Hachette Children's Books
338 Euston Road, London NW1 3BH
An Hachette UK company

www.hodderchildrens.co.uk

In memory of my remarkable Victorian ancestor,
Mary Romilly

Come into the garden, Maud,
For the black bat, night, has flown;
Come into the garden, Maud,
I am here at the gate alone.
I am here at the gate alone.

from a song, adapted from 'Maud' by
Alfred Tennyson (1809–1892)

Part One

The Poison Cupboard

Laudanum: tincture of opium. Used in the Victorian period as a painkiller and to cure a wide variety of ailments, including insomnia. Addiction can develop with prolonged use. Accidental overdose common and death may occur as a result.

One

Maud

'What shall I do, Miss Caseborne? I am penniless. I have nowhere to go.'

I was dry-eyed but my voice faltered. We were sitting in the drawing room of Miss Caseborne's Boarding Seminary for Young Ladies, surrounded by a press of empty chairs and heavy mahogany furniture.

'Come, come,' said my headmistress. She patted her neatly coiled hair. 'We shall find a position for you. I shall write a reference myself.'

'A position?'

'As a governess. At fifteen you are a trifle young but there are others your age in households doing very well.'

'I would rather work in a factory,' I said, in a low voice.

She looked appalled. 'You are a lady and ladies do not work in factories! None of my girls has ever sunk so low. Tomorrow we shall pay a visit to the Governesses'

Benevolent Institution. We shall find you a suitable position and I am sure you will be a credit to the school.'

My beloved father had died unexpectedly. He had never taken out life insurance and there was no money left to pay my school fees; none, indeed, for my livelihood, apart from a meagre annuity from my father's bank.

Poor Miss Caseborne. I think she felt guilty about throwing me out without a roof over my head so soon after his death. It was not her fault, after all, that the next two years as a governess would be the worst of my life:

Verney Place, that dilapidated mansion set down in the middle of nowhere;

The Creams of Kensington, with their two feral sons;

Rookyard in Surrey, where I had suffered my shame.

Since I had been dismissed from Rookyard, weeks had gone by with no prospect of work. There were too many governesses seeking employment and most of them older and more experienced than me.

Now I was running out of money to pay my rent, my savings drained. All I could do was traipse daily to the Governess's Benevolent Institution in Harley Street to search the register, riding there in the fug and cigarette smoke of the omnibus. As it trundled over Hammersmith Bridge, I thought how little courage it would take to jump into the dark oily waters of the Thames and let them close over my head.

I believe I would have gone mad with bad dreams and despair if I had not been given the letter that morning.

The Institution was dark on that wet, foggy day, the familiar smell of dust and damp in my nostrils as I opened the heavy front door.

It was usually crowded, but because of the weather there were only two women in there, both as wet and desperate as I was. They were busy writing down their details in the Register.

As I came in, the lady resident, who ruled from behind her glass screen, looked up. It was her job to hand out letters to the lucky ones who had been contacted by potential employers. Today, to my astonishment, I heard my name called out.

'Miss Maud Greenwood!'

I thought I must be mistaken. The lady resident repeated it louder. She had a thin, refined voice that pierced the soft turning of pages, the sighs and mutterings of the two other women.

With my heart beating faster, I went over. She looked me up and down behind the safety of her screen, taking in my dishevelled appearance, my sodden, filthy skirts, stinking from the fog. Ladies did not venture out in the rain.

She spoke with disdain. There was nothing 'Benevolent' about her; not a drop of sympathy warmed her cold veins.

'A letter has arrived for you, Miss Greenwood.'

'A letter?' The blood rushed into my face and I clutched the wood of the counter. Behind the glass I saw the envelope held fast in her hand.

'You have been looking for a while, have you not?' she said. 'You can hardly hope that respectable families will rush to employ you, given your past history, Miss Greenwood. One position abandoned without notice followed by two dismissals!'

How could I divulge the horrors of the last two years to this powerful, forbidding presence? At night those names still rang like a hideous jingle in my head, haunting my dreams.

Verney Place.

The Creams.

Rookyard.

'None of it was my fault,' I said, in a low voice.

She continued as if I had not spoken, still holding the letter, 'In my view it is most generous and forgiving of the Institution to let you display your particulars in the Register again. A kind reference from your old school cannot protect you for ever.'

I bowed my head. 'May I have my letter, please?' I muttered, and at last she passed it through the opening.

'Miss Maud Greenwood, c/o The Governesses' Benevolent Institution.'

The writing was clear and elegant, with long loops to the capitals. I sat down on a chair and opened the envelope with hands that trembled with cold and anticipation.

It was dated a mere two days previously. The address meant nothing to me but I saw to my astonishment that the surname on the bottom of the letter was my own.

Greenwood.

Windward House
Rending
Suffolk

10th March 1867

Dear Miss Greenwood

You may not know who I am, since there was no communication between your father and my step-father for many years before their deaths. He and my late mother married when I was a child.

I have been trying to trace you since your father died. Eventually I discovered the name of your old school from Mr Odbury, your father's solicitor. The headmistress, Miss Caseborne, told me that when your father died you became a governess. She suggested that I might be able to contact you through the Governesses' Benevolent Institution.

I shall come to the point. As your only living relation, even if only by marriage, I feel responsible for you, orphaned as you are. I do not care to think of you having to earn your living and at such a young age.

I should like to offer you a home here at Windward House. I live alone apart from a few servants, and my health is failing. Young company would do much to cheer me in my last years.

I should be grateful if you would give me your answer by writing to me at the address above. Then at least I shall know my letter has reached you.

Yours sincerely
Juliana Greenwood

Perhaps I should have read between the lines and wondered. Perhaps I should never have gone to Rending at all. Then what happened afterwards would never have happened.

But I would have ended up on the dark corners of London streets, living a life of degradation and danger, offering my body so I would not starve.

At the time there was no choice.

Two

John

John Shawcross. I sign my name with a flourish on my new painting of Paddington Station. The black paint glistens bravely but I know it will not sell.

When I take it to the gallery in Albermarle Street, Mr Mountford shakes his head sorrowfully, as I expect.

'Another of your "urban" paintings, Mr Shawcross? People don't want factories or railway stations on their walls!'

'They are the wonders of our age, Mr Mountford,' I say lightly.

To me there is a haunting poignancy in the sight of hordes of vulnerable humanity disgorged from the monsters they themselves have created. That is why I paint the arrival of trains into stations and the teeming scenes around factory gates at closing time.

'They want cottages and roses, Mr Shawcross,' says Mr

Mountford. 'Hayfields and pretty children playing with dogs.' He steals a glance at my threadbare coat. Unlike most gallery owners, he is soft-hearted, which is why he never makes much money himself. 'Still, I'll take it, just for you, Mr Shawcross. Maybe tastes will change one of these days, eh?'

I know it will join the stack of my unsold paintings at the back of the gallery but I hand it over gratefully.

Portraits are an artist's bread and butter and I have been back in London long enough to fulfil two commissions – the dreary, blousy wife of a local merchant and the small son of another, dressed up in the frills and furbelows of a Cavalier. Neither portrait has brought in much money, for I am a nobody in the art world.

And now I must return to Rending.

At least Mother is stronger. She insists she can manage on her own, so when I go home I pack my bag and go straight to Bishopsgate Station. I am not certain when I shall see her again, for I have not made as much progress on the Doom painting as I should like and must apply myself more diligently. If Juliana Greenwood stops my wages, how will I support Mother?

I don't know why I am being so slow. The Doom is an extraordinary thing – a painting of the Day of Judgement, four hundred years old. I should feel privileged to be restoring it for future generations.

But something about it disturbs me, the subject matter, perhaps – the Last Judgement, the end of time, when human souls rise naked from their graves and are destined for heaven or hell, presided over by an aloof Christ and a merciless Devil. The village of Rending's church, St Mark's, where it belongs, is claustrophobic and cold, despite the wood burner donated by the vicar's wife, and my fingers are numb to the bone by the time I finish my day's work.

As I board the Great Eastern train bound for Suffolk, I find myself dreading my return.

The gas lamps are already lit in the carriages, for it is a dull afternoon and dusk will not be long in falling.

Outside it is damp and windy. As the door of my carriage is slammed shut and the train draws out of the station, the wind comes in at right angles through the partly open window. I pull on the leather strap to shut out the cinders, for steam is billowing past in the gusts.

The old gentleman opposite, wrapped to his chin in a travelling rug, nods his thanks at me as I sit down again on the hard wooden bench. The train is not crowded this afternoon, even in third class.

I begin to think about eating the pork pie I have bought from a vendor on the platform. It is then that I become aware of a child sitting in the far corner.

At least at first glance I think she is a child, for she is so small and finely built. But then I look at the delicate features framed by her bonnet and see that she is not a child at all but a young girl. Although her black mantle is shabby, she sits upright like a lady, her gloved hands resting either side of her hooped skirt. She has lain her battered suitcase on the floor at her feet.

'Let me put that in the rack for you, miss,' I say above the sound of the wheels on the track, and I jump up again.

Startled, she gazes at me wide-eyed. Her eyes are dark – I cannot tell their colour – and her face very pale and tense. She shakes her head without a smile.

'Thank you, sir, but I shall not be able to lift it down again by myself.'

'As you wish,' I say sheepishly.

Her voice is high, girlish, educated. I sit back, trying not to watch her. Indeed, I pull out my book, a collection of Ruskin's lectures on art, and endeavour to read it. But I find that I keep glancing up so that I can see her averted profile. It swims, elusive, in the glow of the gaslight. Fine dark strands of her hair have caught on the brim of her bonnet.

Who is she? Why does she gaze out of the window at the darkening flatlands of Essex with such a haunted air?

At Ipswich I must change to the branch line and fear I will lose her, but no – I watch her board the same train and leap in after her in triumph.

But to my disappointment in a moment we are no longer alone. A couple climb in, laden with baggage and much given to chattering loudly at one another. As we leave the station, darkness falls outside and the moon rides fast through turbulent clouds.

The couple grow silent, defeated by the noise of the cinders knocking on the roof and the wind rattling the pane. I see the glint of water, the Woodbridge estuary. We stop at the station, and the couple with much pother retrieve their bags from the net racks overhead.

I am alone at last with the girl. But she is staring out with such intensity, her manner so repressive, that I find myself tongue-tied. Any conversation is clearly unwelcome and, indeed, not appropriate when a woman is travelling alone.

But as the train wheels churn into Marsham, she stands up. She is alighting at my stop!

'Let me carry that for you, miss,' I say eagerly. 'This is my station, too,' and I put a hand on her suitcase. In my other I have my own bag.

I think she is about to refuse but then a hint of a smile crosses her face. 'Thank you.'

The suitcase weighs nothing. I wonder what is in it, if anything. I let her go before me and the stationmaster helps her down the steps on to the platform. I follow and set down her case. I think she may say something, but she merely nods and looks about her in distraction.

There are gas lamps lit along the length of the platform but they give off a feeble glow. An elderly lady is struggling down from her carriage with her case, so I have no alternative than to help her. When I turn back I see the girl's black skirts disappearing into billowing clouds of smoke and steam as the train begins to pull out. Idiotically, I raise my arm but her dark figure has already dissolved away, as insubstantial as the smoke itself.

I doubt I shall see her again.

But since that journey, I believe I am half spellbound in love, as if that fairy creature has laid an enchantment on me.

Three

Maud

My journey to Marsham was uneventful and we reached the stop in good time. I stepped down on to the platform, my heart beating nervously. A man in the employ of my cousin Juliana was being sent to meet me, a Mr Tiggins.

I looked around in the gas-lit gloom, wondering if he would be waiting for me, as Cousin Juliana had promised. I made my way to the exit, and there he was, a burly little man sitting in a canvas-covered trap, the sides flapping in the wind. The pony was uneasy, shifting about between the harnesses and munching the bit.

'Excuse me, sir, are you Mr Tiggins?'

He nodded. 'And you be Miss Maud Greenwood.'

I thanked him as he threw my suitcase, without ceremony, into the back of the trap. He motioned me to climb up behind him, which I did. At first I leaned forward and tried to make conversation.

'Have we far to go?'

''Bout four mile.' His accent was strong.

'Have you worked for my cousin long?'

'Long enough, and Mr Greenwood before her.'

The trap was not comfortable, a wooden seat covered with sacking. 'Does my cousin ride in this?' I asked, in disbelief.

He gave an abrupt laugh. 'Lord, no, miss! There's the Windward carriage for her. Shaft's broken and Sly be mending it, if his poor brain can work it out.'

Sly. A strange name. I fell silent as the pony pulled away and the trap swayed over the cobbles.

It was a dark night, the moon hidden by clouds. There was little of Marsham to be seen and no light anywhere, save for the lamp on the seat beside Tiggins. I retreated further into the canvas shelter as we left the station behind, for the wind was getting up, gusting coldly across open countryside. We jolted along a sandy track, on which the pony's hooves made no sound.

I leaned forward and asked timidly, 'Shall we reach Rending soon, Mr Tiggins?'

'We don't pass through it,' he said shortly, and sure enough the track soon branched, one way disappearing over what appeared to be heathland, dotted with the dark shapes of heather and gorse. We took a right hand turn up a long hill between black trees. Birds flew up from their roosts with a hoarse clacking. I recognised the noise of rooks and immediately thought of my time as governess at Rookyard, where the rooks had watched and mocked my degradation.

The memory made me more apprehensive still.

At the top of the hill we passed a high fence of wooden boards. On our right the countryside fell away. I could see little, but sensed vast acres of space over which the wind cut sharply.

We came to some open gates and the wheels crunched over gravel. A short drive led to the dark mass of a house, with tall chimneys and crenelated gables, black against the sky. The ground floor windows had light behind their curtains and as we approached, a pale face appeared at one of the windows between the curtains and stared out directly and unnervingly at me before it vanished.

I had arrived at Windward House at last.

The woman who answered the bell introduced herself as Miss Potton, the housekeeper. She was a plain woman in a dark grey dress and starched apron, keys jangling from a belt around her waist, her hair screwed back, her eyes puffy.

She shut the front door smartly on the gale and on Tiggins, staring inquisitive from his trap. There was something in her superior manner as she looked me up and down that reminded me of the lady resident, that all-powerful, disapproving personage at the Governess's Benevolent Institution.

I was dazed by the light and my legs trembled as I fumbled with the ribbons of my bonnet; I had not eaten since a mouthful of bread at seven that morning.

'Madam has been waiting for you, miss,' Miss Potton said. She picked up an oil lamp from the letter table. 'I will take you to her, then show you to your room. Madam is waiting for the vicar's visit so we must not linger.'

I wished I might have had a chance to wash and see to my appearance before meeting my cousin, but Miss Potton opened a door off the hall immediately and motioned me in past her. It was my cousin's parlour and I was soon to become all too familiar with it.

'Miss Maud, Madam,' Miss Potton said, and I entered uncertainly.

The parlour had a thick, close atmosphere despite the draught under the floor-length velvet curtains. A fire burned brightly in the grate, guttering now and then as the wind rattled the panes. Pictures hung in rows on the walls and there were little tables everywhere to trip me.

A woman lay on a day bed reading a book, her face turned away. I had imagined an old woman with grey locks, but the rolled hair that showed over the back was fair. She turned her head as I came in.

'Why, Maud! That train is always late. I have been expecting you a while.'

In the yellow light of the oil lamps Juliana Greenwood was a strikingly pretty woman, not at all the elderly invalid I had been expecting. She was neither old, nor young but somewhere in between.

'Come here. Let me look at you.'

She did not get up herself. She was wearing skirts of dark blue silk that hung down over the edge of the day bed; a plaid rug lay over her feet and a paisley shawl was folded over her shoulders.

I ventured closer, awkward in my shabby clothes, aware that my hair smelled of cinders and smoke and that my face might be dirty. 'Come,' she said, a little impatiently.

Should I kiss her? I stood beside her, overcome with shyness, and waited for her to embrace me first. She did not, but reached up and took my face between her hands, examining it closely.

Instinctively I drew back. No one had touched my face since Papa. It was a strange sensation, oddly intimate; her blue eyes, disconcertingly sharp and bright, gazed into mine.

Her smile died. A look of displeasure crossed her face. What was the matter? Did she hope for some resemblance to her late stepfather, my uncle?

'Take off your mantle, Maud. Sit by the fire. You may read to me a little while I wait for my visitor. I find reading to oneself such hard work, don't you?' And with that she thrust her book at me.

Obediently I took the book and tried to pull off my gloves, hoping she wouldn't notice that my hands bore the red marks of rat bites. Then I struggled to take off my mantle, fumbling with the clasp with one hand while I held her book in the other, feeling most horribly clumsy under her gaze.

I glanced at the book's spine and the words blurred. *The Rules and Exercises of Holy Dying*. I looked at my cousin, startled.

Miss Potton was still standing by the door. She cleared her throat. 'The vicar will be here any moment, ma'am, and I have had Dorcas put some supper by upstairs for Miss Maud. It will be getting cold.'

There was a pause. Juliana looked at me through narrowed eyes. 'Oh, very well. I dare say you are hungry?'

I nodded, trying not show my eagerness. 'Yes, indeed, Cousin Juliana.'

'Just Juliana, for heaven's sake!' She seized the book from me and lay back on the day bed. 'Take her away if you must, Potton. We shall keep the reading for tomorrow.'

'Good night – Juliana,' I said humbly, for I thought I should say something. I felt I had offended her.

Without looking at me, for answer she put up a pale, delicate hand, its fingers glittering with rings, and waved me away carelessly. The gesture discomforted me; I had hoped for so much more from our first meeting

'I have put you in the usual room,' said Miss Potton. She held her lamp high to light the first-floor landing. Later I was to discover that there was another floor above us, where Miss Potton had her rooms, and above that the attics, where the maids slept.

She informed me, importantly, that there were the new water-closets on each floor and bathrooms with hot running water, while she looked with some significance at the grimy hem of my skirts. 'Madam is most particular about cleanliness.'

I flushed and thought of the time I had spent scrubbing my collars and cuffs in my landlady's sordid little sink.

My bedroom was not lavishly furnished but after the last years spent sleeping in cramped, greasy quarters, it was luxurious. Someone had lit a fire in the little grate with its flowered tiling and there were chintz curtains at the window. My suitcase had been placed by the bed and there was a new candle on top of a small table.

'We're not fitted for gas here like you are in London,' said Miss Potton, with a curl of her lip. 'Nasty smelly stuff, and dangerous too. We use candles upstairs.'

'What a pretty room!' I murmured to mollify her, for she sounded defensive.

She looked around, expressionless. 'Apparently it were madam's room when she were a little girl.'

'Where does she sleep now?'

'In her late stepfather's study downstairs. She's a bedroom on this floor but she won't be having any of it, has got to be downstairs in that old room we can never keep clean.'

'Why did you call this the "usual" room, Miss Potton?'

She looked wary for a moment. 'It was my mistake, miss. I was forgetting that you weren't here as madam's paid nurse, not like all them others. Now, if you'd follow me, I'll show you to your sitting room.'

It was next door and furnished with an armchair and a fern beneath a glass dome on the mantel. A fire burned in the grate and a tray with several covered plates was set on a round table in the corner.

'I hope the food won't be too cold, miss.' Miss Potton said, as if challenging me, her voice gruff.

'I am sure not. Thank you, Miss Potton.'

She nodded, her mouth tight, and looked at me sideways. 'You'll be staying here permanent, then? As you're a relation?'

'Oh, yes,' I said.

Something came into her flinty little eyes. 'I hope you're strong,' she said mysteriously, with that same doubtful look up and down, before she reached to light the candles at either end of the mantelpiece.

Below, the door bell jangled. 'That will be the vicar,' she said. 'I must see that Dorcas shows him in,' and she bade me goodnight without grace and turned, with a chinking of the keys at her belt.

'What time does Miss Greenwood take breakfast?' I asked quickly, before she should leave. 'I would not want to keep her waiting in the morning.'

'Madam always has it in bed. Never rises till noon. You'll find your breakfast laid in the dining room from eight.' She picked up the lamp and her shadow jerked away behind her.

I believe I felt sorry for Juliana that first night, that she should have such an ill-tempered housekeeper.

As I wolfed down the boiled beef, I stared around the candlelit room that was now to be my very own sitting room. The heavy clock on the mantel, louder than the rattle of the window pane, ticked in time with my chewing. There was no sign left of anyone who might have stayed here before me. They had been completely cleaned away.

Or so I thought.

When I had finished, I took down one of the candles and went round examining everything minutely, peering into empty cupboards, touching the rather ugly china ornaments.

I shall add my own touches, I thought. I shall do some sketching in the countryside and cover the bare walls with my drawings; pick bunches of wild spring flowers and arrange them in jars on the mantel.

Another gust shook the window. I went over, curious about what lay outside, and pushed aside the curtain, my candle flame stretched back by the sudden draught.

There were bars stretching across the glass.

At once I felt shaken. They had locked me in at Rookwood.

I tried to calm myself. The bars stopped at a small child's head height. This room might have been Juliana's nursery once, since it was next door to her former bedroom. No one had been imprisoned in here. As for the view, I could only see a few dark trees tossing against the stormy sky.

But at Rookyard I had also faced a view of trees.

To distract myself from my darkening thoughts, I went to look at the books in the small bookcase. They were novels, stacked untidily together, perhaps read by Juliana when she was about my age. I pulled out Emily Brontë's *Wuthering Heights*, an old favourite, for I was not as brave and independent-minded as her sister's Jane Eyre. I thought to read it again in bed to quieten myself.

Something fell out from between the pages. A folded piece of paper, a marker, perhaps. When I opened it out I saw it was a drawing, crudely executed but exuding a disturbing power.

The head of a giant fish, with teeth lining its vast open mouth, was in the process of swallowing a human whole. The figure was childishly drawn, a stick person, with a circle for a face, dots for eyes and scribbled hair. There was no mistaking, though, the round hole of a mouth, open in terror.

I refolded the paper, stuck it in *Wuthering Heights* and put the book back on the shelf.

I wouldn't read it after all. Somehow it seemed tainted.

Under the china knob on my bedroom door there was a brass arm and hook, with a corresponding catch on the door frame. As I hooked the arm into the catch I noticed that the catch had been clumsily fixed and was a little loose in the wood.

I thought nothing more of it at the time.

I climbed thankfully into bed, after going through the bedclothes, a piece of damp soap from the bathroom raised and ready in my hand. But I could find no trace of bed bugs or their tell-tale droppings, those minute black dots. The sheets were starched and smelled of lavender, the blankets soft.

My mind was too tired and busy to sleep. I listened to the wind keening around the house, rising now and then to a shriek and all the while shaking the windowpane, and felt a most painful loneliness that brought tears to my eyes.

For what? I didn't know. I had everything I wanted, now.

But I knew I would not sleep without nightmares unless I had help.

I reached for my thick brown bottle and squeezed the dropper into a glass of water I had set by ready. I waited until the water turned milky and drank, grimacing at its bitterness. When I ran out of my precious potion, I didn't know what I would do. I had no money to buy more. My train fare had taken my last penny.

In the dark I waited for oblivion to take over, as I knew it would.

But before that, the horrors came back.

Verney Place.

The Creams.

Rookyard.

Verney Place is a big house to clean. It is crumbling, filthy.

After my first week I protest at last.

'You employed me as a governess.'

'You will teach in the morning and clean in the afternoon,' says the mistress. 'I am short of staff.'

I don't dine with the master and mistress but have supper in my room alone.

Tonight I have been given a potato. Nothing else.

I am so hungry. I have been so since I arrived.

The next day at luncheon the mistress catches me in the nursery, eating the leftovers on the little girls' plates.

She strikes at my hands with my own ruler.

Four

John

The carrier who has collected me from Marsham drops me at the lane to my lodgings. There is scarcely enough light to see my way without a lantern but even if I had one, the wind would blow it out. I am thrust upon a great shelf of air that I lean on as I struggle to walk against it.

Above me the driven clouds rage. I hear the wind cleave the reeds across the marshes with a sound like tearing paper and the boom of the waves on the shingle shore.

The wind sucks all the air from my lungs, scours my face, rakes through my hair. Then at last it hurls me, breathless, against the door of Marsh End.

There is no one in the cottage kitchen. The oil lamp gutters wildly on the table until I force the door shut. Mrs Brundish and her daughter must be in the tiny living room and not wishing to disturb them, I take my bag upstairs.

I have been lodging with a widow, Mrs Brundish, and

Edith, her fourteen-year-old daughter, while working on the Doom. Juliana Greenwood arranged it for me, for Mrs Brundish is cook up at Windward House. Their small holding is some two miles' distant from Rending and its church.

At first I thought it tiresomely inconvenient and would have preferred to stay at The Magpie, the public house in the village. However, I have grown comfortable here. I like returning to the expanse of seashore and marshes after a day spent in the confines of the church. Besides, I know the money is useful to Mrs Brundish, and she gives me the fresh eggs I need each day to make my tempera paints. Edie brings me my supper and we have a little conversation.

During the early days I asked Edie what she wanted to do when she grew up. I thought she might say 'marry and have children', for there is little else open to her.

'Not go into service!' she exclaimed. 'I will never be like my mother and work for a tyrant!'

I knew she meant Juliana Greenwood and thought it best not to dwell on that.

'What *do* you want, Edie?' I said, intrigued.

She looked down. 'I should like to be a pharmacist but it's not possible for a woman.'

'But I have seen you helping in Quilter's apothecary, have I not?'

'Yes, sir. I write the labels for the prescriptions if Mr

Quilter's busy measuring out the drugs. It's a dull task.'

Another evening I said, 'Remind me how the Doom painting was first discovered, Edie. You were there, I believe.'

'Oh, yes, sir! I saw it happen with my own eyes!'

Apparently Rending had experienced a miracle.

The rains that spring had been heavy and the roof began to leak, so Edie said. During a service one Sunday the lime-washed boards above the roof beam, that separates the choir from the nave, began to drip. The faint outlines of the Virgin Mary and John the Baptist, like ghosts beneath the limewash, were slowly revealed to the awestruck congregation.

As the whispering increased, the Reverend Wissett was forced to stop his sermon, something of a minor miracle itself, I thought.

Shortly after that, while the roof was being repaired, the boards were taken down and examined by art historians and specialists, with much excitement. They found that concealed beneath the coating of limewash, put on during the Reformation when all such paintings were destroyed or painted over to hide them, was an ancient painting of the Day of Judgement.

Money was raised for its restoration but not enough. That was when Juliana Greenwood, encouraged by the Reverend Wissett, offered to make up the shortfall for the good of her soul, and to find a restorer.

'And then you arrived, Mr Shawcross,' Edie said. She flushed. 'And we are so glad of your company, my mother and me!'

'Are you glad the Doom was discovered?' I asked. 'It will make your village famous in time, you know.'

She hesitated and twisted her hands in her apron. 'To be honest, sir, we've had one miracle already and I'm not sure we need another.'

'You mean Quilter's Restorative Powder?' I swallowed my smile hastily, for I could see her round, childish face was solemn.

'*That* is what will make Rending famous, sir! As for the Doom, it gives me the creeps, for all that you're making it look good as new again.'

Soon after that she stopped calling me 'sir' all the time. I have asked her to call me 'John', as her mother does, but she will not. I am sure she must think me very old.

Tonight, as I open my bedroom door, I see Edie standing by my bed holding my nightshirt close to her face, presumably to fold it but seemingly lost in a dream. The candlelight outlines the curve of her cheek and gleams on gold strands in her long chestnut hair; the pale cotton stuff of the shirt she holds is almost translucent.

It strikes me as a pleasing picture. I arrange my fingers to judge how it will look within a frame, and gaze through at the colours and shapes.

But she has already heard the floorboards creak and jumps around like a cat, dropping the shirt. Even in the candlelight, I can see she is blushing.

'Mr Shawcross, you startled me!'

I lower my hands. 'I am sorry, Edie. I was thinking you looked like a painting by one of the pre-Raphaelites.'

'Oh,' she says, flustered but not displeased, though I am sure she doesn't know whom I am talking about. 'I was turning your bed down.'

'There is no need for that,' I say gently.

'I thought it would be nice for you to come back to – you must be tired after London.' She comes towards me, eagerness in her face. 'How are you? It has been a long time. Three months and five days! Is your mother quite recovered?'

I am touched that she has counted my days away. 'Yes, indeed, thank you.'

I can see that she has tidied me up in the meantime. My books and sketches are neatly stacked; my pair of thick-soled country shoes, their mud brushed away, arranged under the chair; my bed made with clean sheets turned neatly over the smoothed coverlet. Even my old brushes look docile and orderly in their jars.

I am amused to see how snug it all looks in the

candlelight, like an idealised version of an artist's garret. 'It is good to be back,' I say, and find myself meaning it.

She smiles. 'Let me bring you some supper.'

I begin to protest. 'I had a pie on the train—' but she has already darted out and I hear her feet skip down the stairs.

I ask Edie how her own mother is, when she returns with soup and bread and cheese on a tray. Her face, which shone when I thanked her, clouds over. 'She's to bed early tonight.'

I know Mrs Brundish always looks exhausted on her return from Windward House, though she gallantly tries to hide it.

'She's not well,' Edie exclaims. 'I know she's not! She never used to be like this – not when Father was alive. She was happy then, and strong.'

'She must miss your father,' I say. I think of my own mother, a widow of only two years. 'It can depress your spirit.'

'It's working for Juliana Greenwood that exhausts her,' Edie says bitterly. 'How Mother puts up with all the mortification, I don't know.'

I have suffered myself. Juliana Greenwood has exacting standards. She inspects the Doom on Sundays after the service and questions me until my head buzzes. Each time she sounds dissatisfied with my progress. But then she is investing a good deal of her money in it – and me.

I expect Edie to go, now that I have my supper. But she

lingers, and as I look at her a transformation comes over her features.

Her pretty face twists so that she looks ugly. I am shocked to see such an expression on one so young. She says in a low voice, her eyes averted, 'There are times when I'd like to murder Juliana Greenwood!'

A chill comes over me as the words drop heavily into the little candlelit room.

Then almost immediately she collects herself together. Her face relaxes into its curves, her mouth softens, her voice becomes matter of fact.

'I am sorry, Mr Shawcross, for talking so. You must drink your soup before it gets cold.'

Five

Maud

Someone was knocking at my door.

My drops always made me drowsy and dull when I first woke, but gradually I became aware of a voice asking anxiously, 'Miss Maud? It's past eight o'clock and your breakfast is ready.'

It was a young voice. One of the maids. She must have been calling for some time. I tried to reassure her, my voice mumbling through thick lips.

When I drew the curtains at last and peered out, I saw that my window was on the back of the house, looking down on a garden bordered by holly bushes and a dark yew hedge; the tall lime trees behind, with rooks' nests in their topmost branches, were still bare of leaves. The wind had not yet completely died with the night and it was a blowy morning, the clouds scudding above the garden.

As I looked out I saw the bulky figure of Tiggins, with a

wheelbarrow and rake, clearing the gravel path of fallen twigs and leaves. With him was a tall lean man with his back to me, who dragged one leg behind him – an under-gardener, perhaps.

I dressed with care. Mindful of what Miss Potton had said, I had sponged away the dirt of the train on my clothes before I went to bed the previous night, and once I had parted my hair and looped it in braids around my head, I hoped I was looking the best I could for my cousin.

My *cousin*, I thought. She is not my cousin at all, not related by blood. I should not be surprised that she doesn't wish to be called 'Cousin' Juliana.

But I recalled the sense of abandonment I had felt when she said so. I wanted her to like me; I wanted her to *love* me, as a true relation might, for I had no one else.

The mirror on the dressing table showed me my face, heavy-eyed from sleep and tense with apprehension. I tried to smile but could not; it was a long time since I had smiled.

My feet made a clatter on the stairs as I went down, echoing through the house as if it were empty of any life other than my own. I remembered where the dining room was, for Miss Potton had pointed it out to me the previous evening. A maid was silently sweeping the passage; as I passed, she made me a nervous bob.

The dining room was large and gloomy, and though a fire was lit, it was still chill. Dark oil paintings hung on the dusky crimson walls – a few murky landscapes, but mostly portraits, presumably of my ancestors.

I went along the length of the mahogany sideboard where a row of silver covers sat gleaming, and lifted each in turn. My eyes widened to see the quantity of ham, eggs, bacon and kidneys beneath.

I helped myself and went to sit at the single place laid for me, spreading the linen napkin on my knee and picking up my knife and fork. The utensils were heavy silver; my plate was the finest bone china, almost transparent, and within a circle of leaves on its gilt-edged rim was painted a 'G' for Greenwood, as was the fashion for those who did not have a coat of arms.

It came to me, suddenly, all unbidden: There is only one true Greenwood in this house and that person is me. Then I banished such a thought quickly; it was most ungenerous when Juliana had offered me her own home.

But it set me wondering why my uncle had left nothing to his own brother, my father, when he died. There seemed a terrible unfairness in it. Perhaps there had been some quarrel between them that I knew nothing about, for Papa had never mentioned him, nor had he ever come to London to see us. As a young child I was hardly aware of my uncle's existence.

Now I looked around at the furniture, at the silver candelabra on the table, at the rich Persian rug on the floor, at the solemn portraits of my ancestors on the walls – genial men with wigs and cravats and stiff-backed, unsmiling women, draped with children.

Why had all this gone to my uncle's stepdaughter, Juliana, when it should have been shared with Papa? And after my father's death that share should have come to me.

I did not understand.

I only knew that if I had inherited my rightful share, I need never have suffered as a governess.

A girl entered, wheeling a trolley. 'Shall I clear, miss?'

'Please do.'

I watched her, not knowing what else to do with myself. Every now and then her eyes would slide up to stare. They were slightly protuberant, which gave her an astonished look as she moved about the room collecting the dishes. I judged her to be about fourteen, a stolid, lumpish girl with big arms.

'What is your name?'

Her eyes bulged at being addressed. 'Dorcas Copping, miss.'

'Do you live in?'

She nodded. 'I didn't at first, living so close, but then Madam said she needed me more hours.'

'Do you know what she suffers from, Dorcas?'

The girl shook her head. 'She's right poorly sometimes.

After the last nurse left, it was too much work for Miss Potton, by herself in the evenings, so I had to live in.'

'Is there no other staff living here?'

She shook her head. 'The other maids – they've come recent to replace the last lot. They're from the village and they go home at nights.' She sounded resentful.

'What about the cook?'

'Mrs Brundish lives out, too. The supper is kept warm in the range and then I serves it to Madam.'

'No one else? There must be so much work!'

She was warming to me; she spoke more confidently.

'Well, there's Mr Tiggins outside, of course. He does the garden and drives Madam's carriage. And then there's Sly.'

'Sly?' That name again. I remembered Mr Tiggins the night before saying Sly was mending the carriage shaft.

Dorcas tapped her head. 'Sly's as mad as a fish. He looks after the horses and helps Mr Tiggins in the garden. He helps with the downstairs fires, too.'

She put her hand to her mouth. 'Oh, miss, I was meant to tell you, you are to go to Madam. She asked me when I took in her breakfast.'

I jumped to my feet, pleased that Juliana had asked to see me so soon. 'Thank you, Dorcas.'

She smiled. 'Now you are here, miss, I am sure Madam will be in more agreeable spirits.'

* * *

I knocked on Juliana's bedroom door. Silence. I knocked again, more firmly.

This time an irritable voice called out, 'Come in, do.'

There was a heavy, fusty smell in the room. I took a few steps over a thick rug and stopped.

At first I couldn't see Juliana, for a large screen shielded her bed from draughts under the door. My mother had had one, though hers was not as fine. There was a round table covered with a clean white cloth at the foot of the bed, holding medicine bottles and poultices, a kettle for blisters, a jug and several small glasses on a tray. There was also a large jar of boiled sweets and a pile of slim books bound in leather. They looked as if they might be prayer books, for the topmost had a gilt cross tooled on the front.

My gaze moved back to the medicine bottles and dread seized me.

I remembered vividly my mother's sickroom. Those endless days and nights smoothing her pillows, changing her bedding, measuring out her medicine, tempting her to eat, even a mouthful. To keep up her strength, to keep her alive – for a month, a week, a day, longer.

I had prayed with Papa that she would get better, until he stayed away, unable to see her suffer. I don't think he realised how much he asked of me. All the nursing left to me, a twelve-year-old girl. I was old for my age, even then. But no twelve year old should go through what I did.

Mama did not get better, but with my help she was free of pain, at last. Papa was shut away with his grief in his own room. He never asked me about her last hours.

'Who is it?' said Juliana's voice fretfully.

'It is Maud,' I said, disconcerted that my voice trembled.

I came round the screen. The room was candlelit still, the heavy curtains at the windows drawn against the daylight. Juliana lay in bed, a brass half-tester with red fabric curtains edged with gold that matched the ones at the window. She was propped on pillows, staring – you might say glowering – at me, though it was difficult to see which in the poor light.

'Good morning,' I said nervously, still uncertain how to address her. 'Shall I draw the curtains? It is a fine day outside – that is, it is not raining.'

'If you must,' she said, sullen.

She watched me silently as I went to the windows. Daylight flooded the room as I pulled back the curtains, showing the large wardrobe, the washstand in birchwood with its tiled back, the dressing table with its needlework cloth crowded with jewel boxes and ring trays, the walnut desk.

Juliana's bedroom, like her parlour, was cluttered with possessions, the windows tightly closed. The air was clouded with minute dust particles and as the beams of light shimmered through them, every object appeared out of focus. I wondered if she ever found it difficult to breathe.

'I see you admire the wallpaper,' said Juliana, raising herself from her pillows. 'That design is still very fashionable in London, so I am told. This was my stepfather's study. He had good taste. He had the walls papered the year before he died.'

'I never met my uncle,' I said. I thought it would do no harm to remind her of my relationship to him but she looked displeased again.

I lifted my eyes to the walls, thinking to make some complimentary remark to appease her. They were papered with dark green, making the room darker still, and patterned with peacock feathers. Peacocks, I thought. *Unlucky*.

'The room is quite splendid,' I managed to say.

A satisfied smile crossed Juliana's face and she lay back again. 'I am forced to spend much time in here, of course.'

'I am sorry for that,' I said gently, for a peevish note had entered her voice. 'Is there no good doctor in Rending?'

She flapped her hands about dismissively. They were white, thin, elegant; even in bed she wore her rings. 'Oh, Doctor Biddell comes every now and then to check on me. He finds nothing wrong. Nothing! He thinks he knows everything. And yet I suffer so! I can barely eat!'

In the daylight, her cheeks were without colour and her lips bloodless. Strands of pale hair escaped from beneath her frilled nightcap. She looked small and vulnerable in the big bed.

I found I was laying a hand on hers, as if she needed comfort. It felt bony and resisting under mine.

'I am here now, Juliana,' I said softly. 'I will look after you.'

She looked up at me, her face relaxing.

'Thank you, Maud. I know I was right to write to you when I did. I have suffered a succession of nurses, all hopeless. How difficult it is to find good staff these days!' She took her hand out from under mine and patted my arm – or, rather, tapped it – in a way that was almost admonitory. 'You and I will suit each other very well, I do believe!'

'After my father died—' I began and hesitated. 'Our lawyer tried to contact you. The letter must have been sent to the wrong address.'

Her blue eyes widened. 'Indeed, or perhaps lost in the post. So unfortunate. Thank heavens I found you in the end!' She made a little face. 'Goodness knows what you must have had to put up with as a governess!'

I lowered my eyes so she could not glimpse the dark secrets of those years. 'I am so very glad to be here. Tell me what I must do to help you. For I want to do that more than anything.'

'Do you truly, Maud?' she asked, smiling. 'Then read to me a little and then I shall tell you what you must do.'

I feared she might produce another religious tome but she reached under her pillow and with a great flourish whisked out a novel as if from its hiding place, a gleam in her eyes. *Vanity Fair* by William Thackeray. I wondered briefly if the prayer books might be only for show.

I drew a chair to the edge of the bed and began to read. As my voice echoed in the quiet room against the background of her soft, expectant breathing, I felt we were drawing closer together.

There was a clock on the mantel and after a while it chimed the hour, startling us both. Juliana pouted like a child.

'Eleven o'clock. Dorcas will be bringing in my beef tea before Doctor Biddell comes. You had best stop.' She eyed me approvingly. 'You are quite the little actress, my dear. You may continue later.'

A glow of pleasure went through me. I closed the book and made to get up from the chair but found my wrist suddenly gripped by Juliana, her rings digging into me painfully. She lowered her voice and hissed, 'Wait, I have not told you what you must do!'

She went on whispering, hurried and frantic, while I gazed at her, startled.

'I want you to get me some more Restorative Powders from Quilter's apothecary in Rending. Tiggins will take you. I have an account there. You must not mention this to

Doctor Biddell, do you understand? He does not approve of the miracle cure.' She loosened her grip and lay back, as if exhausted.

'The miracle cure?' I repeated, shaken, not understanding.

She said in a low, rapid voice, 'Quilter's Restorative Powder. It has cured several villagers of their ailments and if it has worked on others, it may work on me. I have taken the powder for a while now and I do believe I feel a little better.'

'It may not be wise to mix it with whatever Doctor Biddell prescribes for you,' I said, alarmed. 'Should you not tell him?'

Juliana frowned. Her voice went cold. 'Are you thwarting me already? It is such a small thing to ask of you.'

'I am sorry,' I stammered, taken aback. 'Of course I will get them.'

'Good girl. I knew I could trust you.' She gazed up at me, her eyes wide and pitiful. 'If you suffered as I do, you would resort to anything to be well again, even to a quack's dubious recipe for a miracle.'

Overcome with sympathy, I nodded.

'Potton tells me that there is no meat left in the larder. She never checks in time, that woman! While you are in the village, go to the butcher's for Mrs Brundish and see if they have any chops. Put them on my account there, too.'

I hurried up to my room and quickly put on my mantle,

bonnet and boots. I didn't know how to find the back door to the garden, so I let myself out of the front and stepped on to the drive.

Windward House was substantial and imposing from the outside, built of the local dark red brick, with tall chimney stacks that I thought must be Elizabethan and later found out had been added by my uncle. He had also added a top floor and a new roof with castellated turrets and gables to the original Jacobean building. I was to discover it was the grandest house for some miles around. Certainly it looked grand to me that first morning, and daunting, rearing up behind me with its many windows.

I followed the drive round to a cobbled courtyard at the back of the house, bordered by stables. The pony that had drawn the trap watched me as I crossed the yard. In the same block the black heads of two horses looked out over the half gates. I peered into a barn, looking for Tiggins, and saw rows of withered apples sitting beneath frames; bales of hay were stacked against the walls.

I found my way through a kitchen garden and stopped. A gravel path led up from some mossy steps to the formal garden I had seen Tiggins in earlier that morning, but he was not among the dark holly and clipped box hedges. At my feet were daffodils, broken by the wind, and there were still a few dying snowdrops left, their white bells tinged with brown, lying limply over the bare flowerbeds. My approach had disturbed the rooks, which began an agitated clacking from the tall lime trees on the slope beyond the garden.

I passed a rockery and came to a shrubbery. A shed was hidden behind the bushes near a compost heap. The door was half open and I hesitated. Perhaps Tiggins was in there.

I went closer and stared through the doorway into the dark interior. The shed was empty, but I was transfixed in horrified disgust and for a moment could not move.

It smelled rank, animal. A straw mattress lay along one side, covered with a tangle of filthy cloths. Above it numerous pelts hung from the wooden beams – mole, rabbit, stoat, squirrel – shuddering noiselessly in the draught from the door. Traps were piled on a shelf, metal teeth glinting. I thought I glimpsed a rotting head in one, oozing darkly. Even on a cold, blustery day it was attracting flies.

A sickness rose in my throat. I stepped back, almost tripping over my skirts, my hand to my mouth.

Then someone tapped me on the shoulder. My heart lurched and almost stopped. I whirled about and gasped.

I was looking into the face of a gargoyle.

Six

It was an ugly face but it was human.

The heavy features and thick lips of a young man loomed over me. His head seemed curiously naked, and after a few terrified seconds I realised it was because he wore a skull cap, its colour so close to his own pale greyish skin that it was hard to tell which was human flesh and which animal. His mouth worked frantically, dribbling spittle. The hand that had tapped me on the shoulder clenched and unclenched at his side, vast, raw and grimy; the other held a rake like a weapon.

I stared at him, my mouth dry, my heart beating in my throat. I thought of Rookyard's master: I was wary of all men now. Then the short, solid figure of Tiggins in brown gardening overalls came up behind him, breathing heavily.

'Sly, you're frightening the young lady. Step away, else I'll box your ears.'

I assumed it was an idle threat, for it would have taken much effort for Tiggins to have reached up so far: the creature was a good deal taller than either of us – and anyway, had he ears?

I looked at him again in horrid fascination and saw that indeed he had: small and neat, like an animal's, showing outside the skull cap. He was still jawing his face, as if he chewed on something tough and grisly, and the ears went eerily up and down with the motion.

Tiggins shook his head. 'He don't speak much, poor fellow. Can never spit it out, can you, Sly? Be off with you now, my boy, before I help you on your way.'

But he said it kindly enough and Sly seemed to understand, for he gave a kind of moan and turned, dragging one leg behind him. It was crooked, bent at an angle to his body.

As he limped away with his rake, writhing the fingers of his free hand at the air until a hedge hid him from sight, Tiggins said, 'You mustn't mind Sly, miss. He's harmless.'

I must have looked as doubtful as I felt, for he added, 'You were a mite too close to his sleeping quarters. He only wanted to know what you were doing. He has feelings like the rest of us.'

I was surprised by the compassion in Tiggins's voice. This was the man who had been so taciturn with me the night before. In the daylight I looked at his weather-beaten face, the dirt-begrimed lines around his eyes, and saw it was kind and mild.

'I am sorry if I upset him.'

'No matter, miss,' he said comfortably. 'You weren't to know. The village wanted to throw him out soon as they saw he were different. Thought he were bad luck. But the master allowed me to bring him to Windward House when he were a little boy. He was a decent, fair man, the master.'

'Was he?' I said, puzzled, thinking of the will again. It did not seem fair to me that he had left my papa nothing.

I pulled myself together and remembered my errand. 'Would it be possible for you to drive me into the village, Mr Tiggins? My cousin said you might take me.'

The open face shut like a box. 'No doubt she did,' he muttered darkly to himself. 'Now her driver's gone, seems to forget the master employed me as a gardener all those years ago.' Louder, he said in a flat voice, 'I'm sorry, miss. I've not had a chance to see to that broken shaft yet. It was too much for Sly's wits last night.'

But the kindness had come back into his face; perhaps he had seen how my own had fallen. 'It's but a short walk if you take the path over the heath, miss. Takes twice the time by horse and carriage.'

It had not occurred to me that the village was so close. I asked Tiggins for directions, thanked him and set off.

I was not to know until later that Sly was following me all the while.

* * *

I came out of the drive and stopped for a moment. Before me was endless space and sky. Beneath the silvery clouds, forming and reforming as the wind tore through them, the land sloped away in a series of undulations, through empty grassy meadows bordered by silver birch and pine to a distant darker line that was the sea. A broad track led down into the trees.

The sea didn't look so far away. I might walk there soon.

The path to the heath led first through old bracken, brambles and thrusting tiny young nettles. It was strangely silent after so long in the city. I was beginning to feel uneasy when I found myself out in a vast open space covered with gorse bushes and dun-coloured heather, and at my feet the bleached roots of gorse that had been cut down for firewood over the years. It seemed only rowan and stunted oak, not yet in leaf, could exist on the poor soil.

My boots sank into dark grey sand. All around me were rabbit holes, and as I walked I could hear a dull echo below me as if the whole land were hollow.

I climbed a low hill. As I came to the top, treading down old heather, the clouds, whirling and dissolving, rent by light, seemed to meet me. I stood under the huge sky and wanted to take off my bonnet, shake out my hair.

I can forget the past, I thought. This is my new life.

But I was not alone.

A figure was sitting on a tree stump, a man. I could only see the back of his head, hatless, and a good deal of rumpled brown hair. He must have heard my footfall for he turned and stared at me, but before I could say anything, even take in his features, I realized his gaze had gone beyond me.

'Sly? Be off!'

In horror I turned.

The creature was capering noiselessly behind me, his eyes reflecting the light of the sky. Then he thrust out an arm to point at me with a long finger, while his mouth chewed on words.

'Doo – ! D-doom!'

John

I rest a moment before going on down into the village, trying to put off the moment when I have to start work again on the Doom. The tree stump is my favourite place to sit and dream.

Someone is walking up the hill close behind me. I hear the soft crumble of the heather beneath feet, and turn.

I see the girl first, then Sly.

He is following her, like a dog after its mistress, and

she all unaware. Why he has fixed on this young woman, I don't know.

'Be off!'

I clap my hands, as one might to scare off a stray, and the girl turns and puts her hand to her mouth. Sly gasps something out at her, then takes to his heels and is off down the heath.

The girl is badly frightened, swaying, her hands to her face. She cannot be a village girl, for they all are used to Sly's ways, nor is she dressed like one. She is in mourning, which is commonplace enough in the village, but her skirts are silk and have a hoop beneath them.

She moans, 'What does he mean?' to herself.

I try to take her arm, meaning to support her to my tree stump to sit down, but she shrinks from my touch, as if I have leprosy.

'Rest a minute, miss. You will feel better.'

She sinks down on the stump, her black skirts a stiff circle about her.

After a few seconds, her breathing slows. She takes her hands from her face and looks up at me beneath the rim of her black straw bonnet. 'Thank you, sir.'

I look into the face of the girl from the train.

I think I am dreaming. I blink, and her face comes into focus again, and it is the same. Her eyes are a very dark grey in a face that is paler still with her recent fright, and fine dark hair escapes in wisps beneath her bonnet.

'Don't be troubled by Sly, miss,' I say gently. 'He means no harm.'

'He followed me,' she says, in a trembling voice. 'He tried to speak. Did you hear what he said?'

'I heard him say something about the Doom.'

I squat down beside her. I want to soothe her as one might a wild creature, for that is what she seems to me. Her arm felt so fragile beneath my hand.

'The Doom is an ancient painting in the village church.' I point over my shoulder to where the village lies beneath the rise. 'You must be new in these parts if you don't know about its discovery in St Mark's. Rending's great miracle!'

'Another miracle?' she says, bewildered.

'It shows the Day of Judgement and dates back to the Middle Ages. I have been engaged to restore it.' I hope to impress her.

'I see. Perhaps I should not have been so alarmed. Is Sly truly not dangerous?'

I laugh. 'Heavens, no! He's not the wit to be dangerous! He lost it when he was born, poor boy. A thief, yes. He is like a magpie – will take anything that attracts his curiosity and is cunning about it. He stole my brushes from the church, though when I caught him at it, he ran off at once, dropping them like spillikins.'

She nods doubtfully and looks at me again. 'You are an artist, sir?'

'That is what I try to be when I have the luxury.' I hesitate. 'You know that you and I have met before?'

She shakes her head and something wild comes into her eyes. 'I don't believe so, sir!'

'We were on the same train yesterday,' I say gently, for she appears much agitated again. 'We sat opposite each other until Marsham.'

Her face calms. 'Gracious, so we did!'

'Is it not a most extraordinary coincidence that we should be both here, in this spot, the very next morning?'

I am beside myself with delight, certain that fate has brought us together. As I watch her face I see that it holds no answering emotion. Instead she stands up abruptly.

'Thank you, sir, for rescuing me, but I must hurry on. I have some purchases to make.'

I am taken aback, helpless. 'May I at least know your name?'

She puts out a small, gloved hand in a formal gesture and says, 'Maud Greenwood,' as we shake hands.

It is a shock to hear that surname. 'Why, Miss Juliana Greenwood is my patron! I am restoring the Doom at her request and, I should add, aided by her generous donation. You are related?'

She shakes her head. 'By marriage only.'

That is a relief to me.

'My name is John Shawcross. Are you staying long at Windward House?'

'I have come to live there.'

My heart leaps. 'Then might I call on you, Miss Greenwood?'

'I do not believe my cousin would approve of me entertaining a visitor so early on.' Her tone forbids me to say anything more.

So that is that.

I watch her flit away from me, my vision from the train, her boots kicking up whorls of dark sand like smoke as she goes down towards Rending; and there is nothing I can do about it.

Seven

Maud

John Shawcross could not be making much money from his painting, for I noticed his coat was patched. He was some years older than me, with a pleasant, honest face you could not dislike and a smile I found engaging despite my mistrust of men. He looked most disappointed when I left.

But I was anxious to reach the village, unsure how long I had been already. I had to find my way to the pharmacy, and to the butcher's.

As I came down from the heath, heading for the church spire, I saw there was only one main street to the village; thatched cottages huddled along the lanes that led to it.

I left the church behind and passed the village green, with its old stocks and cattle pound, and in the centre a duckpond, weedy water ruffled by the wind. The sound of hammering reached me; there was a forge close by.

I came to the main street, avoiding the open sewer that ran down the middle, though I was used to the stench of the city. Some of the shops along the street were built of stone with tiled roofs; it was not the small, insignificant village I had supposed.

I passed a haberdasher's, a bakery, a post office. A sign that said 'Thurlow's' hung above a window piled high with groceries: cheese, tobacco, snuff, jars of sugar and tea.

People stared at me. Old women with brown wrinkled faces whispered to each other, bearded men leaned on sticks to watch me pass, small children pointed.

I had a stranger's face.

I dipped my head and hurried on, until to my relief I spied the butcher's. Dorley and Son was painted above the shop window.

The butcher was chopping meat in a room beyond. I heard the thud of the cleaver and the crack of bone. The bell tinkled as I pushed the door open further and a voice called out, 'Help the customer for me, will you, Jonas?'

I trod over sawdust that was none too clean. A gangly youth stood behind the tiled counter. Carcasses hung on hooks behind his head and I averted my eyes, suddenly and sickeningly reminded of Sly's hut.

'Miss Greenwood asked if you had any chops today,' I said.

'Now what kind of chops would they be? Mutton, lamb,

pork?' He had a crafty mouth that smiled. 'The new lamb is particularly soft and tender.'

There was something insinuating in the way he said it. He had narrow, impertinent eyes and a long pimpled chin. He reminded me of Basil Cream, the elder of the two Cream sons, who had haunted my dreams for so long.

I know your sort, I thought, and dropped my gaze so I need not see his leering face.

'Mutton, please,' I said primly, 'and put it on Miss Greenwood's account.'

He wrote something down in a book and handed over the chops, clumsily packaged. I held the parcel well away from my person while he looked me up and down, first at my dress and then, too long and in a manner I didn't like, at my face. I turned to go quickly, feeling a flush rise in my cheeks.

'You'll be collecting for Miss Greenwood from now on, then?' he said to my back. 'Not the other girl?'

I turned reluctantly. I wanted to get my position straight. 'I am Miss Greenwood's relative,' I said, trying to gather my dignity. 'If she wishes me to make her purchases, of course I shall.'

'Then I'll be seeing a lot of you, no doubt,' he said, with a leer. 'Jonas Dorley's the name.'

I did not divulge mine.

'Strange household, that. No one stays for long. Shall you be different, miss?'

He looked at me mockingly, eyebrows raised, a smirk on his spotty face. I said nothing but hurried to the door. I could not prevent him, though, from leaping in front of me to open it and showing me through with an elaborate and insolent flourish of his hand.

The only way I discovered the apothecary was by seeing the name over the window: 'Samuel Quilter', the letters clumsily painted and dirty, and beneath, smaller, 'Patent Medicines, Drugs and Trusses'.

I was used to my local pharmacy in London, the one that I had visited so often with my mother's prescriptions and where I later bought my sleeping draught. It had had a large plate glass window with a row of tall richly-coloured bottles glowing behind it, inky blue, emerald, amethyst, ruby.

The exterior of this shop held no promise of miracle cures. The window was small and streaked with dust.

I peered through but could see nothing. I pushed the door open and stepped on to a cracked stone floor. Candles flickered in the draught as a thick earthy smell met me, vegetable matter, perhaps, overlaid with chemicals whose sharpness caught in my throat. It was damp and chill, even after the wind outside.

At first the interior was as dark as a cave, even with the candles on the counter, but as I grew used to the gloom I saw it was shot through with light that glinted from every corner. There were glass bottles on the shelves and wide-necked jars for powders that shone in the candlelight. Each container was labelled in black ink and varnished, and their gloss caught the light too and reflected it back again.

On the counter next to a large brass-beam scale, a girl was crushing something in a mortar. She looked up as I stepped in, though she did not stop. She seemed to gleam herself in the candlelight, so vibrant with health that even her rippling chestnut hair sparked with it. She was sturdily built, both strong square hands gripping the pestle as she ground it round and round, her round cheeks pink with effort, a frown of concentration between thick brows.

I stepped closer and saw a mush of small dark leaves in the mortar. She stopped abruptly and her eyes met mine.

'I'm sorry, miss. I have to do this before Mr Quilter gets back. What was it you wanted?'

'I would not interrupt you, but I have a request from Miss Greenwood for more of Mr Quilter's Restorative Powder. I believe she has an account with you.'

'Miss Greenwood? Yes, indeed, but I'm not allowed to dispense and have none set by, there has been such demand. If you wouldn't mind waiting a short while, Mr Quilter will be back.'

She motioned me to a chair near the counter and I sat down, watching the girl as she continued to pound the leaves in the mortar. Then she stopped for a moment to flex her stubby fingers with a sigh.

To break the silence between us, I said, 'Why do you call the powder the "miracle cure"?'

'It seems to give new life to everyone after illness,' she said, earnest and wide-eyed. She was several years younger than me, though her figure was plump and well-formed. 'So far it has cured rheumatism, ague, general decline, mouth ulcers and lethargy after childbirth.' She ticked the list off on her fingers solemnly.

Her gaze fixed on me more keenly. 'Are you by any chance the new nurse at Windward House, miss?'

'I am related to Miss Greenwood by marriage. I am not her nurse.'

'That's good, for no nurse stays long in that house.'

'Why is that?'

'I gather she dismisses them, miss. They are not good enough, perhaps.'

'You have no idea what she suffers from?'

She gave me an odd look. 'I hear she believes she is dying.'

A longing to confide came over me. 'I am not certain it is a nurse she needs, but company.'

It was impossible to read her expression in the candlelight as she looked down at the green mess in the mortar. Eventually she said, 'You will meet my mother, Mrs

Brundish. She is cook to the household. I am Edith Brundish – Edie.'

'My name is Maud Greenwood.' I stood up and held out my hand, and she gripped it, after hesitating a moment. Her fingers were very warm and strong.

'I am sorry if I've said anything I shouldn't, miss,' she said, but seemed proud with it.

I shook my head and said nothing.

I looked around, at the stoppered bottles and phials, trying foolishly to recognise my sleeping draught amongst them.

The girl, as if reading my mind, said, 'They are mostly the ingredients for the herbal remedies that Mr Quilter makes himself. He keeps the drugs and poisons locked up in the back dispensing room. It's difficult to obtain more supplies of those out here.'

'You have a fine array,' I said. 'As splendid as any in London.'

She knew she was being patronised, unsophisticated as she was. 'Folk suffer from ailments in the country too,' she said, coldly polite. 'And sometimes they need their constitutions building up after. That was why Mr Quilter experimented and discovered his miracle powder.'

'And you helped him?'

'I know nothing of what goes into it, Miss Greenwood. I cannot understand the symbols. It's his own special recipe.

He won't let me near when he's making the powder. He does it in the back.' She gestured over her shoulder into a dark room beyond. 'It's secret, in case one of the druggists from Southwold or even as far as Ipswich try to copy it. He's going to take out a patent on it soon.'

'You help Mr Quilter in other ways, though.' I gestured at the mortar.

Edie's face lit up. 'If girls could be apprenticed to apothecaries, then I'd be an apprentice, sure enough. I prepare some of the ingredients, write labels for the bottles, that's all. It's laborious work and my handwriting is ill-formed.'

I would ask Quilter for my sleeping draught when I had the money. But how was I to come by money with my annuity all spent?

Quilter turned out to be a seedy little man, stunted, thin, and somehow grubby, with straggles of grey hair. There was the light of ambition and greed in his eyes behind the smeared spectacles. He knew he had all the village of Rending buying his Restorative Powder.

But I hoped he would be useful to me in the future, and so I thanked him with the utmost politeness when he handed over Juliana's miracle powder in a twist of rice paper.

Eight

There was a carriage outside Windward House when I arrived back, and in the hall Dorcas was helping a man of middle years into his coat. His sandy hair was receding, but he sported a fine pair of bristling sideburns and a cheerful air. He pinched Dorcas's thick red cheek jovially as she smoothed his coat down.

He introduced himself as Doctor Biddell.

'Miss Maud Greenwood? How do you do? I gather you have come to live with your cousin.'

I nodded and we shook hands. 'Pleased to meet you, Miss Maud.'

His grasp was unexpectedly firm and his eyes summed me up. 'Capital, capital,' he said, though whether referring to my appearance, I wasn't certain. 'I dare say I shall see you again soon – very soon, no doubt.' He laughed heartily, with a conspiratorial wink at Dorcas as if it were a joke, and picked up his black doctor's bag.

'Please, Doctor, before you go might I have a word with you – alone?'

He nodded and Dorcas vanished reluctantly behind the door to the kitchen passage. 'Shall we go in here?' he said, waving at Juliana's parlour.

I followed, still in my mantle and bonnet. The fire had not yet been lit and the little room was cold and airless. The doctor settled himself into one of the armchairs, drawing his coat close about him, and gave me a genial look.

'You wish to ask me about your cousin – about Juliana?'

So they were on first name terms. I sat down too and faced him. 'I should like to know what is wrong with her, Doctor Biddell.'

He spread freckled hands across his knees. 'You understand I cannot divulge information about my patients, Miss Greenwood.'

'But might I know something of the nature of her illness? I have lost both my parents. Is that what I am to expect now?'

'Then let me assure you on that count, Miss Greenwood,' he said cheerily.

'You mean my cousin is not going to die?'

'She is not as ill as she thinks!' He sat back in his chair and beamed at me encouragingly. 'You are the very thing she needs to divert her from these morbid thoughts. Young company will lift her spirits.'

'What can I do?'

'Persuade her to take drives and walks with you, so that she breathes the fresh air. Suggest she gives a dinner or two – something to bring her back into society, into the normal world of conversation and gaiety.'

'Will her constitution be able to sustain it?'

'Oh, yes.'

'She eats very little.'

'She has a delicate digestive system. I have tried a number of remedies, and no doubt she will let me know how she fares with the latest one.'

He rose to his feet, grunting. I stood up awkwardly, clutching my hands together.

'Doctor, I have difficulty in sleeping. I have – bad dreams.' I was ashamed to find my eyes welling with tears. He did not appear to notice.

'Then I give the same advice to you as I have given you for your cousin. Fresh air and exercise. You are young and healthy. Those dreams will soon go away.'

He stood aside to let me go before him and as I passed him, he patted my arm soothingly, as if I were a child.

Coming out of the parlour I almost fell over Dorcas, who had returned surreptitiously to listen outside. She had a soft tread for so heavy a girl.

I had to give a wry smile as she took herself off, eyes lowered. During the time I had been a governess, I, too, had learned to eavesdrop at keyholes. That way

I had always been prepared.

Of course I did not need a doctor's prescription for my sleeping draught. If I'd had the money I could have bought it over the pharmacist's counter, as anyone could. Laudanum was in common use and not expensive.

I confess I stole a glance at the range of medicines on Juliana's table when I hurried into her room to give her the packet of Quilter's Restorative Powder, but I could see nothing there that resembled my drops; hers were mostly half-empty bottles of tablets, once prescribed by Doctor Biddell, I presumed, and now discarded, as if she had tried them out and found them useless, for they had a slightly dusty air.

To my surprise, she was not yet dressed but lying back on her pillows, her eyes closed. The fire in the grate gave out tremendous heat. The room felt overpoweringly warm and stuffy after the wind outside.

I laid the packet noiselessly on the medicine table, but Juliana must have heard me come in. 'Is that you, Maud?' she said querulously. Her eyes flicked open and rested on me.

'I have brought you the powder.'

'Thank you.' Her voice was faint.

'Should I summon Dorcas to help you dress?'

'Dorcas? Good heavens, no!' There was nothing wrong

with her voice after all. 'That girl can hardly dress herself!' She frowned fretfully. 'No, this morning I shall rest. The doctor's visit was fatiguing. I have new pills to take, no better than the last, no doubt. I shall get up to take afternoon tea and perhaps you will join me.'

'Of course,' I said, anxious to please. 'Let me open the window a little for you.'

She gave a shudder against the pillows and drew her hands up to her eyes. 'Fresh air is far too enervating.'

'Then shall I leave you to sleep?'

She touched the bed beside her with a limp hand. 'Come and sit quietly with me a while, dear Maud.'

She did, indeed, sound exhausted. I perched there and she closed her eyes as if comforted.

As her breathing became hushed and regular, I studied her face. Her mouth drooped in sleep. I touched the fair hair that escaped from beneath her lace cap and began to smooth it gently from her brow. It was what I used to do for my mother: stroke her hair as she lay in bed. It is an intimate, tender gesture.

Juliana's hair, strong and plentiful, felt different from my mother's, which had been fine and dark like mine before illness threaded it with white; the long curve of Juliana's brow, the sharp shape of her jaw, was unfamiliar. I longed to see my mother's face appear on the pillow instead.

As I rose silently at last, overcome with the oppressive

heat in the room, Juliana's voice said weakly, making me jump, 'Pass me a prayer book from the table before you go, Maud.'

So she had been awake all the time.

Nine

That night I was deeply asleep when I became aware that someone was shaking my shoulder.

I swam up through black layers of sleep and focussed on a shapeless figure dressed in a nightgown and shawl, greying hair in a long plait, a flickering candle in one hand.

I gazed up, frightened, stupified; I scarcely recognised Miss Potton out of her grey dress and apron and with her hair down. The small hard eyes were swollen with sleep, her mouth thin and angry.

'Miss Maud! It's Madam! Have you not heard her?'

There was a tremendous thumping beneath my floorboards. My bed shook with it.

'I've even heard her in my room above you! You must go down to her at once!'

'Me?' I said, bewildered.

'You are here now, miss, and must look after Madam in the night. The nurse always did it before.'

I was dazed with sleep – with my drops – otherwise I might have protested. But the noise beneath my floorboards was not ceasing; it grew more frantic. I swung my legs out of bed in great alarm, fumbled for my shawl, lit my candle with a shaking hand.

My words came out slurred. 'Thank you, Miss Potton. You may go back to bed.'

I staggered out to the dark well of the stairs. Miss Potton's footsteps died away as she returned gladly to her room.

It was very quiet, the dreadful thumping muffled and the only sound my bare feet padding on the wood as I went down. Shadows loomed on the walls and moved in the light of my candle. The air was cold and gusty, so that I shuddered with it after the warmth of my bed.

It seemed to take an age to reach the bottom of the stairs. I was dwarfed by the house, overcome by its darkness.

Juliana's room was lit by a night light that gave only a faint glow. Enough, though, to see her half out of bed, a long stick in her hand. That was what had been making all the noise beneath my floorboards. I was astonished she had such strength in her.

Her shadow was elongated up the dark walls like a spider, the stick an extra limb. For a moment I thought she might use it on me and cowered back. In the light of my candle she looked furious, malevolent, her eyes glittering, her hair streaming down beneath her lace night cap.

'Why have you taken so long?'

'I am sorry,' I stammered.

'You must come at once when I need you in the night!'

'What is the matter? Are you feeling unwell?'

'I always feel unwell!' she snapped, climbing back into bed. 'I cannot sleep. Fetch me some camomile tea.'

I ventured down the shadowy passage that led to the kitchen area. I had no idea how to find the camomile leaves, or indeed how to find a kettle and teapot. I did not know if the range was kept alight during the night, though I discovered it was. I had to wake Dorcas, who slept in the kitchen.

Rubbing her eyes, she grudgingly showed me what I needed and lumbered back to her pallet.

It was difficult to focus as I waited for the kettle to boil. In the red light of the range the kitchen swam around me, breaking like a bubble, to reform. The teapot, cup and saucer rattled on the tray as I wove back down the passage to Juliana's room, brushing the walls with my arms, swaying as I walked, the candle in its holder dripping wax on the clean tray cloth.

I entered Juliana's room as quietly as I could and carried the tray over to the screen. I laid it carefully on the medicine table, anxious not to spill any tea from the pot's spout. I had taken too long; she would complain.

I tiptoed round the screen. Juliana appeared to be asleep, eyelids fast shut over the sharp blue eyes.

'Juliana,' I whispered.

She did not stir, her slight body motionless beneath the lace-edged sheets and heavy bedclothes. Her hand was raised to her face in sleep and there was something between her fingers. A curl of paper.

I lifted my candle closer, puzzled, and then my gaze moved above her head and I saw it. It shocked me, it was so unexpected.

She had pushed back the curtain behind her bed head. There was a long white powdery scar in her stepfather's green wallpaper where it had been torn off, not only tonight but over many nights, gradually, a bit at a time. A little piece of paper, for comfort, like a child, that she could clutch between her fingers, hold to her face. Some of the greyish-white dust – dry wallpaper paste – had fallen on her pillow.

I am not sure what I felt. Compassion, pity, confusion. An adult should not behave like this. Most of all I was uneasy; I wondered if she might be mad.

I turned without a sound and left her, and crept back up to my room. My feet were icy and I tucked my nightgown round them. The room moved about me, even when I shut my eyes.

Then the memories came and I could not escape them.

Coming back to the house from the privy one morning I feel dizzy. I sink down by the garden wall, crumpled and chilled. It is my time of the month and I am weak from hunger.

The mistress passes by with the gardener.

'What are you doing here?' Her voice is shrill. 'Where are the children?'

I stammer out that they are in the kitchen, quite safe; that Cook is minding them.

'What? Consorting with the cook!'

She snatches me up as if I am a feather – for she is a big woman – and I flinch, thinking she will hit me.

'Get to your duties,' she hisses, her spit sour in my face, and she gives me a great push in my back.

Ten

John

My walk to and from the church each day takes me close to Windward House, and in the week after encountering Maud Greenwood on the heath I make a detour so I can pass its gates.

I loiter hopefully for a while under the blowing skies, shivering a little, for the March wind is keen. I yearn to see her again and somehow I am sure I shall.

I do not see her.

Each time the house seems more formidably closed against the outside world than ever. The front door scarcely ever opens to let anyone in or out, and the windows are too small in the mass of dark red brick and appear sealed shut. Darkness lies behind them and darkness rules that house.

What must it be like for a young girl to be shut away in that house, with only a handful of servants and that fractious, self-indulgent woman for company?

* * *

Some ten days after I first see Miss Maud Greenwood on the heath, the wind blows in rain from the west. As I work in the church, I become aware of it pounding on the roof. Earlier that morning I had smelled it, weighting the air with damp, as I trudged over the heath towards Rending.

Inside the church it grows dark, too dark to see what I am doing, even with my lamps, so I sit down in one of the pews to wait for better light.

The church door creaks open.

I turn to see Maud Greenwood enter, breathless as if she has run for shelter, her hems sodden and with a soaking umbrella. She looks about in the dimness, does not notice me and sinks down in the nearest pew, her hooped skirt rising then settling as if it has a life of its own.

For a moment I cannot move. My heart drums as hard as the rain. Then I stand up and move towards her.

'Miss Greenwood?'

I have startled her, a male figure appearing from the darkness, looming over her. She gasps and starts back.

'Forgive me,' I say gently. 'It is John Shawcross. We have met before, do you remember?' Her face looks blank, frightened. Surely she cannot have forgotten me? 'We met on the heath.'

Her face clears. She rises, brushing her skirt down, a shy

gesture. 'Of course. I remember you very well, Mr Shawcross. The artist!'

I nod, smiling, greatly relieved.

'I must not interrupt your work, sir. I came in to shelter.' She hesitates and flushes. 'I didn't wish to remain in the butcher's shop.'

I can understand it. That smirking youth, Jonas Dorley, cheats Mrs Brundish by giving her rancid cuts of meat for Marsh End.

'You are not interrupting in the slightest,' I say quickly, for she looks as if she is about to take flight. 'I have lain down my tools while the rain lasts. It is too dark to work properly.'

She looks around and gives a little shiver.

'You mustn't catch a chill, Miss Greenwood. Here, let me give you my coat.'

I can see that she is embarrassed by the suggestion, coming from someone who is still a stranger, and I feel a fool. She smiles awkwardly and shakes her head. 'It is most kind of you, sir, but there is no need. It is the church. It has such an oppressive atmosphere.'

She seems a sensitive creature, easily perturbed.

'It has no pretensions, certainly,' I say, looking at the bulging whitewashed walls. 'But it has served its purpose for centuries and saved many a soul, I am sure!'

She cocks her head, sensing irony in my tone. 'You don't

sound a religious man, Mr Shawcross.'

'I believe I was until I started work on the Doom. Then I began to wonder, to ask questions, and there was no one to answer save myself.' I look at her mourning clothes. 'Forgive me, but I see you have lost someone close to you. I hope you find comfort in your own faith.'

'I lost my father three years ago, my mother before that.' She twists her gloved fingers together. 'The truth is, Mr Shawcross, I cannot afford new clothes, but nor do I wish to come out of mourning. It is my penance.' She whispers the last words so that I am not sure I have heard them aright.

'I am sorry,' I say inadequately.

She shakes her head, dismissing my sympathy. 'My father didn't suffer, unlike my poor mother some years before him. He died of a heart attack very suddenly.'

'You must have been still at school.'

I cannot work out how old she is. Her face is smooth, unlined and girlish, but she has the gravity and manner of a woman.

'There was no money. I had to leave and seek employment.'

'What did you do?'

Her voice is low. 'I became a governess.' She adds, 'But when I had exhausted all hope, Miss Greenwood offered to take me in.'

'How do you find Miss Greenwood? She has not been to inspect my work for a while.' I do not mention that I am greatly relieved by this, though neither has she paid my wages.

Maud's face clouds. 'I have been trying to persuade her to venture out, but she is not in good health.'

'I confess I can see little wrong with her whenever she comes here,' I say dryly.

Maud's dark eyes meet mine. 'In truth, Mr Shawcross, I believe she sometimes puts on a little fuss to seek attention – especially my attention. She wants me with her all the time, even at night, it seems! Of course I do my best to please her, for she has been most generous in offering me a roof over my head. Even when I do a little shopping for her, I fear she counts the minutes until I am back at her side. She will be doing so now.'

She sighs and looks up at the clear glass windows flooded with rain; the stained glass was destroyed by Cromwell's men.

'Has she no visitors?'

'Only the doctor – or the vicar.' Her mouth quirks, as if she has remembered something amusing.

The Reverend Edwin Wissett is a fussy, eager little man, not yet of middle age, though you would not guess it from his earnest ways.

'I know the Reverend,' I say, hoping to see her smile

again. 'He regards the Doom almost as his own, which in a sense it is – or at least shared between him and Miss Juliana Greenwood!'

'Would you show the Doom to me, Mr Shawcross?' she says earnestly.

I confess I am eager to show off my work and win Maud's admiration, so I lead her to where it lies against the west wall. The best light for working is there. I have a table for my various jars and glass sheets, my brushes and the muller to grind the pigment. Mrs Wissett, the vicar's wife, has thoughtfully donated a stool and a small wood burner to keep me warm.

The painting is across three wooden boards. I have cleaned off most of the limewash with acetone, together with nearly four hundred years of soot and candle grease. The work has been painstaking and delicate.

I have not yet reached Christ, the king and judge, who sits on a faded rainbow. He seems almost unaware of the turmoil far below, where the saved climb a stairway to heaven and the damned are thrust into hell. At the moment I am beginning to restore the right-hand corner – the Leviathan, the great fish whose jaws are the hell-mouth. I have just revealed the small, grinning devils with hooks, clawing at the damned as they are tossed into the flames.

The Day of Judgement.

The subject matter is grim but the figures are crudely

painted and have a cartoon-like quality to the modern eye. That does not take away from the impact of the whole, and I sense Maud feels it as she stands beside me, silently gazing. She is staring at the Archangel Michael, who holds a pair of scales. A tiny naked figure sits in one pan while its wicked deeds, represented by two demons, weigh down the other, condemning that poor lost soul to hell.

A beam of light from the window falls on Maud's face, on her white brow beneath the black rim of her bonnet. Zinc white with rose madder, I think distractedly, a touch of cobalt and Naples yellow, burnt umbre perhaps.

Then she bursts out, 'Why, it is horrible! The most horrible thing I have ever seen!'

Maud

Doomsday, when all souls will be judged.

I covered my eyes to hide the scales that would weigh my misdeeds. I knew how I would fare. I had been the cause of two deaths.

I had killed my mother, I had killed my father . . .

I had committed other sins as well.

I heard John Shawcross's voice say soothingly, 'It is only the artist's imagining. It was painted a long time ago.'

I took my hands from my eyes, ashamed that he should

see me so fearful, and searched for words to excuse myself. 'The image has such power, even after all this time!'

'It had to have power. It was intended to warn the congregation of what awaited them if they sinned, to remind them that they would be judged after death. The good would go to heaven, the wicked to hell and its torments.' He smiled. 'But you, Miss Greenwood, I am sure would have had no such fears. You would have gone straight heavenwards!'

I shook my head. 'Oh, no, Mr Shawcross, you are quite mistaken! I am one of the wicked ones.'

'Surely not!'

He looked amused but quizzical, so I said quickly, to divert him, 'What will happen to the Doom when you have finished your restoration?'

'It will be rehung over the nave. The Reverend Wissett will be relieved to have his congregation reminded of the wages of sin every Sunday!'

'If you have lost your faith, does that mean you don't believe in hell and damnation?' I waited intently for his reply.

'I confess I began to lose my faith even before I began work on the Doom. My beliefs, such as they were, were shaken by Charles Darwin's theories.'

'So you are a follower of Mr Darwin?' I hesitated. '"The survival of the fittest" – is that not what he expounds in his book, *On the Origin of Species*?'

I could see he was surprised that I knew about Charles Darwin. He nodded. 'I went to one of his lectures in London. The audience was held rapt. He argued that the world was not created in seven days but over millennia, everything evolving gradually so that only the most perfectly adapted survived.' He gestured at the Doom. 'If God's creation of the world as described in the Bible isn't true, how can anything else be, including what we see depicted here – the Day of Judgement?'

'I believe I would find that reassuring,' I said quietly. 'To know for certain that nothing will await me in death but eternal sleep. No punishment for my sins.'

'Sins, Miss Greenwood?' he said, and smiled again as if he thought I were joking.

I felt a spurt of anger. 'You know nothing about me, Mr Shawcross! Nothing about my past life!'

'I know you are kind and considerate to your cousin. You must be a good person, Miss Greenwood.'

I shook my head violently. 'I am one of the damned, I tell you!'

He gazed at me, startled by my tone.

I must be careful, I thought. Very careful. There was a gentleness and compassion about him that invited confidences.

'Forgive me, Mr Shawcross, I have talked too much. I

must go. My cousin will wonder where I am.'

'Stay. It is still raining.'

'Listen. You can hear nothing.'

'Then come and visit me here again.' There was pleading in his face.

I put out my hand without committing myself further. 'Goodbye, Mr Shawcross.'

His paint-stained fingers gripped mine as if he did not wish to let go. 'John, please.'

I released myself politely and did not offer my first name in return. I went hurriedly to the main door. As I let myself out he was still watching me.

A figure passed out through the lych gate at the end of the path, a shawl around her head. I thought I recognised the sturdy figure of Edie Brundish, but I did not call out to her. I was too busy dwelling on John Shawcross.

I had revealed too much of myself to him in the church and now I regretted it bitterly. Had I not learnt to be suspicious of all men?

Eleven

In spite of my apprehension, over the next few days John Shawcross kept entering my thoughts.

Perhaps I had been foolish to be so unfriendly. He seemed respectful and kind, not in the least like men I had come across before. If I had the chance I would make amends. Perhaps I might see him at church the coming Sunday.

My heart sank when Juliana announced her own intention to attend. 'You shall come with me, Maud.'

'Are you certain you feel well enough?'

She heaved a great sigh and nodded. 'It will exhaust me, I know, but I must put up with that. I need to see that young man's progress on the Doom. I want the restoration completed before I die.'

I did not protest as I usually did when she mentioned dying. My thoughts were on Mr Shawcross and Juliana looked at me sharply.

'Why do you blush, Maud?'

I put a hand to my cheek. 'It is a little warm in here. I shall move away from the fire.'

As I did so, I remembered that John was no longer a believer. It was most unlikely I would see him at the service.

A curious thing happened at the end of that week.

I came back from a carriage ride with Juliana and went up the stairs, intending to leave my bonnet and shawl in my bedroom. On the landing I paused.

There was a noise coming from my little sitting room. Someone was moving about, there was the tread of feet that paused, then a small sliding sound I could not identify. Was Dorcas cleaning in there? A chill went through me. Could it be Sly?

The door was not quite shut; I pushed it open, hardly breathing.

Mrs Brundish, the cook, was bent over at the bookcase. My heart slowed. I watched her for a moment as she pulled a book out, looked at its spine, then slid it back into its place.

'Mrs Brundish?'

She jumped round, a hand to her heart. 'Oh, Miss Maud!'

'I am sorry. I startled you. Were you looking for something?'

'Nothing,' she said quickly. 'Nothing at all. Please forgive me for entering your room, Miss Maud. I didn't mean—'

'Don't go,' I said gently, as she hastened towards the door in a fluster. 'What were you looking for?'

She stopped, red spots on her cheekbones. She was a thin woman, with a hunted air and dark circles beneath her eyes. When her high colour drained away, she was very pale, pale to the lips. She did not look well.

'It is my daughter, miss,' she whispered. 'Edie.'

'I know Edie. I have met her in the apothecary's.' I smiled to put her at her ease. 'A clever girl. You must be proud of her.'

Her face lightened. 'I am, miss. I'm doing this for her.' She gestured towards the bookcase.

'I don't understand, Mrs Brundish.'

'No, and why should you, miss?' She hesitated. 'If I tell you, I beg you not to tell Madam.'

I nodded, curious. 'It will be between you and me, I promise, but I should like to know.'

She took a deep breath. 'You see, the last nurse and Edie became friendly and the nurse used to allow Edie to borrow books from the bookcase here. She would choose one and take it to Edie at Quilter's.' She clutched her hands together. 'I know she shouldn't have done such a thing, I know it was wrong, but what was I to do? Edie brought home the first book and then I couldn't stop her. She took great care of them, mind. And she's like you said, a clever girl – my own late husband encouraged her reading. And today—'

'You thought you would borrow another one for her?'

She nodded, shame-faced. '*Wuthering Heights*. She was

almost at the end when the nurse was dismissed by Madam and it had to be put back. She pleaded with me to get it for her again so she could finish it.'

I went over to the bookcase and pulled it out. I remembered where it was from my first evening. 'Please take it and give it to Edie with my regards.'

I saw her face register astonishment, relief, delight, all mixed together. 'But Madam? These are her books, the ones she had as a young girl.'

I could not stop the thought: And one day they will be mine.

'We shall say nothing to her. It is our secret, Mrs Brundish. And when Edie has finished that one, she may give it back to me in Quilter's and I shall find her another.'

'Oh, Miss Maud!' She stared at me, as if unable to believe her ears.

I hesitated. 'Tell me, Mrs Brundish, were you working here when Miss Juliana's stepfather was master of Windward House?'

'Oh, no, miss, not then.' She looked sad. 'My husband was still alive. He had an excellent position in a local salt business. I didn't need to work then. But I had known about Mr Ralph Greenwood since I was a child, all the village knew of him.'

'What was he like?'

She frowned a little. 'Everyone was surprised when he

married Madam's mother. She was a young widow, with a seven year old child. He'd met her in London, apparently. I heard the gossip but didn't take much interest: I was only a child myself when he came back here with her. He had a reputation as a bit of a tartar, strong in his opinions. He must have been a hard father –' she corrected herself '– stepfather for Madam. I doubt there was much love in the man.'

'What about Miss Juliana's mother?'

'We never saw much of her in the village, miss. She was only here about two years before she died of diphtheria. And then Madam was left all alone with her stepfather for the rest of her childhood.'

She went paler still. 'I'm sorry, miss. I was forgetting Mr Greenwood was your uncle. Have I spoken out of turn?'

'Not at all, Mrs Brundish. I never knew him.'

When she had gone, I went into my bedroom and took out the crude drawing I had found in the copy of *Wuthering Heights*.

I knew who had drawn it now and what it depicted. I recognised the Leviathan from the Doom painting. And the figure it was swallowing into the jaws of hell? Could it be – though why should it be – *Juliana*?

I didn't tear the drawing up but stowed it away thoughtfully.

Twelve

By now I had managed to persuade Juliana to get up for luncheon, though she returned to her room to rest in the afternoons.

The doctor usually visited twice a week and left as cheerful as he came, unperturbed by Juliana's complaining. She would always make a great effort before his visit, needing a mirror brought to her, fussing over her hair, pouting and sighing. Outside her door I would listen to his murmured reassurances inside and, indeed, she did seem a little quieter after his visits.

The vicar came almost every evening and I would hear his solemn voice raised in prayer through her partly open door. Once I peered in and saw them both kneeling at her bedside very close together, Wissett's bony backside stuck in the air, his voice intoning sonorously. I had to turn away before a giggle escaped me but before I did so, I noticed Juliana's delicate hand creep out and cover his.

The vicar's eyes had shone with a light that I suspected was not altogether holy when he first met me.

'Another Greenwood!' he said. 'How do you do, indeed, Miss Maud?'

We were standing in the hall, for I had opened the door to him, and outside the dusk was falling as we exchanged pleasantries. In the shadows his eyes glowed with fervour. 'You are blessed with your cousin, Miss Maud,' he said. 'Truly a woman of faith! I hope you are one also?'

I muttered something, which he took to be assent.

'That is right, my child.' He was a youngish man, too young for me to be any child of his. His eyes flicked over my mourning dress and he shook his head sadly. 'You are familiar with death. Your faith will sustain you whatever befalls you in this house.'

'What do you mean, sir?' I said, startled.

'Why, that your poor cousin has not long to live. We pray together for her soul in the life to come. I think she takes great succour from our sessions.' His eyes gleamed again. 'Perhaps you would like to join us in prayer tonight?'

I felt instinctively that Juliana wanted the Reverend Wissett to herself, so I shook my head politely.

I could not persuade Juliana to let more light and air into her room, or any of the others downstairs. The ground floor seemed in permanent shadow, the passages a dark twisty maze between candlelit rooms. When at luncheon a single shaft of weak sunlight pierced one of the long dining room windows inadvertently left uncovered by Dorcas, she demanded that the curtains be drawn immediately. 'It makes my head ache so!'

I obeyed reluctantly. As I sat down again, as if sensing a tiny rebellion on my part, she looked at me plaintively across the array of glass and silver, their glitter now dulled in the gloom. 'You must be very bored here,' she said in a sad little voice, 'with only an old woman for company.'

'You are not old, Juliana! Besides, I am happy to be settled and have a quiet life with you.'

'You are a good girl,' she said unexpectedly, and my heart warmed.

She looked up at the portraits, the faces of my ancestors hardly discernible on the shadowed walls. 'One day soon all this will be yours,' she said, in a matter of fact way. 'The house and everything in it.'

I laid down my fork in shock. Such a surge of emotion went through me I could not speak. *I need never be a governess again*!

'As the only surviving Greenwood, all my money will come to you when I die.' She stared at me a trifle impatiently. 'What do you say, Maud? Does the prospect not make you happy?'

'Of course,' I stammered. 'It is only that – I do not wish you to die yet, Juliana!'

She looked pleased, then changed her expression to one of resigned suffering. 'I am prepared for it.'

'Don't say such a thing! Why, your health is much improved lately!'

'My spirits, perhaps.'

'Is there no one else to whom you should leave your money?' I said, wanting to make sure.

'No one. It is right that it should go to you.' She waved her hand dismissively. 'Come, let us change the subject. It is vulgar to talk of money, especially at table.'

I couldn't quite believe my good fortune. I went about my tasks, feeling light as air.

I knew I was useful to Juliana, of course. I had begun to write her letters for her, for she said that she had never had a good hand.

'But I thought your writing very clear when you wrote to me.'

'It is too fatiguing for me now,' she said irritably.

The inside of her bureau was the untidiest I had ever seen when I first opened it in search of writing paper: a jumble of letters; envelopes stuffed into pigeon holes and spilling out, containing bills, perhaps, with the sender's name written upon them in Juliana's hand.

One of them had John Shawcross's name on the top. I held the envelope for a moment, thinking that his fingers had held it, too.

Juliana was always pleased when I finished writing a letter for her, and one morning I plucked up my courage. The level of my sleeping draught was low. Soon I would run out.

'I wonder, Juliana,' I said, 'if I might beg you for a little money?'

'Money?' She stared at me in astonishment, as if I had asked for the most extraordinary thing. 'You have an annuity, have you not?'

I sensed suddenly that this was not going to be easy. 'It is very small and all gone on my lodgings and then my train fare here.'

'My dear girl, you are at Windward House with me now. There is no need for money. You have everything you want, surely?'

'Yes, and I am grateful but—'

'You are not here as a paid servant,' she said, her expression disdainful. 'I offered you a home, not a salaried position. We cannot start conducting a business transaction between us! You must learn to be more careful of money, Maud.'

'I only ask for a few pence,' I said desperately.

Juliana was lying in bed, but at this she raised herself off the pillows. 'When soon you will have my entire fortune in your hands! Can you not wait? Am I to be robbed even as I lie dying?'

This reaction was so unexpected, so out of proportion, that I was dumbfounded for a moment.

'I am sorry, Juliana. Of course I have everything I want. There is nothing else.'

'Is there not?' She lay back on her pillows with a thump and eyed me suspiciously.

I gazed back at her, half mesmerised by those sharp blue eyes. I knew that if I told her I needed laudanum at night to help me sleep, she would complain that my sleep would be too heavy to hear her stick bang upon my floorboards. So I sat silent and uncomfortable.

'Why do you want money?' she snapped out. 'What will you spend it on?'

I shook my head. I could feel a lump beginning to rise in my throat at her probing looks and my own disappointment.

'Drink!' she exclaimed at last, as if she had reached the conclusion she was seeking. 'You want it for drink! Your father drank and you have inherited that terrible trait.'

I was bewildered, stunned. I thought she could not know what she was saying.

A triumphant gleam came into her narrowed eyes. Her mouth puckered with spite. 'You did not realise?'

I shook my head. It upset me that she should say such a thing, with so much malice, as if she wanted to hurt me.

'Why do you think my stepfather, your uncle, left this house and his money to me and not to his own brother?' she demanded. 'Because your father was a drunkard! He would have spent all the inheritance on drink. He drank away any money he had. In the end it was the death of him.'

I began to tremble. 'He died of overwork, of a heart attack. It was my fault. He died trying to pay my school fees because he wished me to make a good marriage.'

'He did not drink in front of you, perhaps. He was careful, as all addicts are.'

I dared not argue. I didn't want to lose my new security by crossing her. But I could trust her no longer. Something shifted in our relationship then and in my perception of her and I think she knew it, for her face changed. She was all prettiness and daintiness again, sighing heavily.

'Poor little Maud. What a beast I am to tell you such a thing! I didn't realise you knew nothing. All these years, the terrible silence between the brothers. I am afraid Ralph disowned your father, wanted nothing to do with him. When Ralph died you must have wondered why the money didn't come to your father.'

'I was only a child then,' I said stiffly; I was cold as a stone.

'I am sorry for what I said, Maud. Come.'

She patted the bed beside her invitingly and held out her arms. Now she had realised what hurt she had caused me and wanted to make it up. But nothing could ever heal the wound she had inflicted.

'Don't be cross,' she said in a small, pathetic voice. 'Come and sit with me.'

I shook my head. 'Now the letter writing is done, I believe I shall go to my room for a while.'

I walked out unsteadily, leaving her staring after me.

I lay on my bed, pulling the bedclothes around me, and tried to get warm, tried to comfort myself. I was filled with a painful doubt.

A picture had slipped into my mind that I had hidden away for so long that I had forgotten it entirely until Juliana's cruel words brought it back.

A twelve-year-old girl, awoken by a terrible, anguished weeping, deep in the night. It is coming from downstairs.

Half-asleep, she tiptoes out in her nightgown to the landing and, looking down into the hall in disbelief, sees it is her beloved father, lying sprawled face-down on the black and white tiles and sobbing – sobbing as if his heart would break. There is an empty bottle clutched in his hand.

There is no worse sound in the world than a grown man weeping, especially if you are a child and that man is your own brave, strong papa.

I did not think about the significance of the bottle at the time; I was too young. Besides, soon after – or perhaps just before – Mama became ill and the whole household was taken up with that, especially me, for it was I who nursed her.

I never saw Papa with a bottle in his hand again, never saw him drunk or indeed taking a single drink in front of me, except on social occasions.

But he spent long hours alone in his study, working – or grieving – so I thought. Had he been drinking steadily throughout my childhood, a habit that grew worse during the long dark evenings of Mama's illness?

Oh, cruel, cruel Juliana, to make me doubt my own father!

I lay numbly on my bed and a creeping fear took hold of my mind. Perhaps Juliana was right and I too would be tempted to drink. What if such an addiction were inherited? Might it lie sleeping in the blood until something – some terrible event or sequence of events – awoke and enraged it?

It troubled me greatly that Juliana should behave to me in such a way, as if she had suddenly revealed a hidden and very nasty part of herself. I could not forget the venom with which she had spoken and so I became wary of her.

As if she sensed my withdrawal, she became a model patient – amenable, charming, affectionate in her manner towards me. For a while our roles seemed reversed.

Her winning ways eventually disarmed me. I so much

wanted things between us to be the way they had been; she was the only person I had.

I didn't raise the subject of money again.

However, soon I would have to obtain more of my sleeping draught, for the images that haunted me at night were worse than ever.

The Creams live in Kensington, a good address. I am to teach little Lizzy only, for the Cream boys go away to school.

They are big boys, both taller than me.

They stare at me as I am introduced, and then at each other, and their eyes gleam.

I know they plan wickedness.

Thirteen

John

Maud Greenwood has not returned to St Mark's. I work in a lacklustre fashion, waiting for a soft footfall that never comes.

Outside the blackthorn blooms, white blossom dazzling against the dark thorns, taunting me with the joyful lushness of spring as I cross over the heath.

I see her again when I am least expecting it.

The restoration of the Doom always causes a certain amount of curiosity every Sunday after the church service, and I am forced to attend to protect it from so many poking fingers.

This Sunday I have taken my seat in a back pew, so that if I doze off during the Reverend Wissett's interminable sermon it will not be noticed, when a figure brushes by.

It is Juliana Greenwood.

She is walking slowly, one hand to her throat, supported

on her other side by Maud, who doesn't see me. They continue at a stately pace up the aisle: Juliana, head erect, looking neither left nor right, apparently unaware of the stir she is causing among the congregation; Maud, her back rigid as faces peer round at them.

A harsh whispering starts.

The strange dark murmuring grows as they advance towards the front pew, and doesn't stop even after they have sat down. Then Juliana makes a great show of kneeling to pray, showing all the watchers what an effort it is for her, invalid as she is, to crouch so low. Maud kneels at her side, one hand supporting Juliana's back. Only then do the whispers die away.

Then Tiggins comes in, pulling Sly behind him on a rope that he has fastened to one of Sly's hands. Faithful Tiggins persists in bringing Sly to church each Sunday, hoping perhaps that during the service another miracle will take place in Rending and God will grant Sly intelligence and the gift of speech.

Tiggins's mild face is set and fierce; he ignores the stares. Sly's eyes roll in his head. His leg drags across the stone flags. He stares at the cross on the altar, at the Doom painting visible behind the pillars, at the people gaping at him; and his tongue lolls in his mouth.

No sooner has Tiggins looked about for somewhere to sit, than Sly collapses, falls flat, almost pulls his protector over. The whites of his eyes are visible. Foam bubbles from his mouth.

Groans and shrieks erupt from the congregation, as if people have been waiting for this moment.

In the front pew Maud turns, puts her hand to her mouth. I think I hear her cry out but it is, perhaps, my imagination.

Wissett and I help Tiggins with Sly, dragging him to the door, for he is still not fully conscious. We leave poor Tiggins alone with him outside while he recovers – as he will do shortly, for I have seen the fit take him before.

All this, alas, does not shorten Wissett's service by as little as five minutes.

I hardly hear a word Wissett says, I am too busy watching Maud.

She keeps her head dipped, as if she is fearful of meeting the vicar's burning eye: his habit is to stride back and forth along the front pew, addressing his words as if personally to each individual sitting there. A tendril of dark hair beneath her bonnet lifts in the draught from Wissett's billowing cassock.

After the service Wissett comes in a rush to take Juliana's hand and help her from the pew with a gallant flourish. She thanks him with a flash of her eyes and a smile. Maud hangs back, a little moth in her dark clothes.

Then her eyes meet mine and widen. A small uncertain

smile steals across her features. It gives me courage.

I walk forward. 'Miss Greenwood,' I say to Juliana. 'I am delighted to see you in good health again.'

'Mr Shawcross, how kind! I am a little improved, it is true.' She puts a hand in a kid glove to her throat, then turns to Maud as if she has suddenly recalled her presence. 'You have not met my cousin, Miss Maud Greenwood.'

'Ah, but we have met before,' I say, smiling.

Juliana whips round to Maud. 'You did not tell me!'

Maud looks startled. 'It slipped my mind, Juliana.'

'I am sure your cousin has had many new things to think about since arriving here,' I say lightly.

Wissett doesn't sense the sudden tension. 'So now we have two Miss Greenwoods, Mr Shawcross. Is that not delightful?'

I agree it is, though seeing Juliana still glowering, the words stick in my throat. 'While you are here, you must see my progress on the Doom,' I say, and thankfully she is distracted.

'Yes, indeed. That is why I am here.' She glances at Wissett. 'That, and to give thanks for my recent recovery, of course.'

'I believe it is you and not the Almighty who has wrought this wondrous change in her health!' I mutter to Maud, as we process slowly behind Juliana and the vicar towards the corner where I work. Maud smiles at my remark and Juliana, turning, catches that smile.

'Mr Shawcross! You must explain your latest work to me.'

She takes my arm and leans on me as we reach the painting, then asks endless questions, exclaiming over each jar of pigment. Her face and body are very close, making me feel hot and embarrassed.

The vicar is bidding his flock farewell at the door and the three of us are left together.

'You have done well since your return, Mr Shawcross,' Juliana says. She releases my arm at last. 'Maud, we should leave. It is almost time for luncheon.'

I look despairingly at Maud, willing my glance to say all that I long to convey; and she looks back at me. I think that perhaps we gaze at each other a little too long, for Juliana says brusquely. 'Take my arm, Maud. You know I cannot walk alone.'

And then, without a farewell, Juliana turns her back on me.

Maud

Juliana was in one of her moods on the journey back to Windward House. 'Why didn't you tell me you had met Mr

Shawcross?' she demanded, as the carriage jolted along. 'I like to know such things. Please tell me in future.'

I looked at her in bewilderment. 'You wish me to tell you each time I meet Mr Shawcross?'

'I do not want you to meet Mr Shawcross at all. Of course, it is different if by chance you encounter each other in the village street, when of course you may bid him good day. But I don't want you to seek him out, or accept his attentions.'

'But why, Juliana?'

She spoke gently and patiently.

'My dear, on my death you will come into a good deal of money and a fine house. You will become an excellent catch. John Shawcross is useful to me now, but afterwards—' She spread her hands and made a little face '—he will go back to being a penniless artist. You can do better than that. One day you will have your pick of husbands and since you will not want for financial security, you may take your time over choosing.'

I felt the colour rise in my cheeks. 'I was not thinking of – why, I scarcely know Mr Shawcross!'

'Then you will not mind cutting short your brief acquaintance.' Juliana patted my knee. 'I am only giving you advice as an older, wiser, woman.'

I bit my lip. Her tone was so reasonable.

She looked into my face searchingly. 'I care about you,

Maud. I don't want you to make any mistakes. If I find out that you have gone against my wishes, I shall be most upset. You do understand that, don't you?'

The implication was plain. *If you see John Shawcross in future, then you will not inherit my money.*

That night I lay in bed, dwelling wistfully on John Shawcross. I had decided I could not risk seeing him again.

When I did sleep, my sleep was shallow. Anxious about the low level in my bottle, I had taken too little laudanum.

Blood seeps from under my pillow.

When I lift it, the glazed eye of a dead rat stares at me.

I scream, I cannot help it.

I hear the Cream boys' laughter outside my door.

I wash and wash the bedding but cannot remove the stains.

I have to sleep in damp, bloody sheets.

I woke in the pitch dark. Something had roused me, a sound outside my door. I thought I heard breathing.

I lay stiffly, not moving, my eyes staring into blackness, every sense straining.

Silence.

Then a soft, dragging noise that moved slowly away from my door.

* * *

‘Sly?’ said Miss Potton the next morning. ‘He’s not allowed upstairs. Besides, the house is locked at night. I lock it myself!’ She looked outraged, as if I were questioning her competence.

‘I only wondered,’ I said meekly, ‘if somehow he might have entered. I am sure it was Sly I heard.’

‘A dream,’ she said firmly. ‘You have plenty of those, don’t you, Miss Maud?’ I felt myself flush and she looked at me closely. ‘I wonder what it is that troubles you so.’

She has heard me moan and cry out, I thought in shame.

She must have forgotten to lock the house up properly that night. I resolved to check the locks myself secretly from now on, from front door to back. Miss Potton went early to bed, so it would not be too great a task.

The following night Dorcas was already on her pallet in the kitchen and Juliana had had her hot drink and was quiet, when I satisfied myself that every outside door was bolted. I went to bed, reassured.

But still I did not sleep.

Fourteen

Juliana was short of Mr Quilter's Restorative Powder.

I offered to go into Rending while she took her afternoon nap and she agreed. I took a new novel for Edie with me – Dickens's *The Pickwick Papers* – in case she had finished *Wuthering Heights* by now, and protected it with a napkin in my basket.

I looked about warily as I walked over the heath but saw no sign of Sly. After my fright that first day, Mr Tiggins had kept him at close quarters in the garden and I had heard nothing more at night since checking the locks myself.

Around the village pond the green heads of cow parsley were massing, not yet turned to white lace by the spring sunshine. The blacksmith, leading a horse into the forge, nodded to me as I passed. The air was fresh, sweetening the stench from the sewer in the street.

I heard Quilter moving about in the back dispensing room as I entered the apothecary. More light was coming in today and Edie was writing labels in the beams. Black ink stained her fingers and her face was screwed up as her hand moved laboriously across the paper. Her letters were smudged and tumbling into each other; her writing was still very childish.

'Miss Maud!' She lowered her voice. 'I must thank you for the book.'

'I have brought you another, Edie.' I produced it from my basket. 'Have you finished the other?'

She nodded and took the book eagerly, stowing it away beneath the counter. She glanced back over her shoulder. 'If you come tomorrow, he'll not be here and I'll give it back to you.'

'I am sorry I didn't speak to you the other day, Edie.'

She looked at me, startled.

'In the churchyard.'

Her glance slid away. 'Not me, Miss Maud.'

I knew she was lying and was puzzled.

The next day I returned to Quilter's while Juliana was sleeping in the afternoon.

In my basket beneath the napkin was the bottle of my sleeping draught, now almost empty. I was beginning to be desperate about renewing my supply and wondered if I might somehow persuade Edie to give me more.

She was alone, still writing labels.

'It is so difficult, Miss Maud,' she complained. 'Mr Quilter wants some of the labels on the bottles redone. I'm doing those as well as the prescriptions, but they are harder. I have to write the formulae and I get the letters wrong and have to start again. I've had no time for reading at work recently.'

'There is no need for me to return to Windward House yet. Let me help you.'

'Oh, I could never do that,' she said, but she looked tempted.

'It will take no time if we do it together. Is there another pen?'

'In the back room. I shouldn't let you, though. What would Mr Quilter say?'

'He will be delighted to see the work done, I am sure,' I said, and stepped through into the other room.

It was much darker in there, for there was no window and no candle burning. I glanced about swiftly.

A shelf of empty bottles and jars waiting to be filled; a sink crammed with black, earthy roots; a chair drawn to a table laden with papers. They were scrawled over with chemical formulae, a pen and inkwell beside them.

I looked up and saw a bunch of keys hanging from a hook. A cupboard was fixed to the far wall and a key stuck out from the lock.

The poison cupboard. That is where Quilter keeps his drugs, I thought. That is where he stores his supply of laudanum.

I could turn that key quickly and help myself.

The thought entered my head so easily that I was appalled and ashamed. It was as if someone else had put it there.

Edie was suddenly behind me. 'There's a pen on the table, Miss Maud. I should have come through myself.'

'I didn't see it in the dark.'

She gave me a curious glance, but soon we were both settled at the counter.

She admired my copperplate. So elegant. She wanted to know all about my school, Miss Caseborne's Seminary for Young Ladies, where I had learned it.

'I had to leave after my father's death,' I said.

Her face was full of pity. 'You still wear mourning dress.'

'It is old and worn now,' I said ruefully.

'Doesn't Miss Greenwood buy you clothes?'

'Perhaps she will do so when she recovers her health.'

She gave me a strange look. 'I am sorry for you, Miss Maud!' she burst out. 'All alone up there in that great big house at night, with an invalid for company and an old man and a lunatic in the garden!'

I tried to smile. 'I have Miss Potton and Dorcas.'

'My mother says that everything there will be very different when Miss Greenwood dies and you—' She put her hand over her mouth.

But I knew what Edie was going to say: 'And you are mistress of Windward House.'

* * *

I was unable to ask Edie for more laudanum that day, for she remembered Quilter was returning at three and hurried me out.

I was in despair as I returned over the heath to Windward House.

At night memories haunted me; I couldn't call them nightmares, for I was not asleep but in a half-awake trance in which horrid visions floated before my staring eyes.

That night I dreamed of Basil Cream.

We are locked in the nursery cupboard, little Lizzy Cream and me. It is dark and stifling. She is crying.

It had begun with a game of hide-and-seek.

The two Cream boys suggested it. It was a wet day and Lizzy was bored. She had wanted to play.

She pulls me into the cupboard with her, to hide. It is very quiet and airless and after a while we try to get out, but the key has been turned in the lock on the other side of the door. I shout and beat my hands against it.

Then at last we hear the boys come into the room.

'You must kiss me, Maud,' Basil Cream calls out. 'I will unlock the cupboard if you promise to kiss me.'

I picked the next time to visit Edie carefully. I went on a Thursday, when Edie told me Quilter worked in his physic garden, and again I took my thick brown bottle hidden beneath the napkin in my basket.

I laid the basket on the floor behind the counter. The top was almost covered with packages of Quilter's Restorative Powder, neatly laid out in rows. Each was to be labelled with the customer's name and Edie was doing this from a list in the register. It was evident that they could hardly keep up with demand.

I glanced into the back room as I entered, but could not see if the key was still in the lock of the poison cupboard. I thought, perhaps today I will be able to persuade Edie of my desperate need and she will take pity on me.

She was delighted to have my help again. I said I would finish her labels for her, and so I set to work. While I wrote and she ground herbs with her pestle, we talked a little. She confided her worries about her mother's health.

'The Restorative Powders make no difference. She gets so tired and breathless.'

'What does the doctor say?' I said sympathetically, for I liked Mrs Brundish.

'Doctor? We cannot afford the doctor!'

For a while we worked in silence. Then I laid down the pen.

'Edie,' I said, in a tone that was solemn enough to make her look up from her grinding. 'Might I ask you something?' I paused, hoping no one would come into the shop to interrupt.

She nodded, surprised.

'If a person suffers dreadful dreams of their past, bad enough to make them terrified to lay their head on the pillow, bad enough to drive them mad, what does Mr Quilter prescribe?'

'Why, laudanum. He sells a lot of it in the shop. It cures all manner of ailments, including sleeplessness.'

'But if that person has no money at all and is in desperate need?' I fixed my eyes on her face. 'Truly desperate need, Edie?'

Even in the half-light of the shop I could see she had gone a little pink. 'Is that person you, Miss Maud?'

I seized her hand. 'I don't know what to do, Edie! I am almost out of my sleeping draught.'

'Can't you ask Miss Greenwood for money?'

I shook my head. I felt tears prick my eyes.

She looked troubled. 'I can't give it to you. What would Mr Quilter say?'

'He need not know.'

'It wouldn't be right.'

I took a deep breath. I hated what I was about to do. 'Is it right that I have been writing labels for you for no payment?'

She went a brighter pink. 'I thought it was to help me.'

'It is, indeed, but there must be give and take on both sides, must there not?'

'It doesn't make stealing right, though.'

I wanted to fall on my knees and beg, to such a pass had I come. '*Please, Edie, for mercy's sake, give me more laudanum*!'

But she was unaware of my torment as she sat prudish at the counter, fiddling with the brass scale and pursing her lips at my low morals.

I steadied myself. I was ashamed of what I was about to do, but do it I must. There was no other way.

'You talk of right, Edie. You know I caught your mother in my sitting room?'

She stopped jiggling the scale, startled.

'She was looking for *Wuthering Heights* to give to you. Is reading my cousin's novels without her permission right?'

'No, but—'

'This wasn't right either, was it?' and I reached down to my basket and found her drawing where I had hidden it before I set out. I held it out to her. 'What would Miss Greenwood say if she knew her cook's daughter had drawn this? It shows her being devoured by the jaws of hell!'

She gazed at me, aghast. 'Don't get my mother in trouble because of me, I beg you!'

'There is no need,' I said gently. 'Listen, Edie. I have helped you with these labels. Now I need your help.'

She seemed at a loss, anxious yet stubborn. I put my head in my hands.

'If you don't help me,' I said brokenly, 'then I don't know what I shall do, for I am tortured by nightmares. I cannot go on!'

I didn't need to act; I thought I might weep.

She hesitated, then put her strong arm around me and held me to her. It was strangely comforting. 'There, Miss Maud, there,' she said, as if to a small child. 'Don't fret. I will help you.'

So in the end it was easy.

Fifteen

Windward House grew suffocating. In three months I had not ventured further afield and found the sea.

When I stood outside the gates of the house and looked down over the slope, I could see the sea in a dark blurred band across the horizon, behind the forest of pine and birch. It could not be so very far away. After all, Mrs Brundish lived somewhere on the shore and walked up through the trees to Windward House every day.

I resolved to ask her.

One fine afternoon in May, when Juliana was taking her afternoon nap, I went into the kitchen. By this time the two maids whose names I never knew had vanished back to their homes in Rending, dismissed by Juliana. Miss Potton remained, of course, superior but lazy – she thought the daily tally of the storeroom beneath her and so we were always short of supplies – and Mrs Brundish and Dorcas.

With fewer staff, the standards of the house had slipped. The silver needed cleaning, the floors polishing. To pass the time I should have been glad to help Dorcas but I knew Juliana would be appalled.

Today Mrs Brundish was scrubbing saucepans at the sink, her sleeves rolled to the elbows over thin forearms that were mottled red with the heat of the water, and Dorcas was wheeling in the trolley from the dining room laden with our luncheon dishes. Miss Potton was up in her room, pretending to see to the household accounts, but in truth asleep.

I looked around in concern. 'You need a new kitchen maid, Mrs Brundish.'

'That would be a fine thing, indeed,' she said wistfully.

Dorcas snorted. 'Just us two now doing all the work round here, same as usual, eh, Mrs B?'

'Dorcas!' Mrs Brundish said, frowning at her. 'Is there something we can do for you, miss?'

I told her and she gave me directions. 'Follow the track all the way and when you come out of the trees, you'll see duckboards going left and right. It's marshy there, so you need to stay on them. They'll take you to the sand dunes and the sea, which ever way you turn.'

My heart began to thrill.

Dorcas had emptied the trolley and returned to the dining room for the glasses. I thanked Mrs Brundish and turned to go, but I heard her say behind me, 'If you don't mind, Miss Maud, there's something Edie wanted me to give you.'

She went to the sideboard and took *The Pickwick Papers* from a drawer.

'Thank you. I'll find her another.'

'She doesn't want another one, Miss Maud. She told me to tell you. Don't ask me why, when she loves them so.'

My hurt at Edie's rebuff was tinged with shame at my own behaviour. But for the last few nights with the help of more laudanum, I had slept without dreaming.

I set off straight away, once I had laced up my boots and put on my bonnet and shawl. There was warmth in the sun now; I didn't need my mantle.

The slope to the trees was gradual, the track clearly marked and wide enough for foresters' carts carrying timber. The sand was silvery-grey underfoot. A lark sang high above the mewling of seagulls and pheasants ran away with alarmed croaks as I walked down. Tiny new ferns curled up from sunlit turf, red with sorrel.

My limbs, cramped and heavy with sitting in hard, high-backed chairs to read to Juliana, or bending endlessly to plump up her pillows and smooth her sheets, began to stretch, to feel loose and airy and young again. I strode on, energy flooding my bones, wanting to run.

The track led into the forest. The sun patched the ground beneath my feet with bright light. It became bumpy with pine cones and there were sandy holes filled with brown needles and dry leaves. The trunks of the pine trees formed long empty aisles either side of me.

The bird song died. I was beginning to wonder how far it was to the sea when ahead of me the trees thinned and the light grew brighter.

A pathway of wooden boards, fringed by reeds, stretched in both directions.

I stood in sunlight, unsure which way to go. Mrs Brundish had said either direction would take me to the sea, so I chose to walk to the left.

The reeds grew high as my head, so I could not see where I was going. There were pools of still black water each side of the duckboards. The sun was hot on the back of my neck where it wasn't shaded by my bonnet and I took off my shawl and carried it over my arm.

As I walked, my boots made a curious thudding sound as they hit the wooden boards and the sound echoed, so that I imagined someone was following and kept turning to stare behind me. But there was only the smooth pathway of wood between the gently waving reeds.

Before I had gone very far, the reeds thinned and scrub took their place, growing in the shadow of sandy hillocks topped with coarse grass. I knew I was almost at the sea and I stepped off the duckboards.

My parents had once taken me on a train trip to Brighton

when I was small, but this was not a popular seashore of sand and donkeys and a pier. This shore was largely shingle, banded only at the water's edge with sand, and there was no one there save me, and a few gulls who took off with harsh, startled cries. The breeze was fresh, pushing beneath my bonnet and cooling my hot face.

The sea was wilder and faster than the sea I remembered at Brighton. Long dark blue waves topped with brilliant white foam chased up over the stones. The stones themselves were not a uniform grey but made up of a myriad of beautiful colours, shining in the sun.

I sat down in the dip of a dune to empty my boots. I unbuttoned them and wriggled my toes in their white woollen stockings. Out of the wind it was very warm.

I stretched out my legs and lay back, and the sand supported and held me.

I was not certain how long I lay asleep.

Something woke me, as if a shadow had passed across my face. When I opened my eyes the sun had gone in and the world had turned grey. It must have been the cold that had woken me, or the sand which had turned hard and damp beneath my back.

I sat up in alarm. Juliana would be wondering where I was. I feared displeasing her; her temperament was so unpredictable.

I buttoned my boots hastily and stood up, brushing loose sand from my skirts. The stones were drained of colour now and the sea, shadowed and darkened by clouds, looked ominous and threatening as it surged up the shore. A chill wind buffeted the tussocks of grass on the dunes.

I began to trudge towards the duckboards. The sand seemed heavy and cloying.

Then above the rustle of the moving grass and the hiss of the waves, I heard a booming sound. Someone was coming along the boards. A heavy tread: a man's footsteps.

At once I knew it was Sly. He was hunting me – haunting me – and I couldn't escape him.

I crouched down low in the dunes. Sure enough, now I could see the dark rounded shape of his head in its skull cap above the reeds, and then though a gap, though indistinct in the dull light, the whole of his contorted body angled forward, seeming to move with inhuman speed. I thought I could even hear the strangulated gurgle that he made.

I was trapped in the dunes, their walls closing in around me, their sand weighing down the folds of my skirts, clogging the soles of my boots. With a moan I began to edge backwards, towards the shingle. On the beach I would be able to move faster. If he came after me, I would see him.

Crouching low, I began to run clumsily, slipping and sliding over the shingle. I had to reach the sand at the sea's edge where the going would be firmer.

I lifted my skirts higher so I wouldn't trip. My breath was coming in gasps of fright which I couldn't hear above the thud of the breaking sea.

Oh, God, rescue me! But why should He rescue a sinner?

The wind tore tears from my eyes as I slithered down a steep bank of stones pushed up by the tide, and on to the flat stretch of beach.

When I blinked them away and looked back, I saw to my horror that Sly had left the walkway and was passing through the dunes, leaping from tussock to tussock in spite of his twisted leg, his figure blurred in the poor light.

My heart was pounding as I reached the sand. I could run no more. I began to walk swiftly along the water's edge, the wet sand giving beneath my boots. When I looked back again the spectral figure was moving over the shingle as if lifted by the air.

I increased my speed. It had reached the shore line now. It scuttled after me with Sly's characteristic jerky motion, half bent to the sand, shadowy limbs spread out like a crab.

I had a picture in my mind. Two figures chasing along that great lonely length of shore, one, a nightmare creature – a devil – gaining inexorably on the other, which was me, tiny and lost. When I looked back, the creature had slowed too. Its dragging leg left grooves in the sand. I thought I could even glimpse indistinctly a swiftly rotating tail.

Horror caught in my throat.

I turned abruptly and headed for the dunes again. If I could reach the duckboards, I could escape into the trees.

I dragged myself up the shingle bank. My feet slipped down in an avalanche of stones. I was mired in them. But fired by panic and revulsion I reached the top somehow and staggered through the dunes with my last breath.

I fell to my knees, crawled like an animal. I reached out blindly. On either side, coarse vegetation. The ground was soft under my boots, under my hands. I began to sink. The water oozed around my skirts, black, stagnant, evil smelling. Mud caught me, held my legs. There was a sucking sound as I wrenched my hands free of the filth. Unbalanced, I toppled forward, half drowned in water.

And then, like a miracle, my fingertips touched wood. It was the edge of the boards.

But he was there behind me, coming back, with his booming tread.

Sixteen

A man's voice, raised, anxious. 'Miss Greenwood? My God, Miss Greenwood, did you fall?'

The next moment I was half pulled, half carried out of the marsh water, and laid tenderly on the boards. I opened my eyes and looked into the alarmed face of John Shawcross.

'Did you lose your balance? Are you hurt?'

I struggled to sit up against his supporting arm and shook my head dumbly. My eyes flicked around, searching. There was only the overcast sky above me and in the midst of it, John Shawcross's head. That was all I could see from my inelegant position.

'Sly,' I whispered. 'Sly was following me.'

'Sly?' He looked puzzled. 'He is with Mr Tiggins, or was when I passed Windward House a short while ago. They were in the front garden together.'

'How can that be?' I said weakly. 'Sly has been pursuing me this past quarter of an hour!'

'I've seen no sign of him. I was on my way to Marsh End

when I saw you half in the ditch.'

I began to shake violently.

'Your shawl is all muddied. Take my coat.'

'Let me stand up and see for myself that he has gone.'

He put his arm under mine and helped me up. I gazed back at the darkening shoreline, at the dunes where I had felt so trapped. There was no sign of any movement.

I shuddered. 'Perhaps he is hiding.'

'He will not bother us now I am with you. Come, let me take you to Marsh End. You must get dry and warm. I will ask Tiggins to bring the trap to the lane to fetch you. It will be dusk soon.'

I let John take my arm and support me. I was thankful not to have to traipse back to Windward House through the twilight, perhaps losing myself among the trees as darkness fell.

We made halting progress along the walkway in the half light. John talked of this and that, trying to cheer me, I think – to wipe the spectre of that creeping figure from my mind.

I began to weep silently, tears coursing down my face. I was filled with shame at my wet skirts clinging to my legs, for I had not worn my hoop that day; at my mourning clothes ruined. They were all that I had, save for my Sunday best. Even my shawl stank; I would never be able to wash it clean.

John Shawcross, gentleman that he was, affected not to notice.

'Don't mention to Mrs Brundish that Sly frightened me,' I said, as we saw the dark shape of a thatched roof and below it a candlelit window. 'I cannot be sure.'

I felt his reassuring pressure on my arm as we passed a collection of hen coops and heard a sleepy clucking from within. 'I will say nothing. No doubt it was a trick of the light. This whole area is full of them. I have been taken in myself.'

Mrs Brundish looked startled by our appearance through the back door, as well she might. She was leaning back in a rocking chair by the fire as we entered. Edie was bringing her a bowl of something hot, for I could see it steam, but she halted midway to her mother.

It was a humble cottage, though warm and cosy, with gleaming copper hanging over the fireplace and candles shining from alcoves in the thick walls.

There were exclamations and explanations. I had missed my footing stepping from the walkway to the dunes, said John, and fallen into the mire.

I was given Mrs Brundish's chair, though I protested. By this time she had banished Mr Shawcross and prised my filthy skirts and shawl from me, hung them on a clothes horse before the fire and wrapped a rug around my legs. The bowl of soup that Edie had been about to give her was given to me instead, taken out of Edie's reluctant hands by her mother.

I hoped I had not taken Mrs Brundish's supper from her. She shook her head, smiling. I stammered my thanks and sipped the soup gratefully.

'Mother, you were resting,' protested Edie. She turned to me, almost accusingly. 'She was late returning from Windward House.'

'Hush, child,' said Mrs Brundish. 'That was not Miss Maud's fault.'

Then I was left alone and fell into a half doze.

Eventually I was roused by the sound of the pony and trap outside. John Shawcross had already been to fetch Tiggins and ridden back in the trap.

He came in and knelt at my side. 'Do you feel recovered enough to return to Windward House?'

I thought of poor Mrs Brundish and felt a fraud. 'A rest has quite put me to rights. I mustn't take advantage of the kindness here any longer.'

But I thought of the house of shadows that awaited me and was chilled.

John saw my expression and laid his hand on mine. It was a workmanlike hand, strong, square, one of the fingers tipped with a trace of red paint but otherwise very clean, whereas my own was grimy with dry mud.

'I should like to know how you fare,' he said quietly. 'Would you consider visiting me at St Mark's again?'

His hand was warm and firm on mine. I smiled suddenly. 'Yes, indeed, John. I will do that.'

I did not tell him what Juliana had said.

At that moment Edie came in through the half open door. John had his back to her and didn't see her, but Edie saw him kneeling before me, clasping my hand, and she must have heard our low, fervent voices, the warmth of our tone, even if not what had been said.

She looked at me and I looked at her, and I knew instantly that she was in love with him, but that it was a secret love and he did not know. Her expression changed in that moment from one of pain and jealousy to intense dislike.

How could I tell in the meagre candlelight? My senses were acute, as they only are when one is about to fall in love. I wanted to say, 'I am no rival, Edie. Think nothing of what you see, for John Shawcross means nothing to me.'

But I knew now that was not true.

Juliana's little bell rang impatiently from the front parlour as soon as I stepped into the hall. She must have heard the trap arrive outside. Dorcas had lit the lamps and Juliana was sitting in a chair before the fire, a tea tray on a table at her side. She put down her cup, stared at my ruined clothes and gave a tinkle of laughter.

I looked at her in amazement. How unpredictable she was!

'We shall take a trip into Southwold tomorrow and see about getting you material for some new dresses,' she said carelessly. 'There is a tailor in Rending who can make them up. Black is such a depressing colour and doesn't suit you. There was little to mourn, after all, in your father's death.'

I was speechless, both because of the deliberately hurtful way she talked of my father, but also because she was offering to buy me new clothes when before she had not wanted to lend me so much as a penny.

However, I was beginning to understand. She liked to control matters herself. She had to be the one to make the decisions.

I found my voice at last. 'It is kind of you to suggest it. Truly I have very little respectable left to wear.'

She was watching the little orange flames reach vainly up the chimney, as if they longed to climb out of the fire and escape. 'You had a fall this afternoon?' she murmured. 'I gather you were rescued by Mr Shawcross.'

'I am sorry, I did not mean it to happen.'

'Remember what I said, that is all.'

She turned, her eyes glinting in the firelight. 'Something

frightened you, perhaps?' She paused. 'I saw a devil on the marshes once.'

I knew she was trying to unnerve me so I would not go wandering again but stay at her side. After my ordeal I could not face a confrontation, so I said nothing and went quietly from the room.

I was alone no longer. Now I had John. He cared for me; I could see it in his eyes, those wide light eyes that could not hide their feelings.

My heart sang as I went about my duties for Juliana. For a while I even stopped resenting her stick on my floorboards at night. I spent hours drawing designs of my new dresses. John will not recognise me, I thought, I shall look so very different! I picked posies of wild flowers to cheer the dark corners of my sitting room and opened the window wide to let in the spring air.

But now I feared Sly more than ever, for I was certain he had pursued me that day by the sea.

I looked out from my bedroom window before I dressed, dreading to see his shambling figure working in the garden. Sometimes he would be alone, kneeling on the gravel paths, his great hands crawling over the damp earth, perhaps searching for worms, to squeeze the life out of them. Once I thought I saw him glance up at my window with a leer.

One morning I came into the dining room for breakfast

early. There was a thick, earthy smell lingering about the open doorway and that should have warned me.

He was crouched before the grate, arranging twigs over old copies of *The Times*. Beside him was an enormous load of logs in a basket that he must have brought in single-handed.

He had seen me. He rose to his full height, giant hands at his side, clenching and unclenching. My hand went to my throat as I took in his brute strength. His jaws moved as if he masticated on something indigestible.

I backed away and muttered, 'I have come too early. I shall return later.'

Then I fled.

Shortly after that we moved Juliana upstairs to her old bedroom, Dorcas and I between us. Miss Potton insisted we should.

There was a nest of mice in the skirting of Juliana's room downstairs. Miss Potton had gone in one afternoon to rewind the clock while Juliana had her tea in the parlour, and thought she saw them running over the bedding, over the pillows. She screeched, bringing Dorcas and me running.

It was the crumbs Madam scattered from her meals in bed, she said. That, and the bits of paper under the bed where Dorcas never swept. Dirty habits bred dirty creatures.

Juliana complained bitterly about the move but Miss Potton threatened to give notice.

Now I had Juliana next door to me.

She did not need her stick; she had a little bell, which she tinkled and tinkled in the night. At least I did not have so far to go.

I tried to cut down on my drops and the memories came back.

The two boys are home from Harrow, and Mr Cream says I must have them in the schoolroom with Lizzy in the mornings, for they are behind in their work.

I ask them to draw a map of India, Lizzy and the boys. I stand over them to appraise their work better.

Basil draws something obscene. Unspeakable.

My whole body burns with the shock of it and he smirks as if he knows.

In a fury I seize the atlas and bang it down on his head.

I went into Rending to collect my new dresses from the tailor's. I might have had them delivered but could not wait.

In the dark little fitting room I cast off my mourning clothes and put on a princess gown in pale grey wool, with a full bustled skirt but no crinoline. The freedom of it! The neat white collar flattered the shape of my face, contrasted with my dark hair. I scarcely recognised myself.

I was weighed down with packages, but joyful. I passed Thurlow's grocery and came to Dorley's, the butcher's.

Jonas Dorley must have spied me through the window. At once he was on the steps, a bucket in one hand.

'Morning, Miss Greenwood,' he called out, eyeing me in my new dress. There was a grin like Basil Cream's in his voice.

At the precise moment I walked by, he flung the contents of the bucket towards the sewer in the middle of the street. Although I stopped, some drops of thick, dark red blood – the blood of slaughtered pigs, sheep, cattle, I didn't know what – spattered my beautiful new skirts.

He had done it deliberately.

'Oops, beg pardon, Miss Greenwood.'

I would have run at him and slapped his face hard, punched him in fury, but something held me back – the thought of Juliana who relied on purchasing Dorley's meat, the conventions of society, the way women must behave with dignity and fortitude at all times.

So I ignored him. I walked on, my head held high, as if nothing had happened, as if it was quite normal to walk through the village with skirts that were spotted with animal blood.

But inside I was seething.

Seventeen

John

She came to me first at the end of May, when the white hawthorn blossom was thick as my arm and poppies flamed along the sandy lane from Marsh End.

She came to the church. She was very shy that first time and said nothing as she watched me work.

Then she began to ask questions.

Now she always comes whenever she is given purchases to make in Rending.

She no longer wears black. Out of the corner of my eye I am aware of a flash of colour in the church moving among the shadows. I look round and see her smile, her dark eyes shining, for me. I take her hands and kiss them. I dare do nothing more.

She seems content to watch me as I scoop pigment on to a glass sheet and grind it fine with the muller, then mix it with egg yolk and water to bind it.

I am restoring Saint Michael at the moment, the guide of the dead. Maud watches my quick, light strokes solemnly.

'Tempera dries so quickly that you must apply it in thin layers,' I say, beneath the mask that protects me from the pigment dust. 'Then the colour won't change over time.'

She nods, watching closely. She has told me that she enjoys painting herself. 'Put your hand over mine,' I say, on impulse. 'Then you will feel the method. It is called cross-hatching.'

I find a fresh mask for her and she puts it on, her eyes laughing at me over the top. Then her hand, tiny and very white without its glove, covers mine and we hold the long-bristled script brush together.

Her touch is as light as a butterfly's. I wonder if she can hear my heart beating. I find it difficult to breathe and am almost relieved when she lets go my hand and wanders over to marvel at my array of jars. Many only hold clear water to wash my brushes, for they must be kept perfectly clean.

She smiles as she takes off her mask. 'What a good housewife you would make!'

I lay down my brush with care; I can concentrate on painting no longer. 'You seem happier now, Maud.'

I hope she will say that *I* have made her so.

'I do believe Juliana may grow to love me a little in time. We do much together.'

I feel such pity for her then, as I see how her face glows.

'Tiggins took us to Halesworth this morning and she shopped a while. She looks well. It must be the fresh air she is getting.'

I know now that Juliana has forbidden Maud to see me, and though Maud is at pains not to tell me the reason, I know it all too well.

The bitter truth is I have no money, no prospects as a husband.

I don't wish to get Maud into trouble but I cannot stop her coming to St Mark's and nor, selfishly, do I want to.

'You do so much for her,' I say. 'Be careful.'

We sit together in a side aisle, with the echo of the past sounding silently around us. We cannot be seen immediately if someone enters the church but even so she looks behind her suddenly.

'What is it?'

'I thought I heard something.'

'Only field mice. They keep me company.'

She shifts closer. 'Do you feel very alone?' Her voice is soft.

'Not now. How could I?'

'I was alone too, and now I am not.' She looks at me, teasing. 'I wonder why that should be so.'

I catch her hand where it lies on her lap and she lets it nestle in mine. 'Once you would have pulled away,' I say. 'You were frightened of me.'

'I thought you were like other men I had met.'

'Have you met many?' I am jealous at once.

'Only those who employed me as governess to their children.' Her face darkens.

'I will never allow any man to frighten you again,' I declare, in the rash heat of my love. 'I will always protect you.' I draw her closer and she does not resist. 'I love you, Maud.'

I know that my mouth has uttered the words that are in my secret heart and have been there so long.

I wait expectantly, yearning to hear her say that she loves me too. But she does not. Something lights in her eyes for a second but then she looks down, hiding her expression. When I lift her face to mine, she pulls away.

'What is the matter, Maud?' I ask, in a frenzy of wanting.

'We should not sit so close, here in the church! It is not right.'

'We are showing our feelings for each other, that is all,' I say, dismayed. 'Is the Christian God not the god of love? I am sure He would not disapprove!'

'You are restoring the Doom and you can believe such a thing?' she says, and slides away from me.

* * *

A few days later, again she is distracted. 'What is that noise?' she whispers. I think I hear something, too, a rustle behind us.

'It must be Sly – spying on us!' she says.

We sit listening, her hand in mine.

I am prepared to chase Sly out with shouts and curses, but as I look around I see only the rows of empty pews and the wide spaces between the arches where particles of dust dance in the light to a silent tune.

'I heard something,' she says, in a low voice. 'I am certain I did.' But now she looks unsure.

Another day we sit in silence. She looks fatigued and strained.

'Nothing will part us now, will it?'

I look intently into her eyes. 'Nothing.'

Tears glisten there. 'Forgive me, John. I am not good company today.'

'Did Juliana call for you last night?'

'Not that – I had a bad dream.'

She gives a shudder and tentatively I take her hand. It lies slackly in mine.

'Oh, John, do you believe in hell?'

'You know I am a non-believer. I cannot accept that there is a place where the soul is tormented. Hell is a state of mind, that is all.'

'Then I shall be for ever in that dark and isolated state, for I am guilty!'

'My dearest Maud, why should you be guilty?'

She loosens her hand from mine. Her face is very white in the gloom.

'Shall I tell you, John?'

'You may tell me anything, my dearest.'

She puts her face in her hands. 'You will not love me any more.'

'I will always love you, no matter what,' I say steadily. 'It cannot be so bad, surely?'

She looks up and takes a deep breath. 'You know I have told you I had to care for my poor sick mother? I was very young, only twelve.'

Tears run down her face. She doesn't brush them away; she seems oblivious.

'I used to measure out her medicine. She was in such pain, I couldn't bear it.'

'Did your father not hire a nurse?' I say, disturbed.

'Papa said there was no extra money, he didn't want someone poking and prying about the house. I accepted that, I wanted to look after Mama myself. We both knew she might not have long to live. Papa shut himself away in his study. He didn't want to see her suffer. Only I saw how she moaned and thrashed and gasped for air.'

I am aghast. 'You poor child!'

'The nights were the worst. She had been given laudanum to help her sleep. I was exhausted myself, I scarcely knew what I was doing. One night she seemed worse than ever. After the doctor left I measured out her dosage. Only—' She halts, the tears still wet on her cheeks. 'Someone is there, listening to me!'

I crane around. There is no one in the church but a breath of fresh summer air flows in through the door, which is ajar. Maud must have left it like that earlier when she came in.

But she has gone already, crushing her skirts along the pew, fleeing down the aisle on noiseless slippers to chase some imaginary eavesdropper.

I realise she doesn't want to tell me the end of her story. She has decided that it is best left unspoken.

I think I know how the story ends. She acted out of compassion and pity. It doesn't change what I feel for her one jot.

When she comes back in a little later, breathless, pink-cheeked, bringing the glow of the noonday heat with her, I ask if she found anyone loitering about, knowing full well there has been no one.

She shakes her head. 'It was a foolish fancy, that was all.'

Maud

I hated having to lie to John but I had to do so.

When I ran outside the church, the heat of full summer hit me full in the face. During the days we had been meeting in the cool and dark of the church, summer had come and was romping away, growing in warmth and ripeness. Around the graves the long grass was thick with buttercups and wild geranium, the trees heavy with leaf.

I screwed up my eyes against the brightness and saw her dress, standing out palely against the black shade of the yews.

I marched over and grasped her shoulder. 'You! You have been spying on us!'

Edie said nothing but looked me squarely in the face. Brazenly, I thought.

'I will tell Mr Shawcross and he will think the worst of you for it!' I said furiously.

'Do so if you wish,' she said, in a low voice, 'but I know someone who will think worse of you.'

My heart beat fast in agitation. 'What do you mean?'

'Miss Juliana Greenwood. What would she say if she knew you were meeting a young man alone in the church?'

I felt my cheeks flame. It made me hot and embarrassed to think she might have seen John's arm hold me close. 'Don't you dare tell her such a thing, do you understand?'

How young she looked with her round sulky face and her faded cotton dress. My anger began to die.

'I understand you are jealous, Edie,' I said, more gently, for I felt some pity for her that she did not have John's love when she so longed for it. 'You want Mr Shawcross for yourself. But you are only a child and he is so much older. One day you will find a boy your own age.'

'It is true that I have feelings for Mr Shawcross,' she said quietly and with surprising dignity. 'But he will never look at me while you are here. I am only his landlady's daughter and as you say, so much younger. But if I told Miss Juliana, she would stop you seeing him.'

'And then you think he would be free for you,' I finished for her, bitterly. 'You would do that?'

She seemed to ponder, the little hussy. 'If you do not wish me to tell her about your behaviour, Miss Maud, then there is something I would ask of you.'

'What is it?'

'Give me my drawing back.'

I had almost forgotten about the drawing. I wasn't certain I had not crumpled and thrown it away.

'Listen, Edie. I will promise not to show your drawing to a soul, including Miss Greenwood herself, if you will say nothing of my meetings with Mr Shawcross. We shall have to trust one another. Will you do that?'

She nodded her head reluctantly. 'I suppose so.'

Could I trust her? 'If talk of my meeting Mr Shawcross comes to Miss Juliana's ears, I will know it is through you, Edie. Then I will tell her how your mother took her books for you to read.'

She stared at me, biting her lip.

'Come,' I said. 'Let us shake hands, as gentlemen do, to show we trust one another.'

I put out my hand which she took gingerly, with distaste.

She left me swiftly then, without further word.

I went back to John after that, but didn't stay long. We talked a little and then I said I must go.

'We should meet somewhere else,' I said. 'The church is too public. Villagers come in to pray, the vicar watches you work. We may be seen together.'

He ran his fingers through his hair. 'If only Juliana had not forbidden you to see me, I could come to Windward House. I could court you in a proper manner. I hate it that we have to keep our love secret.'

'I have been coming here too often, taking too many risks.' I looked around and shivered. 'And this is a cold, inhuman place, too full of righteousness. I feel I am being judged always. I must leave it longer before I come again.'

His face was stricken. 'But you will come again, Maud? How will I see you otherwise?'

Eighteen

John

The summer days go by. I labour on in the church but my heart is not in it. It is with Maud, enslaved by her. Her absence is like a bereavement.

I see her on Sundays, when she comes to church with Juliana, but during Juliana's inspection of my work she remains silent and does not look at me.

I am distraught, caught in a kind of madness.

'Is something the matter, Mr Shawcross?' Edie asks, at Marsh End.

'It is nothing, Edie.'

I envy her as I watch her set my room to rights, picking up the tossed blankets from the floor and folding them. She is only a child. Heartache for her is yet to come, if it ever does. In a few years she'll marry a village lad and have a breed of boys as robust as herself.

She lingers by my little bookcase and casts a wistful

glance at it. I know she likes reading: I have often seen her in the light summer evenings, curled up with a novel. It strikes me that I have not done so recently.

'You like reading, don't you, Edie?'

'Yes, Mr Shawcross. I was wondering . . .' she hesitates 'if I might borrow one of your books?'

I want to repay her for all her little kindnesses. 'Of course. I'm afraid you will find them dull. None of them is a story.'

'I've read too many stories. Stories have mostly happy endings and real life isn't like that, is it?'

I am taken aback. 'I fear you are right.'

'I should like to borrow this, please,' and to my surprise she pulls out my volume of Ruskin's lectures. 'I have seen you reading it. Perhaps when I have finished it, we might talk about it? I should like to know your opinion.'

I have underestimated Edie, I think. She is an intelligent girl who wants to educate herself further. The thought of being a mentor, guiding a young girl through the wonders of art, pleases me and for a moment I forget my suffering.

'I shall look forward to that.'

'There is something else I should like to ask you, Mr Shawcross.' She looks down at the book in her hands and a tinge of pink rises in her cheeks. 'I wondered if you might do a little picture of me for my mother's birthday? I have some money put by—'

'There is no need to pay me. It will be a pleasure.'

She is an ideal subject for oils. Her vivid colouring, her shining, exuberant health. I would paint her in sunlight, her hair sparking in its rays, perhaps lying in a field of corn. She is a child of the sun, whereas Maud belongs to the moon.

'I don't wish my mother to know, Mr Shawcross. I want it to be a surprise.'

'It will be our secret.'

She passes me on her way to the door, holding the book to her breast, and as she does so she shoots me a sparkling glance and her lips curve into a smile.

For a moment I am disturbed. I put that look down to childish glee but afterwards I am not so sure. She had not looked a child at all.

Maud

I was frightened. Too frightened to see John. I let days go by as the summer reached a peak of stultifying heat.

If Edie gossiped in Rending about my secret meetings with John, or worse, told her mother who might then tell Miss Potton, then surely Juliana would get to hear of it. If she learned that I had disobeyed her, then she might cut me from her will, throw me out from Windward House to fend for myself once more.

I could not bear the thought.

John had told me he loved me, that he would protect me. I wanted to trust him. I wanted so much to love him freely. But I did not know what his intentions were, if marriage to me was even in his thoughts.

It struck me then that without marriage to John, I was bound to Juliana until she died, she growing more crabbed and peevish still, and I more careworn. What else would there be in my life but Juliana? What else in hers but me?

One day in early August Juliana called for me. She was in the back garden, sitting on a bench in the shade, wearing a heavily veiled hat in pale straw that shielded her eyes from the sun and her face from flies. Her upper lip was beaded with sweat. Beside her was a little table with a jug of elderflower cordial.

The heat was breathless, the flowerbeds dry as sand, the plants wilting, dust between the blades of grass on the lawn. It had not rained for weeks.

For a while we sat quietly, drinking our glasses of elderflower and watching a sweating, red-faced Tiggins labour up and down the paths, raking the gravel free of weeds. They sprouted everywhere and did not seem to mind the drought. He was unaccompanied, for Sly had had one of his turns and had gone to earth in his hovel. It was only because of his absence that I had dared venture into the garden.

At last I could bear it no longer. I jumped up and went over to Tiggins.

'Mr Tiggins. Wouldn't you like a drink? It is so hot.' And I held out my glass, still half full.

His face went redder still. 'Oh, no, miss, but it is most kind of you.'

When I went back to Juliana, she was scandalised. 'You cannot behave in such a way with the servants when you are mistress here! What are you thinking of?'

'I am thinking that poor Mr Tiggins looks in need of a drink,' I retorted. 'He is not a young man and must be feeling the heat.'

Unusually, she was silent. A wasp crawled around the rim of her glass. She put the glass down quickly, a quirk of annoyance on her lips.

'Shall I fetch you another?' I asked.

'No, leave it,' she said impatiently. 'I have something to tell you.'

At once I was chilled, despite the heat.

'I received a letter this morning from an old school friend, Aveline Dimchurch, who lives in Scarborough. She has invited me to stay and I am minded to go. It will be cooler up north by the sea.'

I looked at her in astonishment. 'Are you well enough for the journey, Juliana?'

She waved a hand. 'The house is well appointed and the

change of air will do me good. I have already discussed it with Doctor Biddell, who has no objection. My health is so much improved.'

A vision of freedom opened up before me.

I need not fear Edie, for Juliana wouldn't be at Windward House to hear any gossip. John and I could wander anywhere we pleased, no longer snatching secret meetings in the church. I saw myself strolling hand in hand with him down secret paths, as the warm dusk filled with the flutter of moths and the moon came out to guide our way.

'Then you must go,' I said, as steadily as I could, though my heart was bursting. 'How long shall you go for?'

'Six weeks, I think. It is a long way from here. I shall take at least a week to recover from the train journey. So it will be autumn when I return.' She looked at me sharply. 'I want you to write to me twice a week to reassure me that all is well here at Windward House. Will you do that?'

I nodded.

'And do not think of allowing any gentleman to court you behind my back.' I could see her eyes behind her veil, piercing, suspicious. 'They must have my permission. When I return, I shall expect to find things just as I left them.'

There was a deeper meaning behind her words, a warning. But I did not heed it.

* * *

After Juliana's departure there was a new atmosphere at Windward House. We drew back curtains, opened windows and let the sunlight into its dark, airless rooms. Dorcas grew slack in her sweeping and dusting, but I did not chivvy her. Mrs Brundish no longer looked as strained, especially when I sent her home early each day; even Miss Potton seemed less gloomy.

When I am mistress here, I want my staff to be happy, I thought. I want them to serve me because they wish to please me, not because I frighten them. I let myself imagine John as an adoring husband, supporting me in all things, constant in his love.

I wandered about Windward House, as if practising for that time, examining paintings and furniture, picking up ornaments.

Although I longed to tell John of Juliana's departure, I waited. I feared she might arrive back on a sudden whim and take us all by surprise, checking to see we were each about our duties as normal.

Then her first letter came, postmarked Scarborough, and I knew that John and I were safe.

Part Two

RESPITE

Nineteen

John

When Maud tells me the news I can hardly speak for joy. We go out into the graveyard and I hold her in my arms in the shadows between the yew trees.

'I never thought we would be together again.' I stroke her smooth pale cheek.

She looks askance at the toppling gravestones. 'Let's go for a walk and leave this dreary place.'

So we go to the heath, where the slopes are vivid with purple heather and the warm air alive with the humming of bees. We sit in the shade of a small oak and I hold her hand. It is almost too hot to breathe. There is no wind and our palms stick together.

'I will take you to the sea tomorrow. There is a breeze there.'

'Not where I saw the devil in the marshes?'

I laugh. 'There is no devil! I want to show you how

beautiful the marshes are in summer.'

We arrange to meet at the gates of Windward House late the next afternoon. I wait at the gates. She floats down the drive towards me in a sprigged muslin dress, her dark hair hidden by a white sun bonnet, a smile in her eyes.

We cross over the road to the start of the track, keeping well apart on the open ground in case anyone should see us. But once we are in the shadow of the silver birch I catch hold of her hand.

She gives a nervous glance over her shoulder.

'There's no one there,' I say. 'Are you frightened of Sly following us?'

She shakes her head. 'I have not seen him for days. I told Tiggins to forbid him to come into the house while Juliana is away. We don't need fires in this heat. No, it is so quiet here I imagine I hear noises.'

I squeeze her hand. 'I am with you now.'

She stops and turns. 'Will you always be with me, John?'

Her face is intense and searching, lifted to mine. I take a deep breath. 'If you want me,' I say thickly.

'Oh, I do! I do!'

I am not certain what I have just promised or, indeed, what exactly she wants of me. I long to kiss her but know I must not. She is walking on, unaware of the tumult inside me.

I show her the beauty of the marshes that first day, the

reeds with their feathered tops, the tall pink marsh orchids rising between them, as if we walk in a garden in paradise.

She prefers the dunes where the grasses and sandy hillocks hide us in our own private room and beyond, the sea murmurs on the shingle, lulling us to sleep; not in each other's arms, for we are too circumspect for that, but close enough for me to watch her breathe, to see how each of her dark eyelashes is separate from the next and how her face relaxes at last under the warm sun.

How, in those hot summer days, I long to run my hands all over her while she sleeps, to wrench open her tightly-buttoned blouse and cover her breasts with kisses. They will be white, I think, whiter even than her face. They will never have been seen or kissed by a man before.

Of course I do not even kiss her. She would think I had no respect for her.

I look down on her cheeks beginning to flush with the sun, her breasts pressing against the thin muslin, the languorous outline of her body beneath the voluminous skirts. She has cast her sun bonnet aside, and her dark head is pillowed on my coat. She has taken off her boots and her feet and ankles are slim and well-shaped. I pull out my sketchpad and swiftly begin to draw before she wakes.

She opens her eyes after a while. Perhaps she hears the scratch of charcoal above the sound of the sea. She smiles lazily.

'It is so hot, I must take my stockings off. Don't look.'

I turn away obediently. I hear the rub of wool against flesh as she pulls them down all the way. My heart beats heavily at the secret femininity of it; I imagine what I must not see.

Finally I have to look around. The discarded stockings are a thick white puddle on the silver sand. She arches and flexes her naked feet. The light shines pinkly through them so that I can almost see the delicate bones; her nails are like slithers of pearl cupped around the tips of her toes.

'Don't move,' I say, in a fever. 'I must draw them.'

'What, my feet?' I hear her giggle in disbelief, but I take no notice for I have already begun.

Later she hobbles over the shingle, complaining all the way, and I, likewise, follow behind, and we paddle in the cold North Sea, shrieking like two small children as the waves swirl slowly about our bare ankles. Her feet, like pale fish, swim in my vision.

Another day I am in despair. I try to draw her, but it is no good. I am unable to reveal the enigma of her on paper. I draw her, but there is no truth in it.

I don't know her, I think bitterly. *Does she love me at all?*

She lies with her hands behind her head. Her breasts rise and fall with her breathing.

'Let me see.'

'It is not finished. Lie still.'

She lies, smiling up at me. I finish and cast it aside. 'It is no good. I cannot capture you.'

'But you have,' she says softly. She pulls me down beside her. 'Rest,' she whispers. 'Lie beside me.'

It is impossible to be so close to her. I feel my heart thud. I put out my hand and lay it on her arm and when she does not protest, I move it slowly to her neck, the soft place beneath her hair, and caress it.

'Undo your hair,' I say.

She sits up and loosens it obediently. At once she looks younger, vulnerable. She stares at my drawing.

'One day you will be famous, John. I know it.'

'I wish I could believe you.'

'*I* believe in you. Is that not enough?'

I smile ruefully. 'It doesn't put bread on my table, Maud. I need to sell my paintings. I can't exist on Juliana's fee for ever. Besides, I have nearly finished my work on the Doom.'

'Go slowly, John! Make it last for ever!'

'Then how shall I live? Besides, what will Juliana say when she returns and finds I have done nothing—' I reach out and stroke her bare forearm where she has rolled up her sleeve, and she shivers at my touch '—and all because of you, my dearest one?'

She lies back down beside me, her hair spread in fine black threads over my coat.

'I didn't realise,' she says at last, in a small voice. 'I did not think, did not *want* to think, that one day you would finish your work and return to London.'

'I cannot remain here once my contract is over, even for you, Maud. But I doubt it will be done before winter has set in.' I turn to her and look into her eyes. 'And winter is a long way off. Let's be happy now.'

She is very quiet the rest of that day.

I try to draw her many times, but her essence remains a mystery to me.

I can mirror the oval of her face, the almond shape of her dark grey eyes, the hair curving down from its straight white centre-parting to loop either side of her smooth forehead. But her expression is changeable and I never know what she is thinking. Even as we kiss, she keeps her eyes open to gaze at me, and physically close as we are, I cannot fathom what is in her head.

But I am content to have her with me for a few hours each day, her hand in mine, her little feet in their button boots keeping step with mine as we walk, as if our minds too are in sympathy with one another. I believe that they are, lovesick fool that I am.

It seems summer will never end.

Twenty

At Marsh End I present Edie with her painting, which I have done in watercolour – a failed attempt to catch her glow – and mounted on paper and card. I have done several pieces of work and chosen the best for her.

I believe she enjoys sitting for me, and as for me, I confess it is a relief to have her as my subject after my elusive Maud, who can be so withdrawn, as if she is somewhere apart.

Edie calls me 'John' these days. She examines the finished painting breathlessly. 'Is that what I look like, John? Truly?'

'It is how I see you,' I say, smiling at her excitement.

'Why, you have made me pretty!'

'Well, you are,' I say awkwardly.

She looks up at me from beneath her lashes. 'No one has ever told me that before.'

'They will do one day, when you become a young lady,' I say gallantly. 'If I had used oils I would have done you proper justice.'

She opens her hazel eyes wide and I see their flecks of gold. 'Why?'

I try to explain. 'The texture of your hair, the exact colour of your eyes – I need the subtlety of oils to show those, and alas, I don't have the time.'

She looks down and a flush rises in her cheeks. 'If you saw less of Miss Maud, you might have.'

I am astounded, alarmed. 'What do you mean, Edie?'

'I know you two have been meeting. Nothing can be kept quiet around here. Miss Potton and Dorcas – they've both seen Miss Maud tripping down Windward's drive to meet you. Even Mother has seen you both, on her way home once.'

'Please, Edie, tell no one. I fear Miss Juliana would not approve. It must not get back to her.'

'You can trust me, John. Only . . .' Her face is troubled.

'What is it?'

'Be careful of Miss Maud. The village say she is a witch!'

'*What?*' I can only laugh in astonishment.

'She has cured Juliana Greenwood. Miss Greenwood was always ill before she came.'

'Miss Maud is a good nurse, that is all.'

'That's as maybe but –' she looks at me directly '– she has bewitched you, hasn't she, John?'

Edie's words make me uneasy; not the words themselves because they are too preposterous, but her motive in saying such a thing to me.

I think back to our sittings. I wonder if I have been foolish and somehow encouraged Edie's affections without meaning to do so. Then I think of her innocent face, her wide guileless eyes, her blithe prattle while I painted, and dismiss the thought as fanciful and conceited. Why, I am years older! I must appear middle-aged to her; and so I dismiss my worry.

Besides, my mind – my whole being – is filled with Maud.

Maud and I meet at the gates of Windward House in the late afternoon when the heat has lessened a little and wander down to the shingle shore.

We give each other stones and pretend they are jewels. We laugh at the squabbling seagulls. Once we see a striped adder on the walkway and marvel at the speed of its escape into the water.

We never see any living soul. The sunlit world is ours alone.

I grow more daring in my attentions.

One day as we walk through the forest, I turn and draw her to me. She stops, her eyes widen. She does not pull away. We stand in the shade, gazing at each other. Around us sunlight plays over the ferns and brambles; otherwise it is completely still.

I put my hand out and touch Maud's face. Her cheeks are cool. I bring my face to hers. She lets me kiss her gently at first, then more deeply, and then to move my hot hands all over her, down from the slope of her shoulders to the swell of her breasts beneath the flimsy material of her dress. Her back is against a tree, her arms loose at her side. Her eyes are almost black in the shadows.

My hands grow more urgent.

I stand back, breathing deeply. It is the first time I have touched a girl in such a way and I am not sure whether I can control myself if I go on. I fear that I may have insulted her but she opens her eyes and smiles at me.

'John,' she says softly, as if practising my name. 'Dear John.'

'I've not hurt you?' I say anxiously.

She shakes her head. 'Kiss me again.'

Her lips are cool, as cool as her cheeks. I want to warm them with the fierceness of my kiss but this time she pulls away. 'Nothing can part us now, can it?'

I feel dizzy with the hammering of my heart. Her eyes are very large and I am drowning. I shake my head wordlessly. She puts her arm through mine calmly, as if nothing had happened between us, and begins walking on.

'Look.' She holds out her hand. She has caught a falling leaf from an ash tree, its little black key attached. 'Autumn is coming.' A shadow crosses her face.

She says it is too hot to sit in the dunes and leads me on to the shingle where the faintest breeze is coming off the sea. The sun is low in the sky, red and angry, and a black cloud, the first I have seen in days, passes across it as we sit down on the stones.

The weather will break soon. The thought of summer's end and Juliana's return fills me with anguish.

Maud is silent beside me, gazing out to sea where hard-edged little waves, gleaming red-gold, look as if they have been varnished on an enormous canvas. They move slowly, stickily, towards the shore and as they reach the band of sand before the shingle, they melt without a sound.

I bite my lip, wondering how best to express the turbulence of my emotions. I long to ask her if she loves me, but am afraid.

'Maud, you know what I feel for you,' I begin. She turns to me at once, as if she senses what I am going to say, has been waiting for me to say it. My mouth goes dry.

'I love you,' I say haltingly. 'I want to make you my wife. If I were rich, I would propose to you now.'

'It does not matter. I will come with you to London, married or not. I can tell Juliana I have decided to take a position there. She need not know we are together.'

I try to smile. 'Think what society would say, Maud! Besides, I cannot afford to set you up as my mistress!'

She says in a low voice, 'Are you telling me that you will return to London without me?'

'I will have to do so in due course, my dearest.'

'You said you would never leave me!'

'Maud, I can offer you nothing there. How can I provide for you?' I put my head in my hands despairingly.

'You said you would never leave me!' she repeats in a higher voice and rises to her feet in a shower of little stones. 'You have broken your promise! You will return to London and once you are there you will never think of me again!'

She is standing against the sun so that I cannot see her expression, but I hear the tremor, the accusation, in her voice.

'You know that is not true.' I stand up on the shifting shingle and try to touch her arm but she turns from me.

There is nothing I can say to excuse myself. No wonder Juliana forbade her to see me. I have wronged her terribly. All summer I have encouraged her to believe we have a future together.

'It doesn't matter to me that you are poor,' she says, as if repeating it will make me change my mind.

'But it will do. You will grow old and weary before your time, scrimping and saving, scrabbling in gutters for rotten potatoes when we are desperate. I have to paint – it is as vital to me as breathing – but I am never going to make any money from it.'

She frowns. 'Don't you understand, John? I will have

Juliana's money one day! Together with your earnings, we shall have more than plenty to live on.'

'But it may be years before she dies! She is not an old woman and her health appears to be improving.'

Her mouth turns down. 'So you are going to leave me to look after Juliana for the rest of my life? You have dallied with me and now you cast me aside. I thought you a fine man, John, but I was wrong!'

Her words pain me terribly but I know I deserve them. I dip my head so that I do not have to face the flash of her dark eyes. She begins to walk away, over the shingle, her shoulders bowed.

'Here you have a home, enough to eat,' I say, as I catch up with her.

'A home!' she says bitterly. 'It is four walls and a roof, that is all. A home should contain love and Juliana feels none for me, I have come to realise that. To her I am merely an unpaid nurse.'

There is little I can say to that, for I have long known it.

'In truth I don't know how I shall tear myself away from you,' I say in despair. 'But I will write, I promise.'

She dismisses that with the contempt it deserves.

'What good are letters, when we have had all this?' She sweeps her hand in a great arc enclosing the shore, the rise of the dunes behind and the forest trees in heavy leaf.

'Listen, Maud,' I say, desperate to cheer her, for I know I

am losing her with my feeble words. 'My fortunes may change. I will work hard for both our sakes when I am back in London. Then I will return in the spring to see you. We shall only be apart a few months.'

But slow tears are running down her face. She looks away from me.

Twenty-One

The next few days are sunless, but beneath the pressing mass of cloud, the heat builds until it is stifling. It is too hot to walk to the sea. We go to the heath, where the heather is darkening as it dies and the turf has gone brown, and sit hidden amongst a circle of gorse.

Maud is listless, preoccupied, her face pallid and moist beneath the yellow gorse flowers, which look garish to me today, though they are the only colour in this overcast world.

'Juliana returns in three days,' she says dully. 'I had a letter from her this morning giving instructions. She wants to move back into her old room downstairs and Dorcas and I must make it ready. Yet in winter she complains how cold it is and wants the fire built up! She wants me to inform Doctor Biddell and the Reverend Wissett that she is ready to receive them. She wants me to purchase more Quilter's Restorative Powder because she has run out. There is no end to her needs.'

Her face is desperate. 'What shall we do? We shall have

no more freedom!'

'We shall do as we did before,' I say steadily. 'We shall meet in the church again.'

'Not that – I couldn't bear it. I feel the eyes are watching me.'

'Eyes?'

'The eyes in the Doom, the devils.'

I humour her. 'Then while Juliana rests in the afternoons, we shall come here, to the heath instead.'

That day I cannot lift her spirits.

The next day, overcast again and with thunder growling behind the clouds, she is in a different mood. She does not smile or greet me but marches in to our secret place and sits herself down with a bump.

I sit beside her, baffled and subdued by the change in her.

'Mrs Brundish came in this morning, full of pride, with a watercolour. It was of her daughter, very charmingly executed. She passed it around to all of us – Dorcas, Tiggins, Miss Potton. I knew before she told me that it had been painted by you. I know your style, having sat for you myself all summer! We said you had a most singular talent to have caught Edie's look so well.'

She stares at me accusingly, her eyes like coals, devoid of any light.

I am at a loss. What is she accusing me of, exactly?

Surely she cannot mind if I take another as my model?

'Edie wanted it done for her mother.'

'You said nothing of it to me.'

'It seemed of little significance.'

'All the time you were seeing me, you were painting her in secret!. You were alone with her, closeted together with no one else present!'

I am exasperated at being made to feel guilty. 'We had a few sittings, that was all.'

'A few? How many paintings did you do?'

I spread my hands. 'I am an artist. My subjects are things around me. Trees, buildings, people. If you are ever to marry me you must understand that.'

They are the harshest words I have ever spoken to her and I regret them bitterly afterwards. I speak to her in the heat of the moment, taken by surprise, wanting to defend my actions. I cannot believe she feels jealous of young Edie Brundish.

Maud rises to her feet. In the gloom of the gorse thicket her face shines out white and glaring. She is suddenly intimidating, a different person from the girl who has lain with me on the beach. There is the coldness of separation between us and I don't want to recognise it.

'I wonder if I shall ever marry you!' she cries. 'I wonder if I even wish to do so!'

'What are you saying? You cannot mean it!'

‘That time seems so far off I cannot conceive of it. For now, I feel you have betrayed me in every way possible.’

‘Maud! I meant nothing by my little watercolour. Edie wanted me to paint it for her mother’s birthday and so I did.’ I reach up and catch hold of her hand but she wrenches it away. ‘How can you believe that Edie is more important to me than you?’

‘I don’t know,’ she says, but her voice sounds broken, defeated. ‘I need time to think about it.’

That night the thunder breaks. As I listen to the clash of it and see the dazzle of the lightning spears as they hit the parched earth, I fear for Maud in Windward House. It sounds as if the world is cracking apart.

It is still raining the next day, the last before Juliana’s return, when I go to Windward House to wait for Maud at the gates as usual. But this is not a usual day; it is as dark as a winter’s afternoon.

I stand in the mud, holding an umbrella intended to shelter us both.

I think, the heath will be too wet today. We shall have to go to the church.

I stand there for a good hour, getting slowly damper and more miserable, while nothing moves behind the windows of the great house. Then I give up and trudge back to the church, where it is now too dark to work but where – fool that I am – I still hope she may brave the rain and come to see me.

She does not come.

Part Three

Corpse Candles

Arsenic: the whitish or steel-grey powder of white oxide of arsenic. Deadly poison.

Twenty-Two

Maud

Rookyard.

The family greet me as I enter after my long dark journey.

Three little girls under ten, who look at me shyly and whisper their names.

A heavily pregnant mother.

Then the father, the master of the house.

He clasps my hand, then moves his hand to my arm, where it stays too long.

He stares at my breasts.

I took too many drops that night, to calm my anguish over John. Could he not see how much he had hurt me?

When I woke in a struggle and a sweat, the window was rattling and a storm raging outside.

I went to the window and opened it, and let the wet air blow on my face. There were sizzling forks across the black night sky and the crashing was very loud. I was soaked but I didn't mind. It cleansed me, that rain and noise, drowning out what was in my head.

'Come, blast me!' I cried to the storm. 'Come, blast me, for that is what awaits me! Oh my Mama, my poor dear Mama! I only did what I did to put you out of your pain.'

The next day it was dusk when Tiggins brought Juliana from the station. The lamps were lit outside the front door and I saw one neat little foot in a kid boot appear on the carriage step, one slim gloved hand on the door that Tiggins held open.

'Welcome home,' I said, smiling as if my face would crack.

'My dear. It is good to be home. I am much fatigued. Help me to my room, Maud.'

'You look so well, Juliana! I think you should stay up for supper. We are to have it shortly. Dorcas is heating up a mutton stew.'

'I am far too tired. Let me to my bed.'

'We shall have no more of that nonsense. I will not put up with it any longer.'

Of course I didn't say such a thing, though I longed to do so. I took her arm meekly and helped her to her old room downstairs, where the curtains were drawn over the closed windows and the fire had been lit by Dorcas earlier. Even so, she gazed about her with lowered brows before consenting to take off her mantle and unpin her hat.

'This room has such a chill to it, you must have let it get damp while I have been away.'

'It can't be damp. The drought lasted until last night, Juliana!' I added, more gently, 'You may go back upstairs if you wish. We didn't think to light a fire in that bedroom but it is easily done.'

She shook her head. 'I am too tired to climb the stairs. Besides, I feel closer to my stepfather in this room. I feel he is watching over me, as if I were a small child again.'

As he never did in life, I thought, and felt some pity.

'It is certainly not so far for Dorcas to bring your supper tray.'

'Oh, Dorcas!' she said, as if Dorcas was of no consequence. Then, 'Can you build the fire up?'

So I laboured in the grate until my face boiled while she stood unmoving, rubbing her hands together, talking of Aveline Dimchurch this and Aveline Dimchurch that. How the Dimchurch household had a butler, a footman, at least six maids and a resident cook.

My head so rang with Aveline Dimchurch's household that I thought I would shout out, 'Aveline Dimwit be cursed!'

Then I helped Juliana undress and climb beneath the covers. She had put on weight; her stays no longer hung on her but were difficult to unlace.

'Sit and talk to me,' she commanded, sitting upright in her bed like a queen. 'Tell me what has been happening in my absence. Your letters said little.'

'You have been much missed by the household,' I lied. 'We have all kept to our duties, as you directed. Nothing has happened in Rending that I know of, save that the summer blew away last night.'

Her mouth turned down. 'The autumn is so depressing to the spirits! And I have no visitors here. I am quite abandoned, save for you, Maud.'

'We shall go on outings together,' I said stoutly, though my heart sank at the prospect. 'They will cheer you.'

'We had guests almost every night at the Dimchurches',' she said, as if I hadn't spoken, 'Several courses at dinner, fine wine and conversation – such a jolly atmosphere.'

I said, 'You could give a dinner party here,' thinking she would protest that she was not well enough. But her face quite lit up.

'I believe I am a little stronger after Scarborough. A small one, perhaps a dozen guests.'

It was a surprise to me that Juliana knew a dozen people to invite. She patted my hand. 'I will need you with me, Maud. I cannot manage on my own.'

She was away in a reverie. 'I believe Grenville Harcourt is returned from London.'

She touched her hair, still in its squashed ringlets, which

I would have to brush out later. 'He is a popular guest, a widower, useful for making up numbers. And we must have the vicar and his wife, an insipid little thing, you will see. Then there are our nearest neighbours, the Ranters and the Garretts. We shall gather up a few couples from further afield and a bachelor or two and find ladies to partner them. I must work out the order of precedence into the dining room.'

She lay back and closed her eyes. 'I will ask you to write the invitations tomorrow. For now, I am altogether exhausted.'

So it began again, the thump of her stick beneath my bedroom floor summoning me to go to her at all hours of the night, the tinkle-tinkle of her bell during the day, sending me on this errand or that.

The day after Juliana's return I wrote letters to her dinner guests until my hand ached; and afterwards she sent Tiggins off in the trap to deliver them.

'I shall rest now I have signed those letters,' she said, yawning like a cat. 'I didn't sleep well last night. I was jerking about as if I were still in the train.'

'You should ask Doctor Biddell to prescribe you some laudanum,' I said casually.

'Biddell would never do such a thing. He believes in fresh air and exercise.'

I had hoped to squeeze some drops into my own bottle when I ran low again, but so much for that.

A few days later she sent me into Rending to get more Restorative from Quilter's and take a new prescription from Doctor Biddell. She had a digestive upset, which he said was the change in diet. She no longer looked in the same good health but peaky and drawn.

The counter in Quilter's was covered with packets of Restorative for collection. I noticed blotched writing on the labels, as if the ink had been smudged by tears.

Edie did not exchange one word with me. She did not need to, of course, for Mr Quilter was there today, with his dirty fingernails and greasy hair. He measured out Juliana's new prescription and shuffled into the back dispensing room to make up more Restorative for her.

While he was gone Edie and I avoided each other's eyes. I stood by the door, looking out into the street. I had to turn when Quilter came back into the shop and saw her expression.

There was a kind of triumph in her look, as if she was saying, 'You think you had John all to yourself, but I was alone with him too!'

She and I sized each other up and it seemed to me that a battle line was drawn between us.

But I was ready to surrender.

You may have him, Edie, I wanted to tell her, for he has betrayed our love and will soon finish his work on the Doom and be gone.

These thoughts caused a dreadful ache in my heart.

I dared not take many of my drops in the few weeks before the party, for Juliana's stick came banging on my bedroom floor at night. I went down through the cold, dark house, guarding my candle that it should not blow out in the draughts and leave me to the ghosts of the house. Often it was to find that she had fallen asleep again, despite the candles brightly lit around her.

She had resorted to her old habit of tearing the wallpaper; there would be a green curl of it in her hand.

I was reminded of my mother at her lying-in, when her corpse lay surrounded by burning candles. After I had climbed the stairs back to my cold bed, my pillow would be wet with thinking of Mama.

A day before the party Juliana received a letter that made her exclaim with annoyance. One of her guests, a widower, had been called away to attend his sister, who had been smitten with congestion of the brain.

'Now we shall be a man short. It is too bad!'

'He cannot help it, it is his sister.'

'Could he not have delayed his visit by a single day?'

And she fell to complaining that the table would look all

wrong with an odd number and there would be no gentleman to take one of the ladies in to dinner.

'There is no need for me to attend, Juliana, then your numbers will be evenly matched.' I found that I could forfeit the chance of sitting next to my promised dinner partner, an elderly gentleman, quite easily.

'I must have you to help; it is so hard for a single woman to act as host! We have no footman any longer and Dorcas is sure to make mistakes. At least with the extra help I have hired from the village, Mrs Brundish should manage.'

She put her hand to her brow, frowning. Her skin looked papery in the morning light, a greenish pallor beneath it. Then her eyes brightened. 'We shall invite John Shawcross to join us! I know he is no gentleman, but he is a single man and will have to do.'

My pulse leapt. *John*!

Juliana broke into the tumult of my thoughts. 'You must write a letter to him from me and Tiggins can deliver it. I am his patron and he cannot refuse.'

So I would see John tomorrow! How would he behave towards me? What would he say?

I had been too quick to judge him: Edie was only a child, after all. When I saw him I would tell him so; I would convey my love for him, my hope—

But Juliana must not suspect there was anything between us.

Twenty-Three

John

I have not seen Maud alone for a long while, and otherwise only on Sundays when she and Juliana attend the service.

I feel I am being punished for my behaviour towards her in the summer and the time I spent with Edie. And perhaps I deserve it, though my feelings for Maud have not changed. I am in despair, wondering if she ever truly loved me, or if she merely saw me as a means of escape to London.

When Juliana's invitation comes, my heart surges with hope. It will be a chance to see Maud, to speak to her alone.

The following evening, dressed in my one dress coat, somewhat shiny and thin, I arrive at Windward House before eight o'clock, not wishing to be late, even by so much as the fashionable quarter of an hour, in case it risks Juliana's displeasure.

There are lamps lit at the entrance but no carriages yet arrived. I hang about a while in the wind and drizzle, trying to see the time on my pocket watch but the slither of moon appears only fitfully between the ragged clouds.

Then the first carriage passes me at last and rolls up to the entrance, followed in quick succession by several more, so I walk uncertainly up the drive, conscious of the drivers' disparaging looks – a young man without his own carriage to bring him, and not even correctly dressed in dark tail coat and white cravat.

It is going to be a grand affair, the first formal dinner party I have been to in my life.

I feel horribly apprehensive, uncertain of the correct way to behave or in what order I should pick up my knives and forks at dinner. When Edie opens the door to me I smile at her in relief, as if we are conspirators.

'Why, Edie, how very smart you look!' She has put her hair up, the first time I have seen her wear it that way – like a young lady. 'I didn't think to see you here.'

She giggles and covers the sound with her hand, looking round. 'I'm not a dinner guest!' she whispers. 'I'm here to help my mother.'

I see then that she has a pinny over her dress. I feel a fool, but smiling, she gently relieves me of my hat and ushers me through to the drawing room.

It is like a hothouse in there, lamps burning brightly, the fire roaring, a press of people buzzing with small talk and exaggerated responses. Some of the ladies are wearing hooped skirts, which makes it difficult for the gentlemen to move, except with great caution.

Juliana greets me with indifference and takes me over at once to my dinner partner, who is to be Mrs Wissett.

I know Mrs Wissett, of course: she will be undemanding company, if a trifle dull. At least she must be a tolerant woman to be married to the Reverend, I think, and will forgive my mistakes. She looks as nervous as I feel, straggles of hair already starting to fall down around her flushed face.

I bow as Juliana brings me to her, and she says something to me I do not catch, for already my eyes are seeking Maud.

There she is, slender-waisted in a dark red dinner dress that shows off her pale sloping shoulders, vivid and delicate as some exotic flower in that room of dry, ageing men, with their paunches and rampant grey whiskers and loud coarse voices.

A flash of her dark eyes as she glances at me and swiftly away.

How cruel it is that she and I, as the youngest there should not be permitted to partner each other! I shall have no chance to speak to her and I begin to despair.

Juliana leads the procession in to dinner, her arm in that of a tall, urbane man I don't recognise, while Maud, following on behind, is partnered by an elderly man with a stick.

It takes a while to seat us all at the long table, with Juliana coming around to show us our places and becoming quite flustered, so that she has to be rescued by Maud, who takes over in the most charming way, although she still doesn't look at me.

We all sit down and the ladies take off their gloves. Juliana's dinner partner is seated in pride of place at the top of the table, with Juliana on his right and Maud on his left.

There is a vast variety of food already laid out: two kinds of soup, oyster patties, a cod's head and shoulders and a number of corner dishes, all set in a bewildering array upon the white cloth. In front of me an unpleasant green arrangement of little boughs stuck with artificial flowers hides my view of the guests opposite.

Mrs Wissett informs me the decoration is quite the latest thing, and is impressed. The silver glitters in the candlelight and around us the dark portraits frown, as if they dislike being disturbed. It is a finely proportioned room, though somewhat gloomy.

I try to draw Mrs Wissett out in conversation but she is loathe to speak about herself and wishes only to mention her husband as much as possible and in the most admiring tones.

Being the least important guest, I am seated in the middle of the table, far away from Maud at the top, who is listening politely to her elderly dinner partner. From time to time I turn and glance over at her covertly; it is easier for me after the first remove, when the boiled turkey and the saddles of mutton take over and we are obliged to talk to our other neighbour.

Mine is a spinster in her fifties, a large daunting lady, very forthright and opinionated, so I let her run on while I nod and smile or frown as appropriate, and gaze at Maud all the while, my view to her being quite open.

She has turned to converse with the gentleman at the head of the table, Juliana's dinner partner, for this course. She must be asking him to arrange her a dinner of her own from the items on the menu, for she is looking up at him in a helpless manner and tapping her menu playfully.

It gave me a pang to see that.

Then he pours her some more wine, and she smiles at him and says something I crane to hear but cannot, and he laughs.

He is a handsome fellow, with a well-fed air, fleshy in the face and his eyes small and half-hidden, but his thick springing hair is hardly grey though he must be in his mid-forties at least.

After the second remove, when the puddings are brought in by a red-faced Dorcas, he continues talking to Maud, their two heads close together, rather than turning back, as is the convention, to Juliana Greenwood.

I notice she is looking somewhat peeved to have to

continue conversing with the vicar on her other side. For my part, I am altogether perturbed, and the sight of the blancmanges, the jellies and the cabinet pudding makes me suddenly queasy. I am forced to tear my eyes away from Maud then, in order to talk once again to little Mrs Wissett.

She regards me kindly. 'You seem much distracted, Mr Shawcross. It is your artistic nature, I am sure. You are thinking of your work in the church, longing for the morrow when you may resume it.'

'That is so,' I agree. 'It is difficult to think of anything else.'

'The Doom is very extraordinary –' she gives a tiny shudder – 'I find it almost frightening.'

I look at her, forgetting for a moment the sickness in my throat but she blushes then and says, 'You must not tell Mr Wissett I said such a thing! He will be very cross with me!' She casts around for a safe topic. 'You find the wood burner useful?'

'Yes, indeed. I am most grateful for it.' I take a great gulp of the pudding wine; the sweetness of it steadies me.

'The other guests here, do you know who they are? Who is that gentleman, for instance, who sits at the head of the table, on the right of Miss Maud Greenwood?'

She glances beyond me. 'Ah, that is Mr Grenville Harcourt. He is a widower. His local church is Walberswick, not Rending, but Edwin and I have met him on occasions.

He gives money to church charities.' She gives a surprisingly mischievous smile. 'I believe he likes to be thought of as a benefactor!'

I think to myself, Mrs Wissett would have qualities of her own if she were not married to the repressive Reverend.

'So he is rich?'

She nods her wispy head. 'He is one of the biggest landowners around here. It all came from sheep. They made his family's fortune in the middle ages.'

A rich widower who is enjoying Maud's company.

I see his hand on her arm as he whispers something and she laughs again. I suspect something coquettish in her behaviour and I grind my teeth.

I begin to drink more than is wise.

After the dinner is finished, I, being the most junior of the guests and therefore seated nearest the door, have to hold it open, while the ladies file out to the drawing room, leaving the gentlemen to converse amongst themselves and drink their port.

To be honest, I am glad of the door frame to clutch. I am feeling decidedly unsteady on my feet. I think at least Maud will acknowledge me on her way out but she does not. Afterwards I down a couple of glasses of port but don't feel any better for them. I find myself unable to say very much to the gentlemen.

We rejoin the ladies afterwards in the drawing room,

where they are seated in a circle fanning themselves and talking in a desultory fashion, Maud among them. We are expected to seat ourselves in the empty chairs between our dinner neighbours but I see immediately that there are two chairs close to Maud that have not yet been taken.

Since I am one of the first men to enter and Juliana is out of the room for the moment, I lurch towards the one immediately next to Maud with perhaps unseemly haste and collide with the large, softish figure of Mr Grenville Harcourt.

He raises his brows as I throw myself into the chair without an apology.

'I believe that is my chair, young man.'

'Why should it be yours, sir?'

'Miss Maud Greenwood was on my left side at dinner.' Harcourt bows his head to Maud, who is looking at us both, wide-eyed. 'The other is for Miss Juliana when she returns.' He points to an empty chair between Mrs Wissett and my formidable neighbour from dinner. 'That, I believe, is yours.'

Most of the guests are now watching. I am in a quandary. I do not wish to hurt Mrs Wissett's feelings, for I have taken a liking to her but I am determined to stay where I am and speak to Maud at last.

'Let Miss Maud Greenwood decide who is to sit next to her – whether it be you, or me!' I say loudly.

Harcourt's face expresses astonishment and disbelief at such a lack of etiquette.

Maud flushes. 'Mr Shawcross, what are you saying?'

I loll back in satisfaction. I have at last made her acknowledge me. 'Well, which of us do you choose, Miss Greenwood?'

My words, I notice, come out rather more slurred than I intend but now I am set upon my course I will not be deterred; it has a fatal inevitability about it.

'It is your decision – him or me.' Yes, definitely slurred but no matter.

Mr Harcourt bends down to me, so close that his cheek grazes mine. 'Young man,' he said softly. 'You are very drunk and shocking the ladies. You had better leave the room before I escort you out myself!'

I have been insulted. I shoot out my fist to punch that smug, fleshy cheek but he catches hold of my wrist in a grip that is surprisingly firm. 'Get out,' he says in his silky, cultured voice. 'Now!'

I focus on his eyes and see that they brook no argument. Next to me Maud has covered her face with her hands.

With an effort I stand up.

The room reels about me. I hear cries and gasps from the ladies as I weave my way to the door and fall over the trolley being wheeled in by Dorcas and Edie, which is laden with teacups and little cut sandwiches. There is a tremendous clatter of china and spoons, a shriek from Dorcas and then I am out in the blessed calm and quiet of the hall.

I rest my head against the softness of the gentlemen's coats. I wish I could stay there for ever, wrapped in darkness and warmth and the smell of damp doggy wool.

A hand touches my arm. 'Oh, John,' says Edie. There is a gurgle in her voice as if she is trying not to laugh. 'You'd best get home to bed.'

I reach Marsh End somehow, staggering along the wet moonlit lane, my dress coat soaked. And the first thought in my throbbing head the next morning is that by my behaviour I have left the field open.

To my rival, Mr Grenville Harcourt.

Twenty-Four

Maud

No one spoke of what had happened after Juliana returned to the drawing room.

But she soon noticed that John was not there. She queried his absence with Mr Harcourt and to his credit and my relief he told her that John had been feeling 'unwell'.

Unfortunately, when the guests had departed, Juliana upbraided Dorcas for the mess on the trolley and Dorcas, fearing dismissal and protesting that it was not her fault, told her the truth. Juliana asked me if that were so. I was forced to say it was and that I was the cause of the quarrel, although I was deeply mortified and anxious to protect John.

'I told you he was the most unsuitable young man!' she said to me afterwards, as I was preparing her for bed. There was triumph in her tone and I hated her.

'He has no idea how to behave in society! What did

I expect from someone who has no class at all? The shame of it! To insult Mr Harcourt so!'

'I believe he can stand it.'

'Now *he* is a proper gentleman. But your manner towards him left something to be desired, Maud. You monopolised him, even after the second remove.'

'I didn't mean to do so,' I said humbly, for I could see she was altogether put out by the evening. I could have pointed out that it was Mr Harcourt who had continued talking to me, but did not. I had suddenly remembered an odd little incident just before the guests arrived that evening.

I had come downstairs in my new magenta dress. Juliana had looked at me with the same expression as when I met her first. She put her hand to my cheek, a touch that held no affection. Then she said ruefully, bitterly, 'What it is to be young and beautiful. I was once, you know.'

I saw suddenly that she was envious of me. She had wanted to be the focus of Mr Harcourt's attentions at dinner.

Now she sighed. 'I must send for the vicar tomorrow. He and I must decide what is to be done about Mr Shawcross.'

I had a vision of the Reverend Wissett devising a special penitence for John, writing a confessional prayer, perhaps, that he must say in church on the coming Sunday, but then Juliana added, 'We shall have to pay Shawcross off, unfortunately, as we will be terminating his contract before his work is complete.'

I looked at her open-mouthed. 'You intend to dismiss Mr Shawcross?'

'I cannot continue to act as Shawcross's employer after he has behaved in such a way! The Reverend will never allow it, he has such high principles.'

I went to bed anxious and upset. As I crossed the landing to the water closet, I could still hear the village girls helping Dorcas far below in the kitchen and making a good deal of laughter and noise. I envied them: to be so carefree must be a delightful thing.

Now I was to lose John even earlier than I had thought.

It was strange to me that next morning life at Windward House went on as usual despite the turmoil of my feelings.

Dorcas, sleepy and rubbing her eyes, took in Juliana's breakfast; I had mine alone in the dining room, which still smelled of last night's wine and cigars; and Mrs Brundish arrived at nine, as she always did.

I ate sparingly and rapidly. I had made my mind up. I must go to the church while Juliana was still abed, and tell John to write a letter directly, apologising to Juliana for the upset he had caused. That might mollify her enough to keep him on. I might have him for another month or so.

It was a cold morning, blustery, but after the rain the previous evening the sun was shining outside the dining room window, making it seem darker still indoors.

I went upstairs to put on my mantle and bonnet, meaning to hasten over the heath to the church. However, when I opened the front door I was flustered to find a gentleman already standing on the step, about to pull the bell rope.

It was none other than Mr Harcourt in a heavy greatcoat, and I could see a fly on the drive behind him, a very dashing open carriage drawn by a single black horse.

'Good morning, Miss Greenwood.'

'Mr Harcourt.'

I could not think why he was there; my head was too full of John.

He cut a fine figure in his tweeds, his face flushed from the cold, or perhaps good living. I might even have described him as handsome if he had not been quite so old.

'I came to deliver my letter of thanks to your cousin, and I find you already venturing out. I feared you would be sleeping in this morning and I might miss you.'

'I am on my way to the village, Mr Harcourt,' I stammered, a little embarrassed by his eagerness to see me.

'Then it is both our good fortunes that I am here. Mine, that it gives me a chance to see you again, and yours, that I may save you the trouble of walking there.' He gestured with a flourish at the fly. 'It is at your service, Miss Greenwood, and so am I.'

I looked at the fly and thought that riding in it would be far faster than walking, while he pulled an envelope from his pocket and slipped it, quick as a wink, on to the letter tray inside the door.

'There, that is done,' and he brushed his soft leather gloves together. 'Now, what do you say to a ride, Miss Greenwood?'

It felt very grand to be riding up so high, perched beside Mr Harcourt, who managed his horse with a mere flick of his whip. He didn't say much about himself, but he asked me how I was finding the countryside after London, what my education had been, what my papa had done.

I did not tell him that I had been a governess after Papa's death, I don't know why. I made it sound as if I had come straight from Miss Caseborne's Seminary to Windward House. It was difficult to talk with the wind blowing in my face and my hand held up to stop my hair coming down beneath my bonnet. Last night we had talked of foolish things to do with the dinner and the other guests and he had made me laugh: I could not remember what about.

'Where do you wish to go?' he said, as we approached the village.

I said, 'The church, please,' and he gave me a curious look.

But I was distracted by the sight of Edie Brundish on her way to Quilter's. As we passed her, she looked up; I could not think why she should stare at me so.

Mr Harcourt brought the horse up to the lych gate and halted it. It began to nose the wintry grass.

'I am very grateful, Mr Harcourt,' I said, as he helped me down. 'It has certainly saved my legs.' I could not think of what else to say; I sounded as old as Miss Potton.

'Perhaps I may call on you,' he said, 'at Windward House? You might fancy another jaunt sometime.'

'Thank you, Mr Harcourt,' I said. 'That would be nice indeed.'

Then I scurried up the damp path to the church.

John was in the far corner. I could see his figure dark against the stone, moving about, turning, bending. In the poor light of the church I didn't realise what he was doing until I reached him.

He was packing up.

He was putting his jars and brushes and trays into a large box, folding up cloths and rags, laying them on top. His stool lay against a pillar, its legs crossed into itself.

'John, John! Stop! What are you doing?'

He turned to me. His eyes were red-rimmed, his hair stuck up, unbrushed. 'I must leave, Maud. After what happened last night, I must return to London. I am so sorry.'

'You cannot leave me yet!'

'I have disgraced you.'

'It matters nothing to me!'

'I have disgraced Juliana.'

'You need only write and apologise! She will keep you on. She wants the Doom finished.'

He shook his head. 'She will find someone else in the spring. There are plenty of penniless artists who think they know something about restoration.'

'You cannot go yet!' I repeated desperately. 'You told me you would finish it first!'

'Maud, Maud. I will write to you, I promise. I will let you know how things are with me. I hope that we may meet again one day.'

I stared at him open-mouthed. A dreadful chill encircled my heart. 'What are you saying?'

He spoke slowly, as if wanting to explain. 'There will be others who woo you, far more suitable than I am. I thought long and hard on this in the early hours when I could not sleep. Someone like Mr Harcourt could offer you so much more.'

I was incredulous. 'Mr Harcourt? He means nothing to me! You are quite mistaken. I don't know him and nor do I wish to do so.'

'Last night brought home to me how little I have to offer you. Accept his attentions if they come, Maud. He has money and land. If you stay with Juliana, you will wither away.'

He was serious; I could not believe it. There could be

only one reason. His love for me had died, blighted by our circumstances.

'You mean you don't love me any more?'

'Of course I do. But loving you, I must think of what is best for you. And I know I cannot offer a ha'penny worth as much as Mr Harcourt.'

'John, please, I beg you, don't leave me here! I shall go mad. I don't know what will happen to me!'

'Nothing will happen,' he said coolly. 'You are better off now than if I took you away to live in penury.'

I tried a last time to sway him. 'Write to Juliana, I beg you! She will forgive you, you will be able to remain here!'

'I have already written,' he said, with an icy calm that dismayed me. 'Mrs Brundish has taken the letter up this morning. I apologised, gave Juliana my notice and told her that I would be leaving today. I have given Wissett money for the carrier so that he may send my box and stool on to me in London.'

I went close to him then, clutched his arms, gazed up into his face. Tears filled my eyes. He was a stern, cold stranger to me and I was bereft.

'What has happened to you, John?'

'I have been brought to my senses. I have realised that you and I – we could never be, there is no future for us. You must find a rich husband, Maud, who will provide for you in a proper fashion. That is your escape, not me, and you will find it.'

He removed my hands from his arms gently and bent to strap his box.

I remained in the church as he carried the box silently into the vestry. I was weeping bitterly. But when he returned for his stool he did not once turn to me.

And then he was gone – gone for ever. The church door creaked shut and I was alone in the dark.

And the devil in the corner winked at me.

Twenty-Five

John

I trudge down the lane to Marsh End so I may pick up my bag.

The hedgerows are bare and water-logged fields stretch away on either side. It is a dismal sight and I feel dismal myself as I walk. I begin to regret bitterly the things I said to Maud. I remember her tears and my heart aches. I don't want her to marry Mr Harcourt in the least.

I will write to her now, before I leave. I will declare my love anew.

The cottage is deserted but the door unlocked as it always is. I have already said my farewells to Mrs Brundish and Edie.

I race upstairs. There is not much time. I have to walk to the crossroads to catch the Southwold omnibus to Marsham station.

I unearth my sketch book from my bag and flick through it.

Maud, Maud.

Page after page of her but not of her, for I had never caught her essence, never stripped away her enigma. The girl who gazes back at me is beautiful but bland.

I choose the drawing I think she may like best. On the back I write in a soft pencil:

'My darling Maud

When I heard you weep just now, my heart was filled with anguish. I could not speak, even to bid you goodbye lest I should weep myself. I love you. I want you to know that and I believe you do.

It is my intention to return to Rending in the spring to visit you. If my fortunes have improved, then I will ask you to marry me. I long above everything to take you away and keep you at my side always.

For now we must be patient. And if fate sends you a suitor in the meantime, then let you choose between us.

Dearest Maud, whatever happens, my feelings for you will always remain the same. Please write to me when you have the time and tell me how things are with you.

I am your most fervent and steadfast

John Shawcross

I put my London address beneath my name. I enclose the drawing between two blank sheets and glue the corners together. I write 'Miss Maud Greenwood' across one surface. I will leave a note for Mrs Brundish asking her to deliver it personally the next morning when she goes up to Windward House.

I pick up my bag and take a last look around the room, now strangely empty and unfamiliar, cleared of any mess of strewn shirts, books, jars of pencils and painting paraphernalia, the bed smooth and neat. Then I close the door behind me and descend the narrow wooden staircase.

Edie is standing at the bottom.

I say, startled, 'You are back, Edie, so soon?'

'Mr Quilter gave me permission. I have run all the way to catch you! I wanted to say—' She looks around, as if seeking inspiration. Then she stammers, 'You are a good man, John. You have been so kind to my mother and me. I wanted to thank you properly, that is it. That is the reason I have returned.'

I am touched. I try to smile, but the sadness inside me makes it impossible.

'Will you come back and see us one day?' Her voice trembles, from the running, perhaps. She catches her breath.

'I am certain I will.' On an impulse I add, 'Would you write to me, Edie? Tell me of the doings in Rending and up at Windward House?' It is the closest I can come to asking for news of Maud. 'Your mother knows my address in London.'

She looks overcome. 'I'll do that and gladly, John. Is your mind quite made up to leave?'

She sounds wistful. I know the extra income for my room is helpful to them, that it will not be easy to find another lodger, being situated out of the village as they are.

'I am afraid it is, Edie.'

She hesitates. 'It is not because Mr Harcourt is courting Miss Maud, is it?' She sees my face and her eyes flick away.

'Mr Harcourt?'

She fiddles with her buttons. 'It is only that I saw him giving her a ride just now. He's a quick one all right! He met her only last night and they're out driving this morning.'

I shake my head for I cannot speak, my throat is so filled with despair and a dreadful sense of fate. No sooner am I out of Maud's sight than she is accepting drives with another man. But then it is my fault. I have told her to welcome Mr Harcourt's advances, to forget me.

I go to the kitchen table, meaning to write a note to Mrs Brundish on a clean sheet from my sketch book.

Edie watches me. She is agitated, evidently wanting to be rid of me and return to Quilter's. Her hands clutch her breast.

'Should we not bid each other farewell now, John, and be done with it?'

'You must return to work, of course.' I gesture at Maud's package. 'I was intending to leave this for your mother to deliver for me. Perhaps you could ask her for me, Edie? It is for Miss Maud Greenwood. It is confidential, do you understand? I don't want Miss Juliana to know of it.'

'Give it to me. I'll pass it to my mother and explain.'

I hand it over, and as I do so, Edie catches hold of my other hand, takes it to her mouth and kisses it. It lasts only a second but I feel the soft fullness of her lips. I stare at her and her eyes fall.

'I didn't mean to shock you, John,' she whispers. 'I wanted to thank you. Come back to us.'

I believe I nod, mumble something; it was a charming gesture, though its unexpectedness has disconcerted me oddly. Then I pick up my bag and leave.

Edie stands stock still as I go out of the door. In the dimness of the kitchen her face is as white as the glued papers I have given her.

Twenty-Six

Maud

I did not hear from John, though he had promised he would write.

I must give it time, I thought. But what was there left to say? He had said it all.

I slept fitfully; my drops did not seem to be working.

During the week that followed his departure I felt strange in the daytime: hollow and drained, as if I did not exist. Around me the walls seemed insubstantial, bulging and retreating, or floating above the floor as if made of gauze. On my way down to breakfast I would blunder about like one of Mr Darwin's creatures.

Frightened, I reduced my dosage. The level in the bottle was growing lower and I had no idea how I would refill it.

'It is no use going about with those despondent looks,' snapped Juliana. 'Mr Shawcross has gone and good riddance to him!'

I believe she was peeved that John had given her his notice before she had had a chance to give him his. She was in a sour mood until the vicar told her that she was well rid of such an ungodly man. They prayed together for the saving of his soul.

One afternoon in early November, Grenville Harcourt came calling again.

I had heard a carriage draw up and, glad of some distraction for we had so few visitors, I opened the front door before the bell rope was pulled and Dorcas heard.

Mr Harcourt was standing with his hat in his hands, a smile stretching his plump cheeks. His hair was smoothly brushed back; I could not help thinking of John's tousled locks and a pang went through me.

'You must want to see my cousin, Mr Harcourt. I am afraid she is resting.'

'It is you I have come to see, Miss Greenwood. I wondered if you would care for a little drive?'

There was something suddenly humble and beseeching in his pale blue eyes, surprising for so confident a man.

Why not? I thought. It was so very dull in the afternoons and I was in sore need of diversion.

Mr Harcourt looked after me most courteously, wrapping me in thick rugs, for the afternoon was cold, though this time we were in a covered carriage, with his driver outside. He enquired about my welfare in a fatherly manner from time to time – whether I felt the slightest chill or sickness from the motion.

He said little about himself but commented on the weather, the state of the animals grazing the poor grass, farmer so and so's land as we passed it, and the new railway extension to some local market town.

They were not topics of great moment, but he seemed eager to put me at my ease, to fill the empty air with talk so that I should not need to do so. I enjoyed listening to his pleasant, well modulated voice; all I had to do was to nod while I thought about John.

Mr Harcourt continued to visit.

He always arrived when Juliana was resting in the afternoons. I would open the door, for by now I recognised the particular sound of his carriage wheels on the drive, and there he would be, doffing his hat and bowing.

'Do you fancy a ride, Miss Greenwood?' he would say, and I, having nothing better to do, would tiptoe off to fetch my bonnet and mantle without disturbing Juliana's rest. Then off we would go in his carriage, bowling along the lanes with their bare hedgerows, in which the berries showed richly red.

He was a cultured man, interested in the arts and science, but also a man of the land, a farmer at heart. I felt young and foolish in his company but when I did venture a comment, he listened to me in the most gentle, polite manner.

Gradually I felt more at ease with him, though I still wondered why he bothered with me when there must be single ladies of his own age who would be glad of a wealthy widower's company.

Early on he had told me that he had no children. I believed he must think of me as the daughter he had never had, for he was forever fussing over me with furs and rugs as my own papa might have done, and tempting me with seed cake and little sugar biscuits.

I began to look forward to our drives together. It was most delightful to ride so high above the country lanes and be cocooned in warmth and comfort after the bleakness of Windward House.

I didn't tell Juliana of my drives with Mr Harcourt; she was such a sour puss I feared she would not wish me to have any diversion. I felt sure she would forbid me to go out alone with him, for of course we were never chaperoned: it never occurred to me that there was anything in the least bit improper about our driving out together, him being so old and his manner so paternal towards me.

On the afternoon of Christmas Eve Mr Harcourt came to the door of Windward House. I had not expected him, thinking that he would be entertaining over Christmas.

It was a gloomy afternoon, already turning to dusk. It had been overcast all day, with no wind to blow the steely clouds away. I had wandered about the house all morning, at a loss to know what to do with myself, too restless and unhappy to settle to reading.

I had heard nothing at all from John.

Every time I attended church with Juliana it was to see the Doom unfinished in its dark corner and be reminded of how he had left me. I remembered how I had loved to watch his fingers holding the brush so gently, so tenderly, as he restored each figure in the painting to its original brightness. He had never finished Christ, sitting aloof and apart among the clouds in heaven and paying no attention at all to the poor naked humans crawling on the earth below Him as they waited to be judged.

And I thought, too, of how, when John drew me among the dunes, his eyes would open very wide as he gazed at me, so that they seemed filled with light. His concentration was absolute, as if to record on paper everything about me. I was the sole focus of his regard and nothing else mattered to him.

Oh, to have that same attention from him again!

Juliana was being particularly demanding, full of complaints. Christmas should bring joy and gaiety; there was none at Windward House.

So when Mr Harcourt stood before me on the doorstep, beaming expectantly and Juliana slept in her room all unaware, what could I do but jump into the carriage beside him, smiling in relief at being freed, if only for an afternoon?

'I have a little surprise for you,' he said mysteriously. 'We shall be a little longer today.' But he did not divulge more, telling his man to whip up the horses instead, so that we drove off at a fine speed.

We didn't turn into Rending but drove on, so that I lost count of the long straight lanes bordered by endless flat brown fields, ploughed over and empty.

'I must be back by four,' I said anxiously. 'That is when Juliana takes tea.'

'I will return you by then, Maud, never fear.'

On his insistence we were on first names terms by now, though it felt too familiar to me to call a man of his age 'Grenville' and I avoided it when I could.

He glanced at me. 'I take it you do not tell Juliana of our drives?'

I shook my head.

'Good. I would not wish her to know, Maud.'

This remark puzzled me and made me somewhat uneasy, but I did not feel I could ask further; there was something in his face that stopped me.

We were driving past extensive parkland, leafless oaks standing proud in the gloom. We came to a splendid pair of wrought iron gates and the driver drew up the horses. An elderly man doddered out of the lodge and doffed his cap.

With a great effort he drew back the gates and we rolled through.

A broad sweep of drive, grassland to either side of us with sheep grazing, their winter coats starkly white against the dark ground, then arrival at a great house built of white Suffolk stone that gleamed like marble in the dusk. I was overcome by the size of the place, and nervous.

'This is Rusholme Hall, Maud, my home.'

Mr Harcourt helped me down and led me up to the front door, his hand beneath my elbow. I was wondering all the while, and not a little frightened, I don't know why. For the last few years I had been apprehensive of new places.

I began to prattle. 'It is so very large. You must be lonely, living all by yourself here.'

'I am indeed. Most of the time I have only the servants for company.'

He took the bell pull and tugged, and I heard the jangling within. Presently another elderly servant opened the door and bowed to us both, and we entered into the warmth, into a vast shadowy hall, with a fireplace in which a fire burned merrily beneath an ornate marble mantelpiece decked with holly; there were garlands of holly and ivy around the framed oil paintings on the walls.

My eyes were drawn at once to the Christmas tree which dominated all that space. It was the sole light in the place. No other was needed, for it was a tree lit by stars.

Or so it seemed to me, when I came in from the dusk outside and saw it rising up before me, so tall its top touched the high ceiling, with tier upon tier of gleaming golden light against the dark green branches of the fir, going upwards for ever.

It was a magical tree; unearthly.

I felt a soft, plump hand take mine and press it.

'This is what I wanted to show you, Maud,' said Mr Harcourt's voice.

He didn't let go of my hand; he had never held it before. This was greatly daring and I wondered again. Then I thought, he is showing off the Christmas tree, as a father might to his daughter, to take pleasure in her awe.

'It is very beautiful,' I whispered.

'I didn't feel you would have many Christmas festivities at Windward House, so I wanted to bring you here.'

'Thank you. I am truly grateful – Grenville.'

'This house needs more young people to appreciate it. It needs a young, lively mistress.'

He sighed and looked about him as if conjuring one up from the shadows beyond the tree. Perhaps he was looking for the ghost of his dead wife, asking her opinion. All of a sudden he turned to me, letting go my hand.

'I have a present for you, Maud.'

I was disconcerted. 'I was not expecting – I have nothing for you.'

'Of course not. This is a token of my feeling for you. You could say my gratitude for tolerating a lonely old man's company these past weeks.'

He smiled wryly and bent to take something from beneath the tree. It was an oblong box tied with ribbon and he presented it to me almost shyly.

'I wish you would open it now, Maud.'

'Then I will do so.' It was so long since anyone had given me a present, not since our last Christmas together, my papa and I.

It was a gold heart-shaped locket on a chain, gleaming in the candlelight as it nestled into the palm of my hand. 'Such a pretty thing!' I said, in delight.

I felt I should not accept it, but Mr Harcourt was looking so pleased and proud of himself that I had not the heart to refuse it.

'It was my wife's,' he said quietly. 'I gave it to her just before we married, when she was much your age, and she loved it too. If you open it you will see that it has two halves and in each half there is a lock of hair, hers and mine.'

The thing was suddenly repugnant to me and I wanted to drop it.

I clicked the locket open in dread. Behind the clear glass of each half a tiny strand of hair was curled, the dark brown of Mr Harcourt's, no threads of grey in it then, and in the other, a lock that was black as night, lustrous, as if it still lived.

'You may wish to remove my wife's hair,' Mr Harcourt said awkwardly. 'I know it must seem strange to you to see it there, when she is dead. If you do, perhaps you would return it to me?'

I swallowed. 'Of course.'

'Let me fasten the clasp for you,' he said.

I felt his fingers touch my neck for a moment, damply. Then he had done up the clasp and the locket lay above my breasts, over my blouse. His hands slipped to my shoulders and he gently turned me to face him. 'You see, Maud, you remind me so very much of my wife. Come, let me show you.'

A shiver passed over me as he walked away down the dim length of the hall, beckoning me to follow.

What was I to see? Not – a corpse?

I imagined the dead body of his beloved wife laid out on the marital bed upstairs, her rotting hair spread out around her. The image was so dreadfully real that I had to shut my eyes to blot it out and almost stumbled.

I should not have imagined such a horrid thing, for it was a portrait that Mr Harcourt showed me; and he took a lamp from the table nearby and held it up. A beautiful young woman in a white satin dress, holding a yellow rose in languid fingers, as if she were bored with the sitting and longed to return to the sunlit garden where the roses bloomed. She looked vivid with life and health, not in the least as if she would die before her time.

'She was painted in her wedding dress. She was your age when I married her, Maud, with your pale skin and black hair and your dark eyes.'

I stared up. It was true, she did resemble me in colouring. 'What was her name?'

'Florence. She came from one of the great families of Norfolk. She died in childbirth. It would have been our first child, but the boy died too.' Mr Harcourt's eyes were fixed on mine and he blinked them rapidly.

'I am so sorry, Grenville. You must miss her.'

'I have accepted that she is gone. She died fifteen years ago.' He sighed. 'It is a long time to be alone, Maud. She was such a very good hostess. I still do entertain but it is not the same.'

It was a strange thing to say of one's dead wife. He did not talk of his love for her; I supposed that to be a private thing he would keep to himself.

He went on laboriously, as if trying to explain, 'I miss female companionship, Maud, but not Florence herself any more. You are so very young. You may not understand that.'

'I believe I do,' I said, wishing to reassure him of my maturity in such matters. 'My father came to an acceptance of my mother's death eventually. She had been ill so long, though, perhaps it was different.'

'Ah, your father.' Grenville sighed again. 'I imagine I must seem much the same age to you. I am so much older, I know. May I ask your age?'

'Twenty,' I lied at once, without thinking. I thought that would seem old enough to satisfy him, but he looked downcast.

'Our ages don't signify,' I said hastily. 'Other things have brought us together. I have been lonely myself since coming to Rending. You have given me so much, Grenville.'

'Maud!' He seemed overcome. He took my hand again and clasped it. His eyes were moist.

'I should go,' I said, suddenly apprehensive of I knew not what. 'I know Juliana will wake before long and demand my presence.'

I believe I was rather quiet on the way back to Windward House. I had dropped the locket beneath my bodice so that Juliana should not see it, and it lay very warm between my breasts. I was conscious all the time that inside it lay a lock of hair that had belonged to Mr Harcourt's late wife. And now he had given it to me. Was it possible that I had misinterpreted his feelings for me?

I stared out at the darkening landscape and my thoughts churned.

Twenty-Seven

In church on Christmas Day I kept my eyes on my prayer book and did not allow my gaze to stray to the Doom. I thought about John, though.

He might as well be dead to me. I must accept it, like a death.

In the pew next to me I felt Juliana's hand clutch my wrist for support as she rose to sing a hymn. Her fingers felt like manacles.

I thought of Mr Harcourt then, of how he never made any demands of me and seemed content with my small conversation. I remembered the warmth in his eye when he gave me the locket and when we parted company after our drive the evening before.

Grenville Harcourt . . .

There was a way to free myself and it had been suggested to me by John himself. He had said that if I married Mr Harcourt, I would have both financial security and a means of escape.

I could feel the locket burning beneath my bodice. I had

taken out the dead black hairs and shuddering, put them into a screw of paper to return to Mr Harcourt as he had asked. His own hair still remained in the other half of the locket and that now lay between my breasts. I imagined his damp hand touching me there, as it would do if we married, and that hand moving across my delicate naked flesh, fondling, squeezing, pressing, with his podgy eager fingers.

To lie beneath his plump, ageing body would be repellent. But he took care of me, he was kind and cultured, even handsome in a fleshy way, and he was rich. He offered me an escape from Juliana's endless demands. And I never need worry about my future again if I married him.

However would I meet anyone else, with the secluded life I led?

And so despite my qualms I began to encourage him.

The mild weather lasted through January and the beginning of February and Grenville continued to take me for drives.

When he laid a fur across my shoulders or tucked rugs around my legs, I wondered if he had done the same for Florence and with those same wraps. I thought, at any moment he will mistake me for her and murmur 'Florence' in my ear.

I felt I was becoming her – indeed, that I needed to become her – and I endeavoured to act the part, chattering gaily, as I felt she must have done, for she had looked most vivacious in her portrait.

So I laughed at Grenville's little jokes. I let him lie his hand over mine, though I disliked its sweatiness. Once I even squeezed his fingers, fingers that were surprisingly firm as they gripped me in return.

He was a cultivated man, always well groomed and immaculately dressed. I tried very hard to grow fond of him, but all I felt was admiration for his conversation and pity for his loneliness.

Was that enough? It had to be.

'Maud, Maud,' Grenville murmured one afternoon, stilling my chatter as we bowled along. 'I feel I know so little about you.' He sounded troubled. 'You are quite a mystery. You never talk of yourself.'

'There is little to know,' I said lightly. I was wary of revealing too much about my past until I was sure of him.

'You are so delightfully modest. If our future is to be together, then I dare say I will learn more.' There was suddenly doubt, a question in his eyes.

'You will do, Grenville.'

He looked at me and smiled, the doubt gone. 'Is that a promise?'

I saw security in those pale blue eyes, security and comfort for the rest of my life.

'Oh, yes,' I said, and made myself press his fingers again.

Another time he asked me if I liked children.

The word 'children' brought up nightmare memories. I think my face must have shown my feelings, for he added gravely, 'It is an important question for me, Maud.'

I swallowed and the words came out, a black lie curling up into the roof of the carriage. 'Children? Why, I love them dearly, Grenville.'

It sounded false and I hated myself for it, but he relaxed and sat back satisfied. 'I want to have children running all over Rushholme Hall.'

He spread his hands in enthusiasm, as if envisaging a collection of little heads between them, fair and dark, and his eyes shone. 'I need an heir, a boy who will take the house over from me and inherit the land.'

So I would be a breeder for him, producing a child a year. A shudder went through me. Then I thought, we shall employ a nurse and a nursery maid. I never need see them, save for an hour after tea!

I thought Grenville might propose that very second, such a light was in his face. But he started on about something else entirely.

'I wonder if I should write to your cousin.'

I felt a flutter of disquiet. 'Why should you do such a thing?'

'To ask her formal blessing on our courtship. I feel uncomfortable that I have been seeing you these past weeks without her knowledge and permission, when she is your only relation and responsible for you.'

'She is not my cousin. She was my uncle's stepdaughter.'

'Ah, I did not know that. All the same, you are so very young—'

'There is no need to ask her permission. She is not my guardian. I have no guardian.'

He looked troubled still, so I said, 'I thought you did not want her to know about us!'

'That was true when I first began seeing you. There were . . . reasons. But now, now we have become so close, you and I, I feel that courtesy and convention demand that I should.'

I laid my hand on his arm imploringly. 'Please, Grenville, do not write! Let it be our secret for a while longer.'

'Why, what is the matter, dearest Maud? You have turned quite pale.'

'I feel she may forbid me to see you, she has such an uncertain temper. She may lock me up – anything!'

He looked astounded, shocked. 'Surely not! What makes you think such a thing of your cousin?'

'She is not my cousin,' I repeated, and tears sprang into my eyes. Seeing them, he looked appalled and put a heavy arm around my shoulders.

'There, there, there is no need to cry about it, little lady. I will do nothing, if that is what you wish.'

I said, 'Oh, it is, Grenville!' and kissed him in gratitude on his fleshy cheek so that his eyes glistened and the colour came up into his face.

I had not realised I had such an effect on him. I thought, when we are married, I believe he will always do as I please.

That was a comfort, at least.

Twenty-Eight

Towards the middle of February the weather turned much colder. The wind came from the north, bringing sleet first and then snow, before it died, leaving freezing days without sun when nothing melted and the world was motionless and white.

Windward House sat rigid, in a carapace of ice. On the drive the snow lay heavy, patterned with dark icy footprints around the front door where Tiggins had attempted to clear it.

During those weeks of bitter weather Grenville didn't come, nor did I expect him to do so, for the route from Rushholme Hall was treacherous in the snow. The afternoons were bleak without my usual jaunts; the nights fell early; the dark pressed down on Windward House by four o'clock.

We were prisoners inside, Juliana and I, and she sat shivering in her little parlour with the fire lit all day, retreating to her bed in the afternoons and lying beneath mounds of bedclothes, a heated stone bottle at her feet.

Miss Potton announced that she would no longer live in at Windward House, that she would only come in the mornings from now on. She wanted to be with her elderly brother in the village in such abominable weather; she was anxious in case he fell over in the snow or slipped on the ice.

It left only poor Dorcas full-time. She was worn out with carrying logs to the fireplaces downstairs as well as upstairs. Afterwards, she had to clean the grates of ash and grumbled all the while. We both had chilblains, itching and painful.

It had been Sly's job to lay the fires downstairs but Sly had been banned from the house after his last fit, which had taken place in Juliana's parlour one morning before her very eyes. She had screamed and called out for Tiggins and cried that she could bear Sly's presence in the house no longer.

I was very glad of this.

With the snow lying all around, there was nowhere for me to go, nothing for me to do except look after Juliana.

Reading, endless reading, and the measuring out of her medicines. We were both bored sick of one another, and she truly did seem sick to me with her paper white cheeks and queasy stomach; and more contrary and demanding than ever.

When Doctor Biddell arrived for his usual weekly visit, he came on foot.

I opened the front door to him. He was well wrapped up

and ruddy-faced, stamping his boots on the step so that little hard lumps of ice flew up, and his breath drifted about him in puffs of white.

'It is good of you to come, Doctor, in such weather.'

He looked surprised. 'Good gracious, Miss Maud! This is nothing! Some winters we have blizzards and deep drifts and I dare say they will be with us before the season is over.' He took off his gloves and blew on his hands, adding cheerfully, 'I grant you, though, it is infernally cold.'

'I am glad you are come. My cousin is not at all well.'

'Ah, many of my patients don't like this weather! I will take a look at her and have a word with you after.'

I hung about in the draughty hall while he strode off jauntily to examine Juliana. I thought, I wish he could give her medicine for her temper.

When he came back he appeared as sanguine as ever. 'Nothing to worry about,' he said. 'Another of her digestive turns, that is all. But it is a cold room and too far for you to hear her in the night.'

'My room is overhead,' I said. 'She has a stick and hits her ceiling with it when she needs me.'

He laughed uproariously at that but stopped when he saw my frown. 'Forgive me,' he said, 'but it is a somewhat foolish arrangement, is it not? She was upstairs before the summer and that room was a good deal warmer. If you could move her back near you—'

'I will do my best,' I said reluctantly, for I hated the thought of having Juliana at such close quarters again, with only a wall to separate me from her moans and groans and noises of sickness.

'Capital, capital,' said Doctor Biddell, beaming. 'I knew I could depend on you, Miss Maud. Then I will leave her in your capable hands.'

I thought bleakly, he regards me as Juliana's nurse.

To my surprise Juliana did not seem opposed to being moved upstairs again – perhaps she was too weak to argue – so Dorcas and I did it that very afternoon after her rest. It was all a great palaver but at least it was something to do. And a few days later she did appear a little recovered, with more colour in her cheeks and a better appetite.

But I could hear her moving about restlessly in her bed close to me as I tossed and turned in my own – for I was not sleeping well, my precious potion so low I dared take only a little each night.

I could do nothing right, even as her health improved. Once she had thanked me prettily enough, shown me a few small kindnesses which had made all my duties worthwhile, but now there was a hardness in her eyes when she regarded me and spite in her fingers when she held me for support. She pinched me quite hard one day when she took my arm to climb out of bed, so that I cried out in pain. She even scolded me for my 'poor' reading.

She began to hark back to her stay with Adeline. It was Adeline this and Adeline that until I could scream.

'Adeline had such a pretty voice,' she said. 'I could have listened to it all evening. She used to read to the family, you know, every night.'

Another time when I tidied her bed for her in the evening, she said, with a great sigh, as she wriggled her back about on the pillows, 'Adeline knew how to make me comfortable. She didn't call the maid but shook up my pillows with her own hands. She would tuck me up too in the dearest, gentlest manner. I was in excellent health, what with all her ministrations.'

'Then it is a pity she is not here instead of me,' I said, exasperated at last.

There was a glint in her eye. 'Yes, Maud, it is a pity. You would learn a great deal from someone as patient and unselfish as Adeline.'

'I wonder how long that patience and unselfishness would last,' I said, and I felt my mouth turn small and mean, 'if she had to do half the things you ask of me, Juliana!'

At that she brought her handkerchief to her eyes. 'Such ingratitude when I have rescued you from a life of drudgery!'

'No more drudgery than I find here.'

'How can you say such a thing? I have taken you in, given you food and shelter out of the goodness of my heart.'

'Perhaps because you desired a nursemaid, one you need not pay.'

I had gone too far, even I realised that. Juliana lay back and closed her eyes. 'Go, leave me,' she said faintly. 'I shall have to reconsider my will. I cannot leave my money to one who shows so little gratitude for what I have given her.'

'Your money!' I cried, in fury. 'It was my uncle's money and it should have gone to his brother, my father! Then after my father's death it would have come to me. Never to you! You had no right to it, and now you have no right to leave it to your dearest Adeline, who is nothing to do at all with our family!'

Juliana waved her hand weakly. 'Leave me. You exhaust me, Maud! You are intolerable!'

And so I left her.

At that moment I did not care what happened in the future, whether Juliana left me her money or not. Married to Grenville I knew I would want for nothing.

One morning I was alone in the parlour with Dorcas, who was thumping about on heavy feet, flapping half-heartedly at ornaments with a duster. It was the only room downstairs where the fire was kept lit, and so I would sit there reading before Juliana was up and try to keep warm.

The snow was starting to shrink back and turn to a hard crust over the ground, though the air seemed as freezing as ever. I was not reading that morning but staring aimlessly out of the window at the drive and the great sweep of snowy emptiness beyond that was tinged with grey under the heavy cloud. My spirits felt as leaden as the sky as I rubbed my cold arms.

Then Dorcas spoke out of the silence.

'You must feel very dull, Miss Maud, not being able to ride out with your gentleman friend in this weather,' she announced boldly, dusting the porcelain mantel clock with vigour.

I stared at her, startled, diverted from my sombre thoughts.

'I seen you out of the window as I go about the house, miss. Nearly every afternoon! He must be keen.'

I didn't want to discuss my private affairs with Dorcas, so I said nothing.

'It's all right, I won't say nothing to Madam, it's not my place. Good luck to you, I say.'

'Thank you, Dorcas,' I said awkwardly.

'He's a fine gentleman, and rich too,' she prattled, reaching up to the mirror with her duster. 'Do you love him, Miss Maud? Shall you be married?'

'I don't know,' I said, and I sat down in a chair for I suddenly felt quite weak and tired. It was a good thing I was sitting down, for she turned and looked at me with her bulging eyes.

'I know I am speaking out of turn, Miss Maud but I wondered—'

'What is it, Dorcas?'

'Well, I wondered if you knew he had once courted Madam. It was before I started here but it was common knowledge in the village. We used to see them riding out together in his carriage. And he came to dinner here at Windward House on many occasions.'

'I see.' My voice had suddenly become hoarse.

No wonder Grenville had tried to avoid Juliana when he first came calling. No wonder he had not wanted me to say anything to her until he was sure of me.

'How long ago was this?'

'Oh, some years,' she said carelessly. 'I don't believe he had any feelings for her. But she . . . Who knows what Madam felt? They must have remained good friends, though, for why else would she have asked him to dinner here before Christmas?'

'That is true, Dorcas,' I said. 'Miss Juliana doesn't know about Mr Harcourt's courtship of me but he means to tell her soon. He will most certainly ask her permission to marry me.'

Dorcas put her chilblained hand to her mouth. 'Oh, Miss Maud! A wedding here at Windward House! That will cheer the old place up, sure enough!'

'I only want her to learn about it from Mr Harcourt

himself,' I said severely. 'It is a secret between you and me, Dorcas.'

'And Mrs Brundish!' She laughed merrily, discomforting me. 'And the rest of the village, too, Miss Maud!'

Twenty-Nine

The snow began to recede at last, as the wind left the north and turned south-easterly. It felt no warmer but somehow the drive turned to slush and my bedroom window was no longer stuck with ice. Now the great thaw had begun, I would be a prisoner no longer. I would be able to walk into Rending or wander where I pleased.

And soon Grenville would come for me again.

Every afternoon as the weather improved, I watched impatiently from the parlour window for Grenville's carriage to roll up. I had a great sense of urgency, like a foreshadowing of some disaster.

Mrs Brundish had struggled up from Marsh End each morning except during the most inclement weather. Shortly after two o'clock Tiggins would insist on driving her back in the trap, for some days it seemed dusk already at that early hour.

He was a good man, Tiggins, kind and thoughtful – which I suppose was why he hoped to find some goodness in

Sly while others merely feared and loathed the creature.

The bitter weather made Mrs Brundish cough. When I took Juliana's breakfast tray downstairs to the kitchen I would see her turn from white to purple and then back to white as her thin chest heaved. When I looked at the hem of her skirts I saw they were soaking wet and steaming in the heat from the range.

'You should not come into work, Mrs Brundish,' I said anxiously. 'You are unwell.'

'That's what I tell her, Miss Maud,' said Miss Potton. 'Still cold enough to bite your head off outdoor.'

She was sitting at the kitchen table sipping a hot drink while Mrs Brundish laboured at the sink, her sleeves rolled up to her raw red elbows in cold water, as she scrubbed the earth away from half-frozen potatoes.

'I must come in. Madam expects it,' Mrs Brundish said hoarsely. 'Who else is to do the cooking? Not you, I dare say, Miss Potton.'

'Indeed not,' said Miss Potton, with a sniff. 'I'm not employed to be a cook! But if you carry on coming up here in this weather, you'll catch your death.'

And, indeed, that is what we thought Mrs Brundish had done, when a few minutes later in the middle of another bout of coughing her face turned blue and she keeled over and lay out cold upon the kitchen floor. Her cap fell off and slid slowly across the stone flags, while Miss Potton let out such a shriek that it brought Dorcas running from the parlour.

'She has fainted, that is all,' I said, kneeling down. 'Help me lift her a little, Miss Potton.'

However, it was Dorcas with her strong arms who helped me raise Mrs Brundish to a sitting position, while Miss Potton cowered in a chair, hiding her eyes from what she imagined was a corpse at her feet.

'She has hit her head,' I said to Dorcas, as Mrs Brundish blinked and the blue faded slowly from her lips. 'I don't believe she should move for a while.'

We propped her against the wall like a rag doll. She looked very vague and out of sorts. 'We should send for Doctor Biddell,' I said. 'I will go.'

'Edie must be told,' said Dorcas. 'She will be at Quilter's.'

'Then I will go there, too. I shall ask Tiggins to take me.'

Under an overcast sky we rattled off down the drive and out on to the road. The horses' hooves crunched over the snow that had drawn back to show a border of brown grass at the verges. On the heath between the black stumps of the cut gorse it still lay deep and woolly and yellowish like sheared sheepskin, and I was glad I had not tried to reach the village on foot.

It was bitterly cold in the carriage, the seat like ice

beneath my skirts, but at least I was sheltered from the freezing air. Tiggins had been alarmed at my news and drove the horses as fast as he dared.

The doctor was at home, fortunately, and threw on his coat and hat while I explained what had happened. Tying his muffler he hurried out to the gig house.

I went back to Tiggins and the carriage, and we rumbled along the village street, where the snow was trampled by black footprints and spotted with horse dung. It had been cleared around the shop entrances but there were icicles melting from the eaves and puddling darkly beneath, where the street was turning to mud.

Tiggins stopped the horses at Quilter's. I jumped down without waiting for him to bring out the step, and landed in a puddle of freezing water.

The bell jangled fiercely over my head as I rushed over the threshold of the apothecary's. Edie looked up startled. When she saw it was me, she turned away, flushing.

'Edie,' I said urgently. 'Your mother has been taken ill at Windward House.'

She stared at me in alarm, then wrung her hands. 'I knew this day would come, I knew it! That evil woman!'

I was shocked by the hatred in her voice. She meant Juliana.

'Doctor Biddell has gone to your mother,' I said, as calmly as I could. 'Tiggins brought me here so I could tell you.'

'Then I must come back to Windward House with you! I must hear what Doctor Biddell has to say!' She looked around the shop in a distraught manner. 'Oh, but I cannot! Mr Quilter is not here today, he is sick himself.'

'Can you not lock the shop?' I thought she would have few customers on such a day.

She shook her head. 'He'd not be pleased. There are prescriptions to be collected and paid for.' She gestured wildly at the counter, where several white packages were laid out in a row.

'Then let me stay in your stead,' I said.

It was as if a stranger had made the suggestion for me and I had not had to think. I listened to the words coming out of my own mouth and was filled with admiration at my ingenuity.

She shook her head. 'Mr Quilter would never allow such a thing!'

'Mr Quilter is not here.'

She looked at me in a distracted way.

'It will only be for a couple of hours at most,' I went on, in my most persuasive voice. 'Let me take over for you until your mother has been seen by Doctor Biddell.'

She nodded at last. Her eyes turned to the door and she flew out, without thanking me, grabbing her bonnet and shawl on the way.

And then I was alone.

* * *

I wandered about the dank little shop, looking at the labelled bottles on the shelves, with the names I did not understand. Then I stepped down into the dark back dispensing room with its locked poison cabinet.

The air was dense with the smell of fatty tallow and the strange, sharp ingredients that Mr Quilter used for his medicines. It caught in my throat; for a moment I thought I would choke.

It was very quiet. I knew I would be alerted to anyone entering the shop by the jangling of the bell by the door.

On the table were a couple of bottles, labelled with the customer's name, as if Quilter had mixed them just before he was taken ill and not put them on the counter in the main shop. There was also an open packet of Restorative Powder, labelled with Jonas Dorley's name.

I gazed at the shelf of empty bottles and jars ready to be filled with medicines and salves, the sink jammed with cut herbs and strange plants. There was a jar of curled brown eel-like things on the washboard that seemed to move as I looked at them, and next to it a dish of bloody meat.

The key to the poison cupboard was sticking out of the lock again. Quilter was a careless man, or had been feeling too ill to hang it back on the hook.

It took only a second to turn it. I didn't feel as if I was Maud Greenwood at all at that moment but someone else entirely: a wild, desperate girl, willing to risk anything to get what she needed.

The door to the poison cupboard opened. I stared at the bottles and jars within. The garish red borders around the labels warned of the contents. *Poison*!

My heart was thumping as I read the labels. They meant nothing to me. But I remembered where Edie had found the laudanum.

I reached in and took the bottle out. Then I found an empty bottle on the shelf behind me, poured a good quantity of the red-brown liquid in and stoppered it. Then the bottle was in the pocket of my skirt and no one had seen.

It was almost as if it were not stealing at all. Besides, it had been taken by this stranger who was not me.

I slid the first bottle of laudanum silently back into its place. As I did so, I noticed that on the bottom shelf there were several unlabelled glass jars grouped together. I glanced at their contents but they were a mystery to me. All save one.

I recognised the whitish powder from a packet our old housekeeper in London had kept to deal with the beetles in the kitchen.

Arsenic.

How very dangerous not to label it.

* * *

I went back into the front room and looked at the names on the packages that lay on the counter. There was Sly's packet of Restorative but Tiggins would not be collecting it that day. I shall take it back with me, I thought. It will be a kindness for Tiggins and he can pay any time.

Near two hours passed and only a couple of customers came in to collect their prescriptions, both elderly and either too blind or too sick to notice that there was a stranger behind the counter. I was feeling very odd, the shop expanding and contracting around me. When I spoke my voice came from outside myself.

Then the bell jangled violently and Jonas Dorley sloped in.

He was half bent over with his cough and the flesh eaten from his face with illness, so that he looked an old man almost, and grey about the lips.

However, his eyes held the same familiar gleam when he saw me. There was something knowing about those eyes that made me vulnerable; he looked at me as if he could see me through and through, even to the strange girl who was now inside me.

'If it isn't Miss Maud Greenwood. And what do you do here, Miss Greenwood?'

I dared not look into those lecherous eyes. My hatred boiled up as I remembered my spoiled princess dress and I swayed a little and held on to the counter. 'It is none of your business, but I have taken over from Miss Brundish for a while. You must wait here while I fetch your package. It is still in the back room.'

He lounged against the counter, looking me up and down, eyeing the splashed skirts that still clung wetly to my legs, as if he could not stop his lascivious habits though he was so sick. 'I hope this lot works better than the last. What does old Quilter put in his Restorative, eh? Dried pig shit?'

'I cannot tell you,' I said primly. 'I know nothing of the ingredients.'

He was suddenly angry, hitting his hand on the counter, pushing his grey face into mine. 'It's enough to make you cough all the more, and that's what I do, Miss Greenwood, all the time.'

I stood back, away from his sour breath but my heart was thumping. 'Then see Doctor Biddell.'

He gave a dreadful laugh that ended in a vile fit of coughing, thick with phlegm. He put a rag, spotted with old brown blood, to his mouth and I saw new drops, bright red. 'Pay for a quack? Not me.'

'The doctor is no quack.'

He ignored that and leaned over the counter, closer to me. 'I sees you in church every Sunday. Does that mean you are a good girl, Miss Greenwood? I don't believe you are, are you?'

'Go away,' I said, trembling.

'I don't think it would take much to make you bad – really bad – would it, Miss Greenwood?'

I put my hands over my eyes so I need not see him. 'Go!'

'Not before I've got my medicine, miss.'

I said nothing but turned and went into the back room for his package, holding on to the door frame for support. My hands, I saw, were shaking and looked very small and white, searching over the table in the dark like two blind animals.

I heard him call from the front of the shop. 'What's taking you such a time, Miss Greenwood?'

'I must light a candle,' I called back, in a voice that was not mine. 'It is difficult to see in here. You must wait awhile.'

When I gave Jonas Dorley his Restorative eventually, he took it without thanks and looked me up and down a last time. He gave a laugh as he left the shop and it echoed back and mocked me even after he had gone, so that I had to cover my ears to stop it.

He is a devil and I will be rid of him.

Thirty

Dusk was falling when Tiggins brought me back and it had started to freeze hard once more.

Juliana was sitting in the parlour, chafing her hands together and so close to the fire that I could smell the acrid smell of her singed skirts. Her feet were on a hot brick.

'I cannot get warm. Where have you been? I have been waiting for you these long hours. Have you no care for my feelings? Aveline would never allow me to be in such a state.'

I took off my bonnet and sighed. 'How is Mrs Brundish?'

'Oh, Mrs Brundish,' she said petulantly, as if her cook's collapse had been a tiresome interruption to the day. 'The doctor took her down to Marsh End in his carriage and has ordered her to bed. Now I have no cook. It is too bad.'

'It is unfortunate,' I agreed, 'but rest in bed is what Mrs Brundish needs, I am sure.'

'We must manage on cold cuts tomorrow, then goodness knows what we shall do.'

'I will speak to Dorcas. She may know of a girl from the village to come and cook.'

'No one will come,' said Juliana flatly. 'They all hate me. Why, I do not know, when I am restoring the Doom for them out of my own pocket!'

Dorcas told me that Edie had offered to come in place of her mother and would I ask Madam if she would be happy with the arrangement.

'Edie? What about her work at Quilter's?'

'Edie is to leave anyway. Mr Quilter can afford an apprentice now, what with the success of his Restorative.' Dorcas looked earnestly at me. 'Edie Brundish is a good cook, Miss Maud, and a friend of mine. I should be glad to have her company in this big house.'

'Very well.' I was not sure what we should do if Dorcas left. 'Miss Juliana will be delighted, I'm sure.'

But I felt disquieted, I was not certain why.

I was so deeply asleep that night that I did not hear Juliana call out to me. I awoke to see a pale spectre in my room, drifting about my vision, strangely elongated, grotesque, lit by a wavering light.

I screamed but the sound that came out was a grunt. I could not get my lips to move and pronounce anything coherent. I lay fixed in terror in my bed while the apparition moved around me.

'Wake up! Get up! I need you!'

I realised at last that it was Juliana. There was enough relief in that to move me out of bed. I stumbled on to the cold floorboards while the bedroom walls retreated. Her face looked ghastly.

'I cannot sleep. I have been ringing and ringing for you. I need a cup of hot milk.'

She had to light my candle, for my hand trembled too much.

I stumbled downstairs in the dim, flickering light. It was as cold as death in the house. How I found my way, what with the thickness in my head and the darkness, I don't know.

I staggered upstairs at last, the tray unsteady, the milk slopping.

She looked at me askance. 'What is the matter with you?'

The following morning I felt no better, what with disturbed sleep and not enough of it. When I took in Juliana's breakfast tray, she looked at me with narrowed eyes that held no gratitude.

'You are becoming slovenly, Maud. I saw the state of your bedroom last night.'

On the way out of her room I lurched against her dressing table, toppling bottles and potions. One bottle broke and fell to the carpet in shards of glass; a heavy perfume filled the air.

'I am so sorry,' I stammered, while she jerked up in her bed and glared. 'I will fetch a dustpan and brush at once.'

'You are as careless as a calf, Maud,' she spat out. 'I wonder if you will ever learn.'

I must not take so many drops in future, I thought to myself. Just enough and no more.

But it was difficult to judge the dosage.

The master of Rookwood stands at the bottom of the stairs, smiling at me.

He lets me go first, like a gentleman.

Then I feel his hand lifting my skirts.

His breath pants in my ear. 'If you wish to keep your job, say nothing of this to my wife.'

The postman brought weekly letters for Juliana marked with a Scarborough postmark. She told me in great excitement that she had been asked to stay again in the summer. The summer! I could not believe that the sun would ever warm me again.

At least I shall not be here, I thought. I shall be married to Grenville by then.

I had to write Juliana's replies to these letters. They went on at some length and made my hand ache abominably. How I loathed the name Adeline.

* * *

Edie began work in the kitchen. Miss Potton instructed her on what we were to have for our meals, and so I needed to have nothing to do with her.

It was not difficult in a house that size to avoid going into the kitchen area altogether but some days later, Juliana, who had taken to coming down in the mornings and sitting in the parlour, asked me to warm a brick for her feet.

'The fire takes an age to heat this room.'

I was forced to go to the kitchen and encounter Edie for the first time. Her eyes were red-rimmed, as if she had been weeping.

'Is it your mother, Edie?' I asked gently, for I did feel pity for her then. 'Has she taken a turn for the worst?'

'She is much the same,' she said, sniffing. 'I wonder if she will ever be altogether well again. Miss Juliana has driven her to the ground and soon she will be beneath it.' She did not seem to care that she was being rude about the mistress for whom she now worked.

'I am sorry. I hope she will recover soon.'

She said grudgingly, 'I suppose I must thank you for fetching the doctor so quick.'

'I was glad to help.'

'And glad to have the opportunity to have Quilter's to yourself, I dare say!' she burst out.

My pulse beat faster. 'What do you mean?'

'Mr Quilter has accused me of doing mischief in the store while he was sick.'

'Mischief?'

'Tampering with the stock. I never did such a thing!' She suddenly turned on me and her eyes flashed. 'It was you, Miss Maud, wasn't it? I know what you done!'

'I don't know what you mean.'

I pulled the brick from the range, protecting my hands from its heat with a cloth, and stood up. I struggled to speak calmly in the face of her fury.

'I am sorry for you, Edie, for I know you worked hard for Mr Quilter. It is hard to mind a store on your own, as you did all that time. You should not be blamed if you made mistakes.'

She was still glaring after me as I left the kitchen.

Thirty-One

Juliana decided to move downstairs again to her old room.

I was sure it was to spite me, for it took all day to rearrange and heat the room. Even with the fire blazing, it had a dank, sour atmosphere and the oil lamps made the green wallpaper gloomy in the wintry dusk. The torn paper behind her bed was like a wound and I drew the tester curtain over it.

'Why, Juliana?' I said, when she announced the move that morning. 'Why move downstairs when you always complain how cold it is? It is much warmer in here and your health has been better.'

'You know why! It is your fault!'

'My fault?'

'You haunt me at night. You come in and stand by my bedside.'

I was astonished. 'You must have been dreaming, Juliana! The only time I enter your bedroom is when you call or ring for me.'

She shook her head wildly. 'You come in when I have not called for you, though I am awake. You stand in silence beside me so that it chills my blood, then your hand drifts down to the table, to my medicine glass.'

I shivered in spite of myself. 'What happens then?'

'Your hand hovers above it. You make to lift it, then at the last moment you moan a little and step back.'

I studied her. Was this some story to frighten me? To excuse the tedious business of moving her once again?

'My nerves cannot take it,' she said, in a little voice. 'Downstairs I shall be safe.'

Safe from me, when I was her carer, when I had gone to her night after night in the bitter cold, whenever her bell had roused me from my precious sleep!

Rage at her ingratitude and her lies seized me so that I could not speak. I grabbed the bedclothes from her bed even as she lay there and carried them away. I could hear her squawking plaintively, all the way to the top of the stairs.

She hardly said a word to me for the remainder of the day, though in many ways that was a relief.

The next morning Dorcas brought a letter to my sitting room. The envelope was addressed to me in a small upright hand that was difficult to read. There was a heavy seal on the back of the thick paper, the postmark blurred.

My heart began to beat unpleasantly hard. The letter was not from John, for I had seen his careful notes on the Doom colours when I had visited him in the church.

It could only be from Grenville.

Dorcas's eyes gleamed with curiosity. 'Thank you, Dorcas. You may go,' I said stiffly.

I sat for a while holding the letter before I broke the seal, somehow not wishing to read the contents. Perhaps Grenville did not have the courage to see Juliana himself, given their past relationship, and wanted me to tell her of our pending marriage. Perhaps he wanted to delay our marriage until I was older. Perhaps he felt we should know each other for longer before we married.

Or perhaps he was simply setting a date for his next visit.

I sat back in the armchair, huddled into my shawl. Then at last I opened it. The letter was short.

Dear Maud

I hope you are in good health and able to take a walk in this milder weather.

I am being called away on business to London. I cannot tell how long I shall be away. It may be some time, so I fear this letter is to say goodbye.

Thank you for indulging an old man with your company over the past few months. Please keep the locket as a token of my gratitude. I hope the circumstances of your own life improve in the future.

Yours very sincerely
Grenville Harcourt

I brought my hand to my mouth. My stomach churned; I thought I would vomit. Then I forced myself to read the letter again. And again.

I tried to interpret it in a different way but there was no coded message. It was quite clear. It was a letter of farewell, of rejection, couched pleasantly but firmly. Grenville was not going to marry me. He was telling me as kindly as he could that I could expect no future with him.

I took the cushion from behind my back and held it in front of my face so that it blotted out the room with darkness. I pressed it hard against my eyes and mouth. I longed for it to suffocate me, but in spite of myself I had to gasp and hold it away a little so I could breathe. I began to keen into it, rocking myself backwards and forwards.

I think I did that for some time.

When at last I stopped, the letter was still there, where it had fallen on the floor, the small black writing staring up at me as if it was alive and would start to form new letters and words of its own. If only it would say, 'I love you, Maud. I am coming for you. I will take you away from Windward House for ever.'

Why had Grenville rejected me? Was that what he had done to Juliana, also? I should not be so surprised. But Juliana was too old to have the children he longed for, whereas I—

My thoughts chased round in circles until I was exhausted.

Perhaps I had read too much into our relationship. Perhaps he had never intended to marry me at all and I had misunderstood. But he had given me the locket that had belonged to his late wife.

Dorcas came in again, hastily, apologising for not knocking.

'Madam is asking for you downstairs, Miss Maud. She wants you to read to her. Oh, miss, have you had bad news? Would you like a moment to compose yourself?'

I found I had tears standing in my eyes and her figure was blurred. I blinked them away and saw her eyeing me with great curiosity and no little excitement.

'I am quite composed, thank you, Dorcas. I will come down.'

When I stood up eventually I was bent half over, like a dying creature, one whose heart has been shot away. My feet trod over the letter on the floor and I left it there.

Juliana complained about my reading. She said I was not concentrating, that I looked a fright. 'And your words are slurred. Are you taking after your father?'

'What do you mean?'

'I mean, have you been drinking?'

A huge wave of grief and fury welled up in me. 'How can

you say such a thing?' I burst out. 'You know I have not!'

I didn't rush from the room as I longed to do: I was too weak to move, my limbs like cotton. I sat, trapped, while she stared at me, a gloating triumph in her eyes.

'The bad blood is in your family, the devil drink.' The green light from the wallpaper reflected on her face. Her lips twisted. 'You cannot escape the devil, Maud.'

'In that case the devil was in your stepfather's blood too,' I said hoarsely. 'Your dear stepfather's, Juliana.'

We stared at each other in silence, like the enemies we were, perhaps had always been, waiting for the other to surrender. I thought, it will be like this forever now. Juliana will try to hurt me with her harsh words; I will defend myself and I must never ever show her my pain.

The room closed around us both, the walls pressing in on me so that I could not move even if I had had the strength. I raised my hand and tried to push the heavy medicine table away as it slid closer and closer to my feet. Soon it would ride over them, crushing my delicate bones. I backed my chair away but still it pursued me.

'What are you doing?' Juliana said shrilly.

The room stilled. I looked at her and thought, *how many long years will it take before you die?*

Thirty-Two

Before I took my drops that night, I sat a while in the armchair, trying to straighten my thoughts and calm myself before bed. But a terrible vision kept rising before me.

I saw in my mind's eye Juliana and I grown old and crabbed, each as evil as the other, watching to see who would die first. It would be me: she would kill me with her complaints – I so sick and weak and worn out with nursing her.

Before that there might be years of waiting, of closing the shutters and doors of Windward House to the outside world, both of us imprisoned there together, trapped in a deathly pacing of the days by the slow tick of the clock.

What would my life hold but the changing and making of Juliana's bed, the measuring out of Juliana's medicines, being polite and hospitable to Juliana's sole visitors, the vicar and the doctor, carrying endless trays of meals to Juliana's bedside, reading to Juliana from good works, escorting Juliana to church?

And in the church I should only be reminded of my

youth, when I had once known an artist called John Shawcross.

John.

He had loved me. I could make him do so again.

I would have to persuade him to return to Rending, for I had not the money to take a train to London, nor would Juliana allow it. John would have to come to me. I must write straight away.

But how was I to discover his address?

Edie might have it, but I could not demean myself by asking her.

Juliana must have John's address still. I could not ask her for it outright. She would demand an explanation and most likely withhold it from me – a young man who had disgraced himself in her house.

I would have to search for it in secret, in that great cluttered desk of hers.

John, I would write, *Please come. You are my only hope. Please come and save me.*

'You cannot escape the devil, Maud.'

But I would not let it get me, the devil in the corner.

I believe I must have fallen asleep before I took my drops that night, I was so exhausted. It was well after midnight when something roused me.

I struggled awake and realised I was sitting half-upright

in bed, as if about to reach out for my bottle, my shawl still around my shoulders. The candle had burned down and the room was in darkness, so dark I could not see my fingers before my face.

I listened in dread for the knock of Juliana's stick beneath my floorboards but could not hear it. Then a scrabbling, like a mouse, but high up at my door.

I waited, my heart beating heavily against my ribs and shaking my fragile bones fierce enough to break them to pieces.

At last I found the courage to quaver, 'Who is it?'

The scrabbling stopped. For some moments there was complete silence, so that my ears thrummed with listening to it. Then outside my door something slid away.

I relit my candle stub. I took my drops. I pulled the covers right up over my head so that I half-suffocated, and sank into a blackness so deep that nothing could disturb it.

In the morning there was a little pile of sawdust beneath my bedroom door where the hook had jiggled in the wood, as if someone had tried to get in from the other side. Even though my head was thick with dreams and my vision blurred, I saw the little pile of wood dust.

I am sure I did.

'Sly tried to come into my room last night,' I said to Juliana. 'I cannot bear it!'

'Sly?' she said, her eyes wide. She seemed genuinely startled. 'He has no key to the house. He has no means of getting in.'

'I don't know how he does it but it was him!'

'Are you certain?'

'There is wood dust beneath my bedroom door where he pushed at it from the landing.'

I could see that after her initial shock, she had recovered and no longer believed me. 'It is more of your imaginings.'

'It is not, I swear!'

'Then let me see this wood dust for myself.'

And though she was not yet dressed for the day, she flung a shawl around her shoulders and gripped my arm all the way up the stairs, as if she thought I might run away before she had caught me out in the lie.

The little pile of wood dust was no longer on the threshold of my room.

I said helplessly, 'Someone – Dorcas perhaps – must have cleared it away.'

'You frighten me with your stories,' Juliana said, turning on me. 'It is not good for my nerves, so much nonsense. And sleepwalking too! At night I never know if you will hear me, and when you come I am not certain whether it is my stick on the ceiling that has brought you – or some strange whim in your dream.'

My voice shook. 'I attend to your needs night after night.'

Her mouth set. 'Well, perhaps you are tired, that is it. I should get myself a new nursemaid. And perhaps you should go back to being a governess.'

I cried out then. 'Not that! Not that!'

'I shall go into Halesworth today,' Juliana announced a few days later when I carried in her breakfast tray. 'Tell Tiggins to prepare the carriage. There is some business I must attend to there.'

'Shall I come with you?' I said, eager for an outing at last.

'This is private business. I shall manage very well on my own.'

Private business. Something I must not know.

I felt uneasy at once.

I left her and went to see Tiggins. Perhaps he would let something slip.

'I don't know where Miss Greenwood wishes to be taken in Halesworth, Mr Tiggins,' I said carefully, 'but she has set her mind to it. I hope you will be able to take her to the door, for she has not done much walking for a good while.'

He nodded. 'Mebbe her solicitor's.' He shrugged his shoulders. 'I remember that, for it's up a cramped street and another carriage came down at me.'

I went to my sitting room much perturbed. If Juliana were going to her solicitor's, was it to arrange the rewriting of her will?

Later, when Juliana had left the house and I had heard the carriage rattle away down the drive, I crept downstairs to her room. I didn't want anyone to hear me or interrupt what I was about to do.

The passage outside was deserted and noises came from the kitchen, clatterings and voices. They were all in there, Miss Potton, Edie, Dorcas. I opened Juliana's door stealthily and slipped inside.

It was strange to be in Juliana's bedroom when she wasn't there.

The fire lit earlier had died to embers. I had made up her bed that morning and the smoothed sheets and plumped pillows waited for the indent of her body once again. I could see her living ghost lying there in the light that filtered in through the half-drawn curtains, its arms stiffly at its sides, making no mark on the empty bed but staring straight at me as I made my way from the door towards the desk.

The hairs rose on my neck. I turned my back on that accusing gaze, but could still feel it boring through me.

'You are not here, Juliana,' I said out loud and my words echoed back at me. 'I can do as I please.'

Her ghost vanished and light fell on the polished walnut of the desk. I opened the lid and stared down at the bundles of letters, jumbled papers and bills, the envelopes stuffed into compartments, the ink-stained cigar tin where she kept spare nibs. It seemed that for years she had kept almost every letter that had been written to her. I despaired of ever finding it.

I began compartment by compartment, going from left to right methodically, looking for the envelope in John's handwriting. The compartment on the far left contained business letters from years back, mostly from the solicitors Smallbone and Bagge of Halesworth, dealing with my uncle's will.

I pulled them out, looked through them and was about to stuff them back in when I saw a letter pushed right to the back, as if deliberately. I thought, there it is! and I pulled it out in triumph, setting the others down on the opened lid.

I was so certain the letter must be from John that I was taken aback to find it was not.

The letter was much crumpled but the ink was still clear. I recognised the address and the name signed at the bottom, Frederick Odbury, my father's solicitor, the small, fussy man who had come to see me at Miss Caseborne's about my father's will. It was dated 23rd January 1865 – only a short while after my father's death.

I read it swiftly.

Further to your letter of 20th January inst regarding the future of your young niece, Miss Maud Greenwood, and our previous correspondence thereof, I very much regret that you feel unable to take her in. You are her only living relative and as I have emphasised before in my previous letter, her financial state is parlous. Her father did not take out life insurance and the annuity she has been given by his bank is very small. I fear she will have to seek a living if she is offered no home under your own roof.

The letter continued,

'I beg you to reconsider . . . school reports excellent . . . an amenable, good-natured young lady . . . a talented artist . . . of tender years to go out into the world . . . only profession open to her . . . a trifle young to be a governess . . .'

I thought, Mr Odbury did his best for me and I did not know. Perhaps Juliana destroyed the earlier letter, perhaps she thought she had destroyed this letter, too, but it most certainly did arrive at Windward House, for here it is, in my hands.

She lied to me when she said that it had never arrived.

I found I felt no surprise at the lie, the betrayal of trust. If Juliana had taken me in earlier then I would have been spared the terrible years as a governess. But at fifteen I would not have been able to stand up to her either. What price was a roof over one's head?

It was too high at Windward House.

The letter had reminded me that my annuity would be due now that we were in a new year. I had only to write to Mr Odbury and ask for the cheque to be sent to me direct and I could make my own way to London secretly, to find John – once I knew his address.

I was suddenly filled with hope. I put Mr Odbury's letter in the pocket of my skirts, stuffed the other letters back into the compartment in the same random order and began to work through the next compartment as fast as I could.

It was taking too long. Juliana might return before I found the right envelope and discover me rifling through her desk. There were little drawers beneath the compartments that contained letters as well, so overstuffed they had not shut properly.

The edge of a letter stuck out from one of them. My own name stared up at me.

Maud.

When I pulled it out I saw it was a letter written in Juliana's hand.

I don't think I would have bothered to read it if I had not seen 'Dear Grenville' at the top. Why had she written to him? Why hadn't she sent it?

The letter was much crossed out and the writing over the crossings-out crossed out in turn. It was undated and she had not signed it, had finished in mid-sentence: indeed, it was only half a letter, perhaps a rough copy of one she did eventually send.

For by the time I had finished reading it, I was in no doubt that she had indeed sent a clean copy and perhaps as recently as two weeks ago.

Dear Grenville

It has come to my attention that you have been seeing my niece Maud over the past weeks. I know you are a kind and generous man and no doubt have wished to offer my young cousin some diversion, but as an old friend who keeps your interests still very much in her heart, I feel I should warn you about becoming too involved with Maud.

You must know that she spent some time as a governess before I took her in. I hoped that she would be a comfort and support to me and that we would form a close relationship in due course.

However, I soon realised that though Maud is all charm on the surface ~ as I am sure she is to you ~ she is very different beneath. There is, I believe, some madness in the family, for her father was unstable and addicted to drink.

I have been concerned enough by Maud's behaviour to make enquiries of her previous employers. I tracked them down through the Governess's Benevolent Institution and their replies confirmed what I already suspected. They all described Maud as manipulative and cunning.

She ran away from her first position while out on a walk with her charges and left the two young children quite alone. Another employer said Maud was prone to hysterical outbursts and they were forced to dismiss her after she had been violent to their eldest child.

The third letter shook me in particular. To put it to you as delicately as I can, the mistress of the house informed me that Maud had tried to seduce her husband and that she suspected they had indeed had a liaison~

There was no more to read but I had read enough.

Juliana must have believed those letters, for she had never asked me for my own account of what had happened. She had used them to frighten Grenville away. He would never return to me now. A mad girl with loose morals, who was violent to children.

Juliana's letter was designed to put an end to our relationship and it had done so.

I stood with the letter in my hand, feeling most horribly sick at heart. I closed the desk lid, abandoning my search for

John's address, and blundered over to the bed, thinking I must sit down, for my legs felt as if they would not hold me upright and there was a buzzing in my head.

As I did so, I caught my hip painfully on the edge of the medicine table. I was rubbing it when the door opened.

Thirty-Three

My heart jerked but it was not Juliana returned early. It was Edie.

There was something furtive in her movement as she came across the room. She did not see me at first but then looked most startled, as if she had seen Juliana's ghost standing in my place.

'What are you doing here?' There was accusation in her tone.

'I am Miss Juliana's cousin,' I said coolly, though my heart was thumping and the letter visible in my guilty hand, 'and can enter her room if I wish.'

'You are at her medicine table.'

'I check the quantities from time to time.'

Her eyes narrowed. I could feel dislike and distrust running like an unbreakable thread between us. It was a relief to bend to the dying embers of the fire and prod them with the poker.

'I must warm the room again before Miss Juliana returns.'

I was aware of her hesitation behind me, as if she wished

to say something more, but she did not. Her quick footsteps went to the door and I was alone.

I threw more wood on the fire and thrust Juliana's letter to Grenville into the young eager flames.

There! It had gone, the vile words burned away.

I could not confront Juliana with her letter and betrayal. I knew my position at Windward House was precarious and I did not want to endanger it further. It was at least a roof over my head until I found John again.

The strangeness of Edie's sudden appearance only struck me later.

Why had she come to Juliana's room when she knew very well that her employer would not be there?

Juliana came back from Halesworth and said nothing.

I tried to look for clues in her behaviour to me but could find none. It was almost as if she relished taunting me with what might have happened there. Had she asked to rewrite her will? Had she left her money to Adeline instead? Had she decided that soon she would banish me from Windward House for ever?

She snapped at me and complained but that was her usual behaviour.

Now I found it even more difficult to do the intimate things she demanded of me, even reading aloud to her which I had once so enjoyed.

When I emptied her slop-pot in the night, I wanted instead to pour it over her head. When I gave her her pill from Doctor Biddell and waited with a tumbler of water while she placed it on her long pale tongue, I longed for the pill to stick in her windpipe and choke her. When I turned her pillow in the night to make her more comfortable, I yearned to place it over her sour little mouth and stop her complaints altogether.

I wish you would die.

The day after Juliana's trip, Dorcas came to my sitting room in some excitement.

'Guess what has happened, Miss Maud!'

'I cannot,' I said wearily.

'That rogue Jonas Dorley has upped and died, and I am heartily glad of it and so must be all the other girls in Rending!'

I had not slept well the previous night and my heart began to beat too rapidly. I searched for words.

'How did he die?' I said after a long pause, while she waited for my reaction, pop-eyed with the thrill of it.

'In an agony of coughing, they say. And he'd been taking the Restorative from Quilter's. It can't have done him much good!'

Later that morning, I offered as usual to do some shopping

in Rending for Miss Potton.

I think she perceived she was above such a menial task, for there were always purchases to be made. I wondered sometimes if she smuggled a goodly part of our provisions back home to her brother, for we seemed to get through so much food when there was only myself, Juliana and Dorcas to feed in the evenings.

'We need more candles, too,' she said, pursing her lips. 'Madam lights them in the daytime. Such wastage!'

I was glad of the excuse to go into Rending; I wanted to visit the church. I was now obsessed by the certainty that there would be something left in the vestry that would help me find John – his address on a notice board, the receipt from the carrier that had taken his box, even the delivery note John might have left for him.

I must go and find it, for it would be there.

I took my box of pencils and charcoals with me so I could write John's address down, and a scrap of paper torn from my sketch book, and I took a dose of my potion before I left to still my nerves. I had not done that before.

I set off into the bright, cold morning, taking the familiar sandy path that led over the heath to the village. The sun was slanting across the grass, outlining every gorse bush and tussock of winter-grey heather with light. In the dark earthy hollows beneath the stunted oaks, snowdrops, delayed by the cold weather, were raising their heads to the air.

I was surrounded by the purity and beauty of nature, yet my presence defiled it as my shadow dragged through the light.

Above me the huge skies that had once seemed to offer me freedom, now looked frightening in their vastness. Even as I looked up, a cloud shadowed the sun. It would be overcast by the time I walked back and the cold heavens would press me down into nothingness.

It seemed to me that the villagers whispered together as I walked along the street, craning to watch me as I went into Thurlow's, but perhaps it was my fancy.

'There's been great demand for candles, Miss Greenwood,' said Mr Thurlow, shaking his head glumly. 'Winter and bad weather, you know. You'll have to go into Halesworth.'

I wasn't sure whether I believed him, or if he was lying because Juliana hadn't paid his latest bill.

'Have you nothing left at all, Mr Thurlow?'

He looked at me, sighed, and pulled down two dusty boxes from a shelf behind his head. 'They're green, I'm afraid, miss. Old stock.'

I thought how pleased Juliana would be, that they matched her wallpaper.

'Put them on Miss Greenwood's account,' I said, as I always did, and he frowned and scribbled the new amount in his book.

'I'd appreciate payment sometime soon, miss,' he said, as he always did, and I nodded and left hastily.

The candles were heavy in my basket, together with my own box and the paper, as I retraced my footsteps along the street, past the green at the far end and turned right through the lych gate of the church.

The church door was unlocked as it always was, and dark and deserted inside, the flowers dying at the altar. It was a Wednesday morning, with no service until evensong.

I passed the Doom, my head averted. Even so I caught the little devil eyeing me, the devil in the corner, and I said, 'Go away. I am too busy now. I will ignore you,' and I hurried away up the nave towards the vestry. That, too, was unlocked.

I looked around at the big table with its leather-bound register of christenings, weddings and funerals, at the shelves of prayer and hymn books and mouldering religious tracts, at the several hard little chairs and the row of choristers' surplices hung up on brass hooks.

It was a cold stone room, enclosed, but all the same a little draught came from beneath the outside door and stirred the gowns, so that I saw them move out of the corner of my eye, move and bulge as they came towards me, like an army defending itself against a foe.

I blinked and they were still. Then I began searching.

The single drawer in the table contained only some pens,

the ink dried hard on their nibs, a folded pocket handkerchief and a box of mints. I looked beneath the table in case any note might have fallen down but there was nothing, only my own footprints in the dust. My head felt strange, too big and heavy for my weak body.

It had gone, John's address had gone. It had been here once, I was sure of it.

I sat for a while at the table. Then I picked up my basket and tried the outside vestry door but it was locked.

I went out into the chancel and crossed over to the side aisle. I went up to the Doom in its corner and looked Saint Michael straight in the eye, Saint Michael with his scales that weigh up our good and evil deeds.

'There is no hope for me now, is there?'

And he looked back at me, very upright and grand in his red cloak, and shook his head.

I stood looking at the Doom, thinking of John's square hand moving back and forth across the painting so gently in small, rapid strokes of the long-bristled brush, his eyes intent above his mask. I had lain my hand on his once and felt his strong bones move.

I thought, I should have told him how I loved him, then he would not have gone away.

I thought, *Jonas Dorley*. He should be among the sinners to be judged. He was an evil youth and should be judged for it.

After a while I left. I had done what I had come for.

We heard the news from the vicar.

He came after evensong, it being mid-week so Juliana's soul would not have too long to wait before it was blessed again on Sunday.

I opened the door to him, for Dorcas was having her supper. He set down his lantern and left it on the step. It was a dark night, no stars, and he seemed to bring the darkness into the house with him. He appeared out of sorts.

'I have bad news for your cousin. You had best hear it too, Miss Maud.'

I followed him into Juliana's room. I started when I saw she was sitting at her desk and rummaging through the mess, an oil lamp beside her.

I thought, does she suspect anything? But she rose to her feet when the vicar entered and held out a frail hand to him, which he took and pressed.

'How are you, my dear Juliana?'

How obsequious he was, with his hushed voice and his concern!

She was wearing a dinner gown with a shawl over her shoulders and she pulled it further around herself, hiding her collar bones which stood out sharply, for she had lost weight again.

'As well as can be expected, Edwin. It is this cold weather. It disagrees with me so.'

'It is raw, I agree, but the good Lord will send us spring again soon, as He always does.'

I stood awkward to one side, trying to edge closer to the fire, for I had run out of wood upstairs and my little sitting room was bitterly cold. I waited for the vicar's bad news and my heart beat thickly. I thought, it is my drops. I should only take them at bedtime.

At last the vicar came to the point. 'The Doom,' he said. 'You have not seen it today?'

'Of course not!' Juliana answered sharply. 'You know how exhausting it is for me to get about. But I will be in church on Sunday, as I always am.' She frowned, as if realising the implication of his question. 'Why, what is the matter?'

'I fear it has been defiled,' he said solemnly.

'In what way?'

'Someone has drawn on it. One of the villagers, a child, perhaps – it is a scribble, nothing more. I shall ask in church on Sunday, of course. I hope the sinner who has done it will repent.'

'It must be cleaned off!'

'Best not to touch it. It should be done by an expert.'

'It will be the first task of any restorer I employ.' Juliana sighed. 'I must start looking now, I suppose.'

I slipped away to my sitting room. Later, Dorcas came unexpectedly to see me.

'Why, Miss Maud, it's cold in here! I'll bring you up more firewood.'

I nodded, half in a dream. Her outline was blurred and wavered in the candlelight.

'Miss, have you heard that someone has drawn on the Doom?'

'The vicar brought the news earlier.'

'I looked at it after evensong tonight.' She squatted beside me while I tried to focus on her eyes. 'We were all looking at the Doom afterwards, all us girls and the men from the village too, a crowd of us. It's the strangest thing, Miss Maud, but I would swear the drawing is meant to be Jonas Dorley.'

'The butcher's boy?'

'Him, right enough. The figure's drawn with a butcher's cleaver.'

'A cleaver?'

'I'd swear that's who it's meant to be, and we all agreed. Must be Jonas. And he's been put in along with all the other sinners.' She shivered and put her cold, chapped hand on my arm. 'All them sinners lining up for hell, Miss Maud.'

Thirty-Four

There was sickness in the village. Everyone was going down with vomiting and weakness of limb and high fever. Doctor Biddell was busy with his visits to those who could afford them. He said it was the time of year, everyone's constitution was tired of winter.

A terrible suspicion came to me. There was arsenic in Quilter's Restorative, I was sure of it! Those unlabelled jars I had seen grouped together in the poison cupboard held the ingredients, and I knew one of them contained the tiny white grains of arsenic.

'Juliana,' I said, 'I wish you would not take the Restorative without telling Doctor Biddell. I'm not certain that it isn't the powder that makes you so sick.'

'Stuff and nonsense!' she said, as I knew she would. 'And don't dare mention it to Biddell!'

Sly was the next to go down with the sickness.

I heard nothing more outside my door, nor did I catch him creeping about the house. He stayed fast in his hovel in his bed of rags, with Tiggins tending him.

At last Tiggins brought him to his own room above the stables, carried him bodily there and laid him in his own bed. He looked very distracted and perturbed as he went about his duties in the garden.

I avoided the stables while Sly lay there. I did not like to think of him so close at night, though he was too ill to move.

Not long after, Sly drowned in his own vomit. It happened while Tiggins was out chopping firewood. He said he came back to find Sly dead, his eyes rolled back in his head, his hands clawed rigid on the blanket Tiggins had laid upon him earlier to sweat out the fever.

Tiggins was beside himself with grief and lamentation. Poor Tiggins! I believe he did truly love that demented creature.

And I – I would have slept well after Sly's death, if I had not had nightmares of Jonas Dorley leering by my bed and saying, 'You're a bad girl, aren't you, Maud Greenwood? A bad, bad girl.'

Shortly after Sly's death, another drawing appeared on the Doom; it had also been drawn in charcoal.

It was Sly, the village reckoned, no doubt about it. There he was, with his misshapen leg and skull cap, standing in the line of sinners behind the figure of Jonas Dorley.

I saw it with my own eyes when I took Juliana to church

on Sunday. It was a clever depiction, though it was only a stick figure, better accomplished than the first.

I thought, Sly, you are where you should be, you ungodly creature. You, who terrified me so!

Juliana was most vexed that the Doom had been defiled again.

'It is being done to spite me! They know it will cost me to have the mess cleaned off.'

The village muttered together. 'It is the devil's hand. A child would not do such a thing, not an innocent child from our village! It can only have been drawn by the devil himself.'

This was told to me by Dorcas, whose mother had bustled up to Windward House in a great state to see her. Dorcas told me that some feared to go to church at all in case the devil lurked inside, in the shadows behind the pillars. She looked frightened and said she didn't like sleeping alone in the kitchen.

'Sometimes I think there is a devil in this house, Miss Maud. In the kitchen at night I hear noises in the darkness that maybe are rats, maybe not. Mother said I should give Miss Greenwood my notice but I know she'll create.'

I said, why not move to Miss Potton's old room upstairs? but she shook her head very glum and said that being upstairs was worse than being in the kitchen, which had two doors to run out of if the devil came.

'Look how sick so many are! That's the devil at work, Miss Maud!'

I asked Miss Potton if she would stay on at night as she used to do.

Miss Potton shook her head firmly. 'My brother would not countenance it, not now. He wants me home safe at night.'

'Surely you do not believe there is a devil about, Miss Potton?'

She sniffed and did not meet my eyes. 'There is something wrong, I know it. No one will rest easy until those figures are cleaned away. What a pity young Mr Shawcross is not here still.'

Darkness held Rending in its grip. When the fogs of milder weather came the villagers said they had been sent to hide the devil.

By this time two more figures had been drawn in on the Doom.

Several inhabitants of Rending had died of the sickness, so no one knew who these sinister drawings represented. It was evident to the vicar himself that this was more than a prank.

'You must lock the church!' Juliana cried at him.

Wissett shook his head. He was the only person who could stand up to her. His dog collar gave him the Almighty's authority to do it and even she respected that. 'I cannot, Juliana. God's house must always be open.'

Juliana demanded to be taken to the church and Tiggins took us in the carriage. When we entered and went to examine the two new figures, they could have been anyone – any sinner waiting to be judged – with their anonymous bulbous heads and stick bodies.

'Where is God?' people asked the vicar. 'Why doesn't He stop the devil's work?'

But how can the devil be stopped when he lives inside you? There is no room for God then.

It was strange to walk in the garden without fear of Sly.

I wandered here and there among the wrinkled shrubs and along the narrow gravelled paths, feeling that I was seeing it all anew. I thought, I can come out here whenever I want to escape from Juliana's demands.

Finally I came to Sly's hut.

I looked through the filthy window but of course he was not there. The door was half open and I pushed it open further and stepped in. I wanted to be quick and the stench was enough to drive me out almost at once.

The shelves still held their nasty assortment of jars and traps and dead things, and with the milder weather the flies had awakened and were crawling in a sated, sluggish state over the carcasses.

I was as quick as I could be, then I ran out and returned to the house. I went in the back way, which opened straight into the kitchen.

Dorcas was not there, but Edie was standing by the window.

'I have been watching you,' she said. 'Why did you go into Sly's hut?'

I was taken aback by her rudeness. Recently I had noticed this challenging tone in her voice when speaking to me.

'I was looking for something.'

She pointed to a box sitting on the table. 'It was that, wasn't it?'

I could not lie; I nodded.

'What should you want with a box of Fuller's Solution, Miss Maud? Don't you know it's poison?'

'I intended to fetch it for Dorcas,' I said, with dignity. 'She told me that at night she can hear rats in the cellar. She is frightened they will come up under the kitchen door.'

'She is frightened of that and a lot else beside, here at nights alone. I will put the poison down for her myself, for she doesn't like going into the darkness below.'

I forced myself to say, 'That would be kind,' in what I hoped was a gracious manner. 'Keep it in the storeroom in the meantime, out of the way.'

'I hope we shan't have to buy more, for I see this box has already been opened.'

'It is an old box. Tiggins must have used it in the barn.'

'Perhaps.' She stared at me. 'But rat poison won't keep the devil away, will it, Miss Maud?'

'There is no devil,' I said, but I shivered, though the range was lit and roaring.

Edie went on, 'Now that Mother is so much better and can be left, I will stay on at nights for a while and keep Dorcas company.' She sounded defiant, as if daring me to oppose her.

'I don't think Miss Juliana will like that.'

'I have already asked her and she appeared very pleased. She said she would like to have another person in the house at night, the better to take care of her. And that's what we must do together, isn't it?'

That night I took a strong dose of laudanum and sank into oblivion.

At some point I woke and lay with my eyes open, staring into the darkness, which shifted and moved and pressed on me, as if it contained solid shapes. My neck felt as if it was trapped in a brace but I fought against it and at last succeeded in turning my head on the pillow.

When I did so there was a hand lying beside my cheek.

In terror my gaze followed the hand to the wrist and travelled further up to where the darkness resolved itself into mass – the arm, the shoulders and neck and then the face, the hideous death-distorted face of Sly.

But the voice I heard belonged to Jonas Dorley.

'You're a bad girl, aren't you, Maud Greenwood? A bad, bad girl.'

I cannot lock my bedroom door at Rookyard.

I wake in the night and see the dark shape of the master.

He comes towards my bed. He puts his hand over my mouth.

His voice is low and thick.

'Do not breathe a word, or you will be out on the streets where you belong.'

Thirty-Five

John

In all the months I have been away I have heard nothing from Maud.

I suppose I should not have expected it. I have been busy enough, painting pretty little pictures of cottages and rosy children and spaniels, the kind of thing the public like; and winning two new commissions for portraits. My urban paintings still languish in a stack at the back of the art gallery.

One of my subjects may pay well, for he is a well-to-do young solicitor, with whom I fell into conversation by chance in a public house near the new Charing Cross Station. I had been intrigued to see this wonderful modern edifice and indulged myself all that day, drawing first the facade, then trains and passengers, to my heart's content.

My companion's name in the public house afterwards was Benjamin Goldstone, and he had walked over from

Middle Temple after visiting a clerk of chambers there. I took to Ben, and he to me, I think, for we have become fast friends.

I dwell on Maud often.

I remember the tears that coursed down her face as I left the church that morning, and curse myself for not staying on and insisting to Juliana that I finish my work on the Doom before I left. Whoever has come in my stead no doubt will have ruined it already: the current tendency to over-restore church paintings will undo all my care.

It is not the Doom I mind about, of course: it is Maud. Who has come in my place, to steal her heart?

Edie's first letter comes when I have been back in London for about three weeks, when I have not yet met Ben, nor have any commission. I am feeling altogether low in spirits.

I am surprised and touched to hear from her. I break the wafer and open out the letter. I think she might mention Maud, though why should she?

The paper is cheap and flimsy, the writing round and rather large. Edie writes, very formally:

Dear Mr Shawcross,

I hope this finds you in good health and glad to be back in London.

I am writing to tell you that the carrier

must have been, for your equipment is gone from the vestry. I checked today and thought you would like to be told that it was on its way.

Mother sends her regards and says that she would be very pleased to have you visit in the spring, if not before. She is not well, though she is at pains to hide it from me. I wish she would stop her work at Windward House but she says how would we manage. We have not found a new lodger. I think she misses your conversation and kindness.

The talk in the village is of Maud Greenwood, who is being courted by Mr Harcourt. The rumour is that there will be a wedding in the new year.

With very best wishes

Edith Brundish

I put the letter down slowly, sick at heart. It is my fault. I encouraged Maud to accept Harcourt's attentions and she has done so.

I try to feel glad for her, for she will have the financial security she needs and be able to leave Juliana Greenwood and Windward House. Yet part of me wants to cry out: 'Oh,

Maud, how could you?'

I resolve to shut her from my mind.

It is not easy.

I write back to Edie and thank her for her letter and tell her that my crate has indeed arrived safely and please to write again, for I enjoyed receiving her news.

Shortly before Christmas an American art dealer, rummaging through the stock in the gallery, comes across my urban paintings. He buys two and says he will return.

Mother and I toast each other with Champagne that night and we have roast partridge for supper. I celebrate for Mother's sake. I now have a good sum in the bank, enough to pay for Mother's comforts and more. I rent a new studio in Tite Street and go out drinking with Ben. I say nothing to him of Maud, of course, though I long to unburden my heart. But it is my own private business.

The dealer does come back a few weeks later and, to my astonishment, buys four more of my paintings to be shipped back to Virginia.

The sales have come too late for Maud and me. With the money we could have set up home together. There is no point in telling her the good news. She is lost to me.

Meanwhile, another letter arrives from Edie, longer than the first. She chats of this and that in Rending, repeats that her mother misses me, wishes me a merry Christmas.

And then:

We see Miss Maud out in the carriage with Mr Harcourt. Their heads are close together. I wonder when they will set the date.

Jealousy pierces me so sharply I let out a cry of distress that brings Mother in from the kitchen to see what is the matter.

I struggle to calm myself. I tear the letter up and put it in the fire. 'It is nothing, Mother. Nothing at all.'

She gives me one of her looks and shakes her head.

Christmas comes and goes, and then the new year brings bitterly cold weather and freezing yellow fogs. Even with the gas lamps screwed up high, the light is so thick and sulphurous it is difficult to paint and the choking air seeps in around the window frames.

I finish painting Ben and am pleased with the result. I have caught the flash of his black eyes, the enquiring tilt of his head, his clever mobile face.

All the while I dwell on Maud. I am impatient for another letter from Edie to tell me of Maud's engagement and so stop my pitiful yearnings once and for all.

It doesn't come for some weeks, by which time the snow has turned to grey slush in the gutters and the fogs have been dispersed by raw winds.

This letter doesn't mention Maud at all. It is all about Edie's mother, Mrs Brundish, who was taken ill suddenly at Windward House and is now recovering at home. Edie is now doing the cooking up there in her mother's stead.

I have had a falling-out with Mr Quilter, so will not be returning to the apothecary. It is a pity, for I enjoyed my work there but he has an apprentice starting so I could not have stayed.

I think immediately that it will be pleasant for Maud to have another young person at Windward House, although Edie is so much younger. I give little thought to Edie's own situation, except to wonder briefly what it is that has caused her and Quilter to part their ways. I am concerned about Mrs Brundish and decide that when the weather improves I will make the journey to see her.

I write briefly back to Edie, expressing my sympathy and mentioning this. I think she may press me for a date but I don't hear from her for several weeks.

This latest letter is very different from her others, carelessly written as if in a great rush and crumpled, almost as if at one point she decided not to send it and made it into a ball to throw away.

Dear Mr Shawcross

Mother is progressing well, thank you.

But all is not well here in Rending. There have been deaths from winter fever. You will be sorry to hear about the Church. The painting has been damaged. There are new figures drawn in. Jonas and Sly both died and they are there in the painting, waiting to be sent to hell. Also two others I do not recognise. Some say the devil has drawn them.

At Windward House things are very wrong. Please visit us before too long.

Edith Brundish

I am exasperated to think that my work has been tampered with, for I still feel somewhat proprietorial about it. I suppose that some lout has drawn the figures for a joke.

Above all Edie's comments about Windward House disconcert me. She is a sensible girl, not given to exaggeration. It is out of character.

I write back to her by return, asking for further explanation, but it does not come. As each day passes, I worry the more.

'Go back to Rending then, you silly boy!' says Mother. 'See things for yourself.' She looks at me closely. 'There's a girl in it somewhere, I dare say.'

Then while I am still uncertain what to do, a new letter comes from Edie at last.

Something terrible is going to happen. The devil is with us. I beg you to come.

Thirty-Six

Maud

I had no friend in Windward House. Dorcas no longer spoke to me, influenced by Edie.

Both girls crept about, giving me dark suspicious looks whenever they saw me. It was hard to avoid them, for I had to enter the kitchen for Juliana's needs – to bring her hot drinks, or a warmed brick for her feet, fresh water for her medicine jug – and Edie was always there, watching me in silence. At odd hours I would trip across Dorcas in the kitchen passage, cleaning the linoleum with a rubber – to keep an eye on me, I was sure.

One night when I could not sleep and dared not increase my dosage of laudanum, I thought, I will visit Mrs Brundish tomorrow, while Edie is working here, and ask her for John's address.

I told Juliana I wished to go and enquire after Mrs Brundish's health. Juliana was looking very sickly that day, a greenish pallor in her cheeks as she lay prone on her day bed in the parlour.

'I hope she will be well enough to return to us soon,' she said. 'That child Edie cannot cook! Her food makes me even sicker than her mother's!'

I left soon after breakfast.

The huge sky above me was hung with motionless pewter clouds, for there was no wind. Frost still lay thick as snow in the stiff ruts of the track but light gleamed on the ribbony trunks of the clustered silver birch at the bottom of the slope.

I thought, if I were otherwise – another person altogether, someone as untroubled as Dorcas, say – I might take pleasure in the beauty of this day.

I walked along the track that John and I used to take – that Mrs Brundish used every day – my head bent, lost in my own brooding thoughts. When the silver birch changed to darker trees, I scarcely noticed or cared that they pressed in on me and that the silence was absolute except for my own footsteps, soft in the powdery frost, until eventually I heard the growl of the sea.

The beach was deserted and though the sea further out was unruffled, the tide was driving in in great long rolls and breaking in a shower of white droplets upon the shingle.

I thought, this is where we stood once, close together, and John pledged his love for me. I could almost see us standing by the waves – a girl and a young man, she so full of hope, he so full of promises.

But the sun was not shining today, and as I stood there the light went from the sea. It had taken its colour from the sky and turned the dull, dark grey of steel.

I turned my back at last on that desolate, wintry scene and made my way back through the dunes.

Here was the very dune where we had lain so often together. I believed I could still see the imprint of John's body. When I touched the hollow the sand was firm but my hand burned with the coldness of it.

'I love you, John,' I said, quietly at first, then all the feelings that I had imprisoned for so long rose up in a tumult inside me, so that I repeated it and again, louder still, crying the words across the dunes to the shoreline, as if declaring my love at last might bring him back to me.

But I told my love in vain. There was nobody to hear. Only the empty air.

I was too late.

I began to walk along the duckboards, overwhelmed by an aching sadness.

It was very quiet; the sound of the sea blurred. There was no wind to move the reeds and they stood stiffly upright, bleached and shrivelled by winter. The water was very black at their base and skinned with melting ice that would soon turn hard again.

The boards rose and fell slightly with each step I took, in the way I remembered. Lost in grief, I walked with little care, though they had become slimy with winter weather.

I had not been walking long when I heard the first sound. At first I thought it merely the echo of my boots, which thrummed on the wood beneath my feet.

But there was a dragging noise as well. A footstep and then a scraping along the wood, as if one leg dragged behind the other. When I stopped to listen, distracted at last from my misery, it continued.

Someone was walking behind me.

I walked faster and my heart began to thud. I was seized with terror, all else forgotten.

I knew that sound.

But Sly was dead. *Dead*.

His leg was dragging on the boards, his weight was making them dip more strongly and he, too, was quickening his pace. I could not breathe.

I dared not look behind me. There was a horror behind me and if I turned and faced it, I would be lost.

A hand fell upon my shoulder.

'Miss Maud?' said Edie's voice. 'Did you not hear me calling you?'

I sank down on the duckboards in a fearful state, feeling

very faint. I felt her press my head between my knees. 'I startled you,' she said in concern. 'I am sorry for it.'

I swallowed great icy gulps of air. I could not speak.

'I called your name out but you didn't hear me.'

'What are you doing here?' I managed to say at last.

'Miss Juliana sent me to find you. She said you had gone to see my mother. You have missed luncheon, Miss Maud.'

'Have I?' I mumbled, greatly surprised.

'Yes, it is after two o'clock.'

I lifted my head. She was squatting beside me, her eyes – very green in that colourless landscape – gazing into mine.

'You saw no one following me?' I asked, trembling still.

She shook her head. 'Only me, Miss Maud.'

'There was someone – someone behind me. I thought it was Sly!'

'Sly? But he's dead,' she said, as she might to a child.

I put my hands over my face. 'It was his ghost I heard, then. Or a devil!'

She looked troubled. 'It was your fancy, nothing more.'

'I heard it. I heard something.'

'Come.' I was surprised to hear compassion in her voice. 'Let me take you back to the track. We must return to Windward House.'

'I have not visited your mother yet.'

'You're not in a fit state. I don't want her upset, Miss Maud. Your appearance—'

'Why, what is the matter?'

Then I realised that my hair had come down and was hanging lank around my face and that my skirts were wet and sandy at the hem.

'I must have stood in the sea. I don't remember doing so,' I said, puzzled.

She tried to smile. 'A cold day to go paddling.' But her eyes were afraid. Her grip tightened on my arm. 'Come, we'll walk back together. These boards will be icy soon.'

I thought, A mad woman with her warder.

But I gave in meekly. I was defeated.

I was too frightened to go to sleep that night. The darkness of the house seemed to enter me. I kept my candle burning but it made my room flicker with shadows.

Juliana was worse. Her stick thumped on my floor to summon me, and when I staggered down wearily she was retching and complaining of stomach pains. Her face was ghastly in the candlelight, her fingers, brittle as chicken bones, too thin for her rings now, clutched my arm as I bathed her face.

'I am dying, Maud,' she whispered.

'Doctor Biddell says you will live for years yet!' I said, as heartily as I could.

'Doctor Biddell is a fool.'

'This is one of your digestive upsets, that is all.'

'It is so dark.'

'Let me light more candles.'

'Not the new ones. They have such a horrid smell.'

I took a taper to the nearest lamp and she sank back against the pillows. 'That is better. Fetch me a hot drink, Maud. A mint tea will settle me.'

I took one of the candles with me as I went along the passage to the kitchen area. The house had drawn into itself with the cold and darkness of the night. The walls pressed in on me, crowded with shadows.

I passed the larder and scullery and came to the storeroom. I didn't keep it locked nowadays as Miss Potton used to do, for I never knew what Juliana might demand in the night.

The closed door loomed before me, whitewashed as was all the kitchen area but dull in the candlelight, sucking all the light into itself. Inside on the shelves was the old Coronation caddy which contained the dried mint leaves.

All of a sudden I could not bring myself to open that door. On the other side something waited for me.

I hesitated but there was no sound. I turned the handle, holding my candle higher.

The yellow light glowed over the familiar shelves with their jars of preserves and pickles, their boxes of sugar, starch, rice and soap and the new green candles I had bought the other day. The drawers beneath held cleaning cloths and the brooms and brushes were stacked in one corner. It was not a large room; more like a large cupboard with a tiny window, black with night.

The linoleum was icy under my slippers as I stepped across to the shelf that held the tea caddies and the tins of biscuits.

A figure rose up from under my feet.

I gasped and stepped back in terror. It took me a moment to recognise Edie in a nightgown, her hair down around her face, her eyes wide. We stared at each other in fright. There was a mattress, placed beneath the shelves and I had almost stepped upon it.

'You are sleeping here?' I cried angrily. 'Why aren't you keeping Dorcas company in the kitchen?'

'Dorcas snores so. I waited until she was asleep then I came in here. I'm sorry if I frightened you, Miss Maud.'

My heartbeat slowed. 'Very well. You may stay here. Move your mattress, please, so I can reach that shelf.'

She did not move. I wondered if she had heard me. Then she said, 'What is it you want, Miss Maud?'

A strange question and why should she ask it? 'Nothing you need know. It is for Miss Juliana.'

'Miss Juliana does concern me,' she burst out. 'She is my employer.'

'That and no more,' I said swiftly, 'for I know what your true feelings for her are!'

'And I know yours, Miss Maud.' Her eyes were enormous dark holes in her face that I might fall into if I were not careful.

'Whatever do you mean?'

It was strange, both of us facing each other in the tiny, night-filled storeroom, in our nightclothes, our hair down: two girls each with her own secrets, for I knew Edie had them and she knew I did, also.

'I know you hate her as much as I do,' she said at last. 'I know you wish she was dead!'

My heart began to beat heavily again. 'That is a lie. If I were mistress of this house, I would dismiss you. Now would you please move out of the way?'

And she did so, sullenly, but she did; and moved her mattress with her.

I reached up and took down the caddy. Next to it was a box which most surely should not have been sitting so close to it. I took that down too and showed it to her.

'This should not be on a shelf with the food stuff. Store it away in one of the cupboards until you have finished with it in the cellar,' and I put the box of poisonous Fuller's Solution straight into her hands.

Thirty-Seven

All that week Juliana's health worsened. During the day she sat wrapped in rugs, shivering and ashen-faced, before the fire in the parlour.

Doctor Biddell came to visit her and prescribed calomel. When I questioned him, he was reassuring. 'She has no fever.'

'She has been taking Quilter's Restorative all this long time!' I burst out, for I felt I must tell him, now she was so unwell. 'It must be the powder that makes her ill! I believe it may have made others in the village sick as well!'

He smiled. 'I doubt there is anything harmful in it. There is nothing beneficial either. Let her take no more.'

On Friday Juliana summoned me to the parlour soon after breakfast.

She was very weak and lying on the day bed, which Dorcas had dragged close to the fire. She still wore her dressing-gown and above it her face looked sunken about the eyes.

'You must ask Tiggins to drive into Halesworth and

fetch Mr Smallbone. Tell him it is urgent. I must see him today.'

'Mr Smallbone, the solicitor?' I said, though I knew very well who he was.

She gave a barely perceptible nod over the coverlets that were heaped upon her. 'Give this letter to Tiggins to take with him for Smallbone, Maud.'

To my astonishment her thin wrist and hand emerged from under the coverlets, clutching a folded paper. When had she written it? Why had she not asked me to write it for her?

'Of course,' I said, and hurried from the room.

I went out of the front door, for I hated going out from the kitchen now, with the eyes of the two girls upon me, wary and spiteful. I had not bothered to put on my mantle and bonnet, and the chilly wind that had blown all week dragged at my skirts.

Juliana had not sealed her letter, merely folded it. I tried to see what she had written but the wind played with the paper in a maddening way. I had to go into the barn to read it.

I stood by the bales of hay and smoothed it out in the close, sweet-smelling half-dark. The handwriting was even more untidy than usual, the strokes jagged but the message was clear.

'I wish to make an amendment to my will. Please

come at once. I am dying. My man will convey you to Windward House.'

'Can I help you, Miss Maud?' came Tiggins's voice.

I started, looked up guiltily. In the shadows of the barn there seemed to be two of him, Tiggins and another. A tall dark shape, one leg bent crooked.

I gasped and fell back against a wooden post.

'Miss Maud?'

I folded the letter with trembling fingers. 'Mr Tiggins, Miss Greenwood has asked if you could take this at once to Smallbone and Bagge in Halesworth.'

Mr Smallbone was brought to the house about an hour and a half later. I took a glass of Madeira and a slice of seed cake into the parlour, hoping to catch something of his conversation with Juliana but he stopped talking when I came in.

There were papers covering the little table beside him and he was sitting close to her day bed. He was business-like and without sentiment. He thanked me briskly and said he did not wish to tire Miss Greenwood and his work would be soon done.

I closed the parlour door gently behind me and stood listening. The windows were rattling and I felt the draught in the hall about my ankles. The house was gathering itself together for another onslaught from the east wind.

There was a mumble from the parlour.

I strained my ears. I could pick out a few words, but what with the thickness of the door and the wind noise in the house, could make no sense of them. Juliana's voice was too weak to be heard at all.

Then in a short gap when the wind died I heard the name 'Adeline Dimchurch' mentioned distinctly by Mr Smallbone. Afterwards, nothing more.

I don't know how long I stood, hoping to hear something else, growing colder and more despairing. I was certain now that Juliana was changing her will in favour of Adeline.

Dorcas came out of Juliana's room with a pan full of ashes. She gave me a curious look.

'I am waiting to show Mr Smallbone out,' I said quickly.

She wrinkled her nose. 'There is a strange smell in Madam's room.'

'The wind will blow it away.'

She frowned, looked over at me again but said nothing more.

Mr Smallbone did come out shortly afterwards, with his black overcoat on and his lawyer's case under his arm.

I went to the front door with him. 'I believe Mr Tiggins is waiting to take you back to Halesworth.'

'Kind, most kind. I am sorry to see your cousin in such poor health. I hope to see her improved on Monday.'

'Monday?'

He nodded. 'I shall be returning then with the amended

papers for her to sign.' He gave me a little bow and went out through the front door, which I was holding open to the gale. 'Thank you, Miss Maud.'

Juliana was worse the next day, Saturday. She remained in her room and lay passively in bed while I read to her until I thought I would swallow my own tongue with dryness. She took her calomel obediently only to retch it up again. She ate very little otherwise. Dorcas made her a calf's foot jelly and she had a spoonful.

'We shall have to put off Mr Smallbone coming on Monday if she is no better,' I said in a low voice to Dorcas, who gazed at me silently, pudding-faced, and made no reply.

Then Juliana called out in a surprisingly strong voice, 'No, Smallbone must return!'

I hurried over to her, for she had raised herself off her pillows. She subsided, muttering, 'It is the will, you see. He is bringing the new change to the will.'

Later Dorcas and I left the room to allow Juliana to sleep.

'It would suit you, miss, would it not, if Mr Smallbone didn't come?' Dorcas remarked once we were out in the draughty hall.

'Whatever do you mean?'

'I think you know, miss. I should tell you this: Edie and me, we know too.'

There was something horrid in the way she said it. I stared at her, at her closed stolid face, as she folded her arms and faced me.

The two girls were united against me and I must tread very carefully indeed.

Thirty-Eight

I was unwell myself that night and brought up the small amount of supper I had managed to eat. I had stayed in Juliana's stuffy room all day, with its drawn curtains and candlelight, without the chance to wander outside for air.

The next morning I felt weak and light-headed but no longer nauseous. I crept down the stairs like an invalid, holding on to the bannisters for support.

It was Sunday and Edie had the day off. She would have already gone home to her mother. I was glad, for I was not certain I could stand up to her today.

Juliana was in no fit state to go to church. She lay against her pillows, her cheeks as bleached and stiff as the starched linen. She put her hand out and it lay on mine, no heavier than the picked backbone of a dead fish and as cold, so that in revulsion I wanted to draw my own warm young hand away but could not.

The room smelled oddly, and this morning I recognised it as garlic, probably from something Edie had cooked.

'You should go to church, Maud,' Juliana whispered. 'We must keep up appearances.'

I didn't want to go alone into that church where the Doom would accuse me with its images, where I would be reminded of John. But all respectable households attend church on Sundays and Windward House must be seen to be respectable.

So it was that Tiggins came for me at the usual time and helped me up into the carriage, and we set off into the wind under heavy, rolling clouds.

The path to the church door was crowded with people from the village, their dark clothes blown back, like so many ruffled crows. Edie and Mrs Brundish were ahead of me and I quickened my step.

'Mrs Brundish? I am so very glad to see your health improved.'

She turned to me, Edie looking awkward at her side, but I didn't care about that. I was glad to see colour in her mother's cheeks and brightness in her eye. She greeted me warmly while Edie stared at me sullenly, yet seemed to simmer with a secret excitement. This I only remembered afterwards, when I was casting my mind back over that terrible day.

'I'm very much better, miss,' Mrs Brundish said. 'See, I've had the strength to walk to church today! I hope to return to Windward House before the month is out.'

I said, but the words choked me and I felt my mouth go sour, 'We are grateful to Edie for coming in your place, Mrs Brundish. You must not come back until you are completely recovered.'

She smiled at me and then they were blown into the stone porch and so was I, behind them.

As I went past the bench for the elderly and the notices stuck on the board and through the open door into the church, the air struck chill. People were gathered about the Doom, murmuring. Pale faces stared from the pews.

I slipped into our usual pew at the front, with my head bowed. When the usual mutterings started I tried not to listen. They were not about me, after all, but about Juliana, for the congregation had noticed she was not with me.

It was very dim in the church that day, with only the altar candles burning and such grey clouds overhead that the windows were darkened by shadows. The organ played; the vicar came in. I remember very little of the service until he began his sermon. Then some word chimed with something in my head and made me listen.

He looked at the congregation gravely.

'Do not be swayed by what you have seen, my people. It is not the devil's hand at work. Rather, it is someone here who has allowed the devil in himself to take charge. We are all vulnerable and can work mischief if we choose. It is a matter of choice and God has given us that right freely. Do you choose Good or Evil to have the upper hand inside you? Someone here has chosen the latter.'

Afterwards, at the church door when I led the congregation out – as I had to do because of Juliana's standing in the community – and therefore was the first to shake the vicar's hand, he murmured to me: 'I am sorry for it, but you must convey the bad news to your cousin. I hope it will not endanger her health further.'

I looked at him in bewilderment.

'Did you not know?' he said quietly. 'A new figure has been drawn on the Doom.'

For a moment I could not breathe. I stared at him and his face seemed to dissolve. He put a hand on my arm. 'Miss Maud?'

I pulled myself together. 'I didn't know.'

'Perhaps you had better take a look for yourself, so you can decide whether or not to inform Miss Juliana.'

There were a few people around the Doom, Mrs Brundish and Edie among them, but they fell back as I approached.

'Oh, Miss Maud, it's happened again!' Edie said to me, her eyes very bright and agitated.

It was there: a new figure among the sinners destined for hell, a stick figure like the others but this time unmistakably a woman – I could tell by the hair, which had been represented by straight lines, and a kind of long garment about the figure. It held something: a bottle?

A dreadful feeling assailed me. I knew without any doubt.

The figure was intended to be me.

I was certain of it the more I stared at it. The charcoal was fresh, lying thick and black on the colour beneath, as if it had been drawn recently. There I was, with the other sinners, my hair down and in my nightgown, administering with a medicine bottle.

But I was not dead.

Not yet.

I felt sick with horror. The image shifted, and from the corner the devil winked at me.

'What a thing to happen when Miss Juliana is so ill,' Edie said. 'There's wickedness abroad in the village. The devil is lurking somewhere among us, sure enough!'

Around her people muttered in agreement. Her mother tutted and pulled at her arm, but Edie stood closer still, with her round, bright eyes.

'Shall you tell Miss Greenwood about the new figure, Miss Maud?'

'When she has recovered.'

'And when do you think that will be, Miss Maud?'

Mrs Brundish put her hand on my arm. 'Miss Maud,' she said gently. 'You look pale. Should you not sit down?'

'Thank you, I believe I will,' I said.

I sat in a pew as far from the Doom as I could, while the

people who had clustered around it left and the church fell silent and cold about me.

The vicar passed down the side aisle and out to the vestry without noticing my still, bowed figure. I was trying to pray. 'Oh God, save me' – but from what, exactly? Further words did not come to me, merely those, running round and round in my head in a manic way.

At last when I was sure everyone had gone, I rose stiffly to my feet, smoothed my skirts down and left.

My head was bent and at first I did not see the figure coming through the lych gate towards me.

I was looking blankly at the dead leaves that scurried over the path in the wind. I thought that soon dead leaves would blow over my grave, just as they had over Papa's, and Mama's too. They had not deserved to die, whereas I—

Footsteps were coming towards me. The wrong way. Why should someone come to church when the service was over?

I looked up.

The sky pressed down on me and under the dark clouds I saw the darker shape of a man. And then the clouds whirled faster and I brought my hand to my throat and gave a gasp, for I knew that figure and had thought never to see it again.

John.

Thirty-Nine

He took off his hat and bowed. 'Miss Greenwood.'

I thought, so stiff, so formal in his address. He does not call me Maud. He no longer cares for me, I must remember that. His long, long silence.

I wanted to reach across and touch him but the gap between us was immense, insurmountable. 'Mr Shawcross.' My heart beat so that I could hardly speak. 'I didn't expect to see you again.'

'I said I would come back and here I am.' He smiled but it was a grimace.

'What brings you, Mr Shawcross?' How I longed for him to say, It is you, Maud. It is you.

'I hear there has been damage to the Doom.'

Of course. That is what has brought him.

I nodded, my throat constricting. 'There is a new figure drawn today that has set the village to gossip.'

He nodded, then he looked at me, a grave, considering look, his wide eyes filled with light in the way I remembered. 'You are well, Miss Greenwood?'

'Perfectly, thank you.'

He persisted. 'You have not been ill recently? I rather thought—'

I shook my head. 'And you – you look in good health.'

It was true: his face had filled out a little and it suited him. His coat was new. His hair, though, was blown about by the wind and he had to brush it from his forehead in the old way.

'I have had some minor success in London.' He always was a modest man.

'I am glad!' I cried in genuine pleasure and clasped my hands together.

His expression lightened. For a long moment we gazed at each other, then both spoke together and stopped, embarrassed. He let me speak, gesturing politely.

'You have returned just in time,' I said. 'How did you hear about the damage to the Doom?'

'I have been in correspondence with Edie Brundish. She said that all was not well in Rending. She told me about the figures drawn on the Doom.'

'Edie Brundish?' I felt something inside me that had begun to blossom again, shrivel and die a bitter death. 'You have been writing to Edie Brundish?'

All this time and never a letter to me!

He nodded. 'She has given me news of the village, yes.'

'And no doubt you are staying at Marsh End cottage?'

He nodded, his voice neutral. 'I am glad to see the Brundishes again.'

'I do not doubt it.'

If he noticed my tone, he did not show it. I could not think of what else to say and fell silent. I had a lump in my throat and talking was difficult.

He tried again, however. 'I am sorry to hear your cousin is unwell again.'

I flared up. I wanted to hurt him with words. 'I cannot believe that, sir, knowing full well how much you dislike her!'

He dropped his gaze and hesitated. 'But you, Miss Greenwood? Has your life become any easier?'

'With Juliana?' I gave a dry, brittle laugh. 'How could it be?'

'She must be distressed by what has happened to the Doom.'

'The Doom?' I said scornfully, my lip curling. 'I don't believe she cares a jot for the Doom! She wanted to buy her way into heaven.'

'You have become very harsh, Miss Greenwood. I hope you remember me kindly.'

'How could I remember a man kindly who made me false promises?'

'I never intended—'

'No, you never intended anything at all!'

'That is not what I meant. My circumstances—'

Then once again he was interrupted, this time by the vicar, who came hurrying out and almost fell over us both.

'My dear Mr Shawcross!' he cried, in a great fluster of good will. 'God has brought you back to us at a most opportune time! Another figure drawn on the Doom today! No doubt you will want to see what has happened to your work.'

What with greeting John and requesting that his good wishes for Juliana's recovery be passed on to her through me, he was too taken up with pleasantries to notice that neither of us were best pleased by his presence. At last he went on his way, shaking John's hand vigorously and bowing to me.

'I will be up tonight, Miss Maud, to see how the dear lady is, never fear.'

'I hope you will not have to administer last rites one of these nights, vicar,' I said smartly. 'She is failing fast.'

He looked horrified, as much at my tone as at my words. 'Gracious, I am quite devastated to hear it! I knew she had taken a turn for the worse, but this! Let me know whenever you need me to give comfort and succour.'

'I will indeed, Vicar.'

'So you see,' I said bitterly to John, as finally he left us, 'little has changed since you were last here. Juliana still has her two faithful visitors, the vicar and the doctor.'

'And you? I hear from Edie that Mr Harcourt is an admirer.'

'No longer,' I said shortly. How dared Edie tell him of Mr Harcourt's visits!

There was a long silence. John fiddled with his lapel, his head bent. 'Maud,' he began.

I felt very cold and it was not from standing in the wind. I could not accuse him of not writing to me, for it would be most immodest. Besides, I could not bear to hear his excuses. It had taken all my strength during our conversation not to weep and rail, not to beat my hands against his chest and beg him for a last time to take me away.

I half turned so that he could not see my despair.

'With Juliana so ill I must get back to Windward House, Mr Shawcross.'

'Of course. I must not detain you,' he said, all politeness. Then he added and his voice changed, 'But I return to London tomorrow morning.'

'So this is farewell then.' I put out my hand and he took it and dropped it swiftly. Then he bowed.

I began to walk away unseeingly down towards the lych gate. I heard him call after me, 'Maud, Maud!'

I turned back quickly, hope beating high and hard in my chest. He came striding down towards me.

'What did you mean when you said I had returned just in time?'

'Did I say such a thing?' I said, as carelessly as I could. 'I meant nothing by it, nothing at all.' I waved my gloved hand vaguely in the direction of the church. 'Merely that now you are here you can assess what needs be done to repair the Doom.'

He laid his hand on my arm and his touch made me tremble. I tried to hide it from him while he looked gravely into my face.

'I gather from Edie they are saying in the village that the devil is behind the drawings. You don't believe that, do you, Maud? Not you?'

I shook my head.

'I am glad of that, at least. I would not like to think of you frightened by superstition.'

My mouth twisted. 'Edie believes it, you know, the silly girl. She will say as much to you, I am sure.'

He attempted lightness. 'Then I will not listen, I promise!'

'And now, Mr Shawcross, I really must leave you. The wind is very cold. Do you not feel it?'

He bowed his head. 'I should not have kept you standing about. Goodbye, Miss Greenwood.'

I struggled and my mouth formed the words at last. 'Goodbye, Mr Shawcross.'

And I faced away from him into the wind as he left me and let it dry the tears that coursed down my cheeks, as I hurried towards Tiggins and the blessed privacy of the carriage at last.

Forty

John

I go into the church, my steps leaden: I feel dull in spirits, weighed down. I don't know how I can right matters with Maud; it is clear to me now that our relationship is over.

The Doom hardly concerns me; in my head it is Maud, all Maud.

I am shocked by her appearance. She is still beautiful, but now there is a dangerous fragility about her. Only her eyes defy it – those wild, dark, burning eyes take up her entire face. There are bruised circles beneath them and her cheeks are paler than ever.

Once she lost her temper in a cold cruel way; there is a new hardness in her I do not understand.

The church is in darkness, the candles for the service snuffed out, the dying brazier a dull red and the air cold now that the hot, God-fearing breath of the congregation is no longer there to warm it.

I go straight to the Doom and examine it. The new figures are crude, primitive. It will only take a little acetone to clean them off but it needs to be done carefully, then the paint beneath retouched. Someone else will do it under Juliana's orders. I am liberated; I need have nothing more to do with the Doom, or her.

All the same I am curious. There is a figure intended to be female, I think, which has been done more clumsily, and it appears that the charcoal has snapped off at one point, for the line continues thicker.

I search about and discover the broken piece under the nearest pew. Not that it gives me any clue as to who might have used it, but it has certainly been held by a living hand; I can reassure Edie on that. I wish I could also tell the gossip-mongers spreading fear of the devil through the village.

Suddenly I feel very alone, the shadows clustering malevolent about me. Evil has been done in here – if not by the devil, by someone who wishes to spread fear.

And fear now holds me in its grip.

I think I hear something. Even the scamper of a mouse behind the altar sounds ominous – if that is what it is. My scalp prickles. I call out, 'Is anyone there?'

Silence answers me, thick and consuming, like a fog. I pocket the broken charcoal swiftly and blunder my way back to the church door. My heart is beating oddly. I cannot wait to get out of the place. In that moment I feel that

God has abandoned it, left Rending to its own doom-laden path.

When I return to Marsh End, only Mrs Brundish is there.

'Edie has had to go early to Windward. Dorcas came for her once Miss Maud returned after church. Miss Juliana's in a bad way and Edie is needed urgent.'

'I understand,' I say. 'In any case, Mrs Brundish, I think my business here is done. I came to see the Doom and there is nothing I can do for it unless Miss Juliana wishes me to do so. It seems to me that the drawings have been done as a prank, a spiteful one if they are intended to depict individuals, but still only a prank.'

I hold out the broken charcoal. 'No devil has drawn the figures, Mrs Brundish, but a very human hand. This is the proof, and I hope that you will put it about and reassure the village.'

She nods sombrely. She has lain out bread and cheese for me but they stick in my throat, for I cannot forget Maud's frozen white face as she looked at me.

'I am sorry to miss Edie. Would you convey my good wishes to her?'

She stands by me awkwardly as I struggle to eat. I see that the colour has risen in her cheeks.

'John, may I ask you something?'

'Of course, Mrs Brundish.' I take a gulp of beer and it

churns in my stomach.

She twists her hands together. 'It is about Edie.'

'Edie?'

'I know she has been writing to you. I understand you have written back to her. When a letter has come from you I have seen her face. A mother notices these things.' She lowers her head. 'I shouldn't be talking to you in such a way, I know, but I have concerns.'

'Of course, Mrs Brundish.' I frown, perplexed.

'It is that—' She gazes at me in a troubled way. 'I believe my daughter is sweet on you, John.'

'Sweet on me?' I forget Maud for the moment; I am astounded.

Then I recollect my disquiet over Edie's behaviour when I left Marsh End – what I had taken for girlish gratitude might well have been something else entirely. I begin to remember other small instances which perhaps I misread at the time.

I stare at Mrs Brundish in dismay and dawning guilt.

She nods. 'Edie is young, and innocent of the ways of the world. Rending is all she knows. I don't want her hurt.'

'God forbid!' I put a napkin to my lips and try to swallow my last lump of cheese. 'I can assure you I have always thought of her as a child, nothing more! I don't believe I have given her any cause to misunderstand my relationship with her but I am truly sorry if I have.'

'You painted her several times. She was flattered. And you asked her to write to you and have answered her letters.' There is no reproach in Mrs Brundish's voice.

'I know you never thought to encourage her, never had such a thought in your head! To you she must seem only a child and out of your class, but at fourteen one can feel more passionately than at any other time.'

I look down at my plate. 'I never intended—'

'I am much to blame. I should not have agreed to have you stay with us again, but you were good to us, John, and we miss you. I wouldn't want you to think ill of us for Edie's foolish fancies.'

'I would never do that. I am only sorry if Edie believes I have encouraged her in any way.'

I rise somewhat shakily to my feet. 'I shall collect my things and go, Mrs Brundish. I will cause no more distraction for either of you.'

She has great dignity, Mrs Brundish. She stands there gravely.

'That would be best. I am sorry for it – for what I have had to say. I hope you will come again when all this is forgotten.'

Then as I am leaving the kitchen to climb the stairs to my room, she rummages in the pocket of her apron and holds out a folded paper to me that has been stuck with fish glue.

'Edie left this for you, John, and I must give it you, I suppose. When you read it, remember that she is still so young. Please take no notice of whatever it says.'

I take it reluctantly. 'I will not be corresponding further with her, Mrs Brundish. You have my assurance on that.'

She bows her head without speaking, and I go up to my room where I have already packed my bag. I sit on the bed holding the note.

A last message from Edie, which I fear I owe it to her to read.

I open the paper reluctantly. The message is very short, one sentence in the familiar round writing.

The devil in Rending is Maud Greenwood.

I sit on the bed in that little room, staring at those words in shock. Then slowly reason takes over.

It is the kind of melodramatic comment a young girl might make, particularly if Edie is jealous of Maud. In her infatuation for me she must see Maud as a rival. I should have seen that all her letters have been leading up to this and I should never have allowed them to bring me back to Rending.

How can I take any of their content seriously now? She has wanted to see me again and she wants me to think ill of

Maud. Without meaning to do so I have encouraged Edie, and this is the result. I have brought out the worst in her, made her manipulative and malicious.

I bury my head in my hands and curse myself for my blindness and stupidity.

I could have gone up to Windward House then, on my way to the station. I could have had it out with Edie, face to face, asked her what she meant by those spiteful words. Then I might have seen for myself what was truly wrong at Windward House.

But I was too cowardly.

I feared seeing Maud again and suffering some painful new humiliation. My spirit shrank from encountering Juliana with her cold, disdainful eye. And I did not want to engage in conversation with Edie in case it encouraged her further.

I was a shrinking soul, running from three women, and I have never forgiven myself.

For if I had ventured up to Windward House that afternoon, things might have turned out very differently for Maud.

But in the end I abandoned her.

Forty-One

Maud

My cheeks felt stiff with dried tears when I arrived back at Windward House, but I had not disgraced myself in front of John – I had not wept and wailed and clung to him.

There was bitter triumph in that; he would never know how much it cost me.

Now I must control myself before Edie and Dorcas, must oversee the running of the household, must tend to Juliana in her last days, for I did not believe she would recover from this bout of sickness.

And what would become of me after her death, if she intended to cut me from her will?

I dared not think of what Mr Smallbone's revised papers would contain on the morrow. Once again I would be deprived of what was truly mine; it would all go to Adeline Dimchurch and I would be forced into a dark world of grinding poverty and degradation.

I did not have the strength to face it.

When I went upstairs to change out of my Sunday best, the sound of my boots was firm and hard with resolution in the silent house. The light was already fading and from my bedroom window I could see the lime trees swaying in the wind, the rooks sitting fast with ruffled feathers as they watched me.

I took off my bonnet, smoothed my hair into place and saw in the looking-glass that my face was without expression. The eyes stared back at me blankly and I did not know them as mine. I buttoned my day dress to the throat until my pale vulnerable flesh was hidden.

I was myself no longer; there was none of that old self left.

Then I went at last to my bottle. It was all I needed now. A dose to steady me, then I would be fortified both inside and out.

I must leave enough, for I would need it at the end.

As I took the bottle from the drawer the casement rattled in the wind and made me jump. None of that, I told myself sternly.

I sat down until the drops had had their magical effect. I felt the warmth of them seep through my veins, a calm settle on me. The flesh of my cheeks seemed thick and heavy. My eyeballs pulsed and I saw shadows live in the corners of the room.

When I rose and gazed out of the window the slow dragging shape of Sly crossed the gravel path beneath me. I was not afraid; I looked at him with recognition and acceptance.

I thought, you have come to take me to your dark place, but you must wait awhile yet.

I had been mistaken all this time. I knew now that it was not John or even Grenville who would take my hand and lead me away, but Sly. It had been Sly all along.

I could eat little luncheon.

Dorcas made no comment as she cleared away. Her plump red cheeks were unusually pale and she sniffed a little.

'Madam is dying, isn't she, Miss Maud?' she said, as she was about to push the trolley away to the kitchen.

'I believe so,' I said, still calm.

'Should we not fetch Doctor Biddell?'

'Let me see if she is worse, then I will decide.'

She looked at me with a kind of horror. Then she pushed the trolley through the door.

I went and sat with Juliana, my back as stiff as a rod in the hard chair at her bedside. I hardly moved all through the remainder of that long dark afternoon while she lay drowsily and mumbled to herself. I was not sure if she was dreaming, or, if awake, knew who I was.

At one point I took her thin bony hand in mine. It was

cold and purplish and the fingernails were very dark. I tucked it gently away beneath the bedclothes.

I wondered about sending for Doctor Biddell, but he would only disturb her, that maddening little man with his twinkling jokes and jovial laughter. He could do nothing for her, he did not know enough.

It was peaceful, being alone together, she and I, with no one to interrupt with chatter. Our lives had been bound together for such a while, after all.

I studied her face and saw how it had changed and aged over the months I had known her. The wrinkled, papery half-moons of her eyelids were closed over those once-brilliant blue eyes. Her cheeks were sunken and grey. Her beautiful fair hair had thinned so that her scalp showed, pale as dust.

From time to time I stoked the fire. At last I picked up a book and began to read to her. She had always enjoyed my reading aloud and I wanted to do it now, for her.

When dusk had filled the room, I lit the oil lamps. Outside the wind had risen and keened around the house, as if it already mourned her death. The curtains lifted with the draught and when I went to draw them I saw that the sky was choked with black raging clouds.

Something roused Juliana. With an effort she brought a hand out from beneath her bedclothes and held it across her eyes.

'Maud?'

'I am here, Juliana.'

'The light is too bright.' Her voice was very weak. 'I have such a headache. Turn the lamps down. Light the candles instead.'

So I did, though I did not welcome the shifting shadows that now surrounded us, nor the strange smell of those new green candles.

'Would you like some water?' I asked. 'Or something hot? Some tea?'

Her head moved on the pillow, too heavy to shake, and I felt her cold fingers touch my hand. 'Maud, Maud,' she murmured. 'You are so good to me.'

'I am not!' I whispered. 'I am wicked!'

'I am so sorry.'

'For what?'

I had to bend my head to hear her.

'I have never thanked you for all your care.'

I was too surprised and overcome to speak. I shook my head and a lump came into my throat. *This is too late*.

'And there are other things—' Her voice trailed away.

'Don't try to talk, Juliana,' I said softly.

Her lids fluttered open again. 'All the wrongs I have done you – I did them because I wanted to keep you with me. I thought you might leave me – first with John Shawcross, then with Grenville – leave me all alone again in this great dark house.' She was babbling. 'Papa left me, you know, left his little girl alone.'

'Hush, Juliana.' I stroked her poor thin hair.

Her eyes blazed suddenly. 'There is something I must tell you before I die.'

'I am listening,' I said gently.

'I have left everything to you in my will, as I promised. You never need return to working as a governess.'

'But – what about Adeline?'

She frowned, as if she could not remember who Adeline was.

'Adeline Dimchurch? Were you not going to change your will in her favour?'

'I have made her a trifling bequest, that is all – to thank her for her kindness last summer. I felt I must do that. Smallbone has added it.'

I dropped my head. 'Thank you,' I whispered. 'Thank you, Juliana. Forgive me.'

She was exhausted by talking and had closed her eyes. I think she was only semi-conscious at that moment.

'Forgive me,' I said to the empty room, as if the walls could somehow record my feelings and convey them to her. Hard, stinging tears came into my eyes and dropped, burning, on to my hand.

I thought, Oh, Juliana, I wanted to love you so much. Now it is too late.

Forgive me.

Forty-Two

The vicar came to interrupt my vigil. Dorcas let him in and he entered Juliana's room looking most solemn and earnest. He brought the cold outside air with him and there was a prayer book in his hands.

'Don't wake her, please,' I begged him.

He nodded and knelt by her bedside. 'Oh Lord, if it is your desire to welcome your servant Juliana into everlasting life . . .'

Then after several more prayers of this grim sort he left. 'If she should wake and wish for the last rites, summon me immediately,' he said.

I nodded; I had no intention of doing so.

He hovered by the door. 'This is a sorry time, indeed. What will happen to the Doom if Miss Greenwood dies? She was so generous a benefactor.'

He looked at me expectantly. I suppose he had already assumed I would inherit Juliana's money.

'It has survived four hundred years. I dare say it will outlive us all.'

He wrung his hands. 'But the restoration work is unfinished!'

'Perhaps it was meant to be,' I said.

'She is quiet,' I said to Dorcas and Edie later, when they had knocked on the door and entered.

We stood, all three, at Juliana's bedside and stared down at her unmoving form beneath the bedclothes, while the candles flared in the draught.

She might have been dead, she was so fast asleep, but when I put my fingers to her nostrils a tiny air blew out on them.

I felt very nauseous and longed to leave the room. 'We must go to bed,' I said. 'It will do my cousin no good if we are all weary in the morning.'

'I will sit by her for a while,' said Edie. 'I did so with my mother when she was poorly. I will keep her warm, keep the fire going.'

'Thank you, Edie. Let me know if there is any change.'

She did not answer.

I took my drops and went to bed. I had only managed an egg beaten in milk for supper, for I was feeling sick to my stomach. The cold wind in my room made me feel better, and I opened the window further and watched the black feathered clouds, like giant crows, dart across the face of the moon.

In the end I must have been deeply asleep, for I had no idea what time it was when I was wakened by an agitated Dorcas, shaking my shoulder. She held a candle and was still dressed in her day dress and apron, her hair coiled neatly beneath its cap, as if she had waited up for this very moment.

'Miss Maud! Come quick! Madam's took much worse. I've been trying to rouse you these past five minutes!'

I struggled awake. My head felt heavy and my eyes could scarcely focus. I fumbled for my shawl and Dorcas helped me drape it round my shoulders. She found my slippers and fitted them on my feet. Then I stumbled after her down the freezing staircase.

The wind was howling against the house, setting the windows to judder and rattle all around us, as if it fought to break through and claim Juliana for itself. The air up the stairway lifted my long unplaited hair and blew cold on my bare ankles.

Then down the gloomy passage to Juliana's room, where the fire blazed and the candles still burned.

Dorcas stood back and I stepped through the door. A thick miasma met me, of pungent candle smoke and smouldering wood and the fug of sickness.

Juliana lay moaning in her bed, motionless no longer, though her eyes were closed. Her legs twitched and she brought them up in evident agony to her stomach.

Edie pushed the slop bowl towards me, her face averted,

her voice rough and without respect.

'There's blood in her stool. See? And her stool runs like water from her. I can't change the sheets in time. She's been vomiting these past two hours. We can't bring in clean bowls fast enough.'

'Dorcas,' I said, and my voice trembled. 'Rouse Mr Tiggins and send him for Doctor Biddell!'

Even as I stood there, Juliana half raised herself and a spew of liquid gushed from her mouth. Dorcas mopped around her with a cloth, Edie removed the bowl and replaced it. I could do nothing but stare in horror.

Then Dorcas ran from the room for Tiggins.

Juliana vomited out the very essence of her being until there was nothing left but the skin and bone that encased her. From time to time she would convulse, her legs and arms seizing and stiffening as if frozen, her hands rigid claws. An odd brown rash covered her face, her thin chest.

There was nothing I could do, save rub at her limbs to draw the blood back in. She was not aware of me, or Edie.

'Blow out the candles!' I cried. 'We must light the lamps.' I thought that if only we could see more clearly we might save her.

The noxious smell of garlic came back with the snuffing of the candles. I thought that I too might be sick but controlled myself.

We were too busy, Edie and I, to think of ourselves. She

didn't say anything to me but went about her business and so did I, which was tending to Juliana, wiping her forehead, mopping her vomit, replacing the soiled sheets beneath her.

We did it silently together, but a million miles apart.

At last Doctor Biddell arrived in a gust of cold air from the hall, a frightened Dorcas behind him. He was wearing his coat, his clothes flung on beneath, no tie at his throat, his hair windswept. The twinkle had left his eye; he looked old and weary.

'What have we here?' he said to himself, and peered down at Juliana. 'I fear her digestion may have failed altogether.'

He listened to her heart, felt her limbs and peered into her slop bowl. He examined her darkened fingernails with curiosity and rolled back her eyelids. 'Her pulse is rapid and her limbs stiff,' he said to me in an undertone. 'You will have noticed the blood in her vomit.'

'What can you do for her, Doctor?'

At that moment Juliana groaned in her stupor and drew her legs up as if her stomach was in agony. Then her eyelids fluttered open and she vomited again, dark green matter streaked with blood.

'I can give her morphine for the pain but that is all.'

'Do it then!' I cried. 'Give her some relief, I beg you!'

All I could hear were Juliana's terrible groans and the noise of the wind shrieking around the windows.

Biddell did his business with the morphine and we stood helplessly about the bed in the sour yellow light of the oil lamps, all of us as haggard and sallow-cheeked in that light as if we were dying ourselves.

The wind roared down the chimney and made the fire splutter and smoke. Cinders fell out over the rug but none of us bothered to brush them away.

Juliana lay quietly. I believed she had fallen into a coma again, perhaps caused by the morphine, but I was mistaken.

One moment she lay motionless, the next her eyes opened and she half raised herself. Vomit ran from her mouth and she choked. I bent to her at once and wiped her lips with a cloth but I could not stop the trickle of blood coming from the corner of her mouth. Her breath was thick in her throat and rasped horribly. Her eyes wandered round us, unseeing. Perhaps she sensed we were there, I do not know. None of us moved or uttered.

Then she seemed to focus. Her eyes fixed on me.

She struggled to speak.

'Poisoned!' she gasped. 'I have been poisoned!'

We started back from her bed. Doctor Biddell looked startled; the girls were wide-eyed with horror.

'I am poisoned!' she cried out again, more strongly. A bubble of blood burst from her mouth and she choked a last time and fell back.

There was a long time when none of us did anything,

save gaze down. Juliana lay, glaring up at the ceiling but her eyes were dead now and glazing fast, her arms outside the covers already becoming rigid.

Doctor Biddell bent down. 'She has gone,' he said, as if we might not realise it, and he closed her half-open lids. Her upper body was so light it scarcely made a dent in the pillows.

'Poisoned!' said Dorcas, her eyes bulging with fear. 'She said she had been poisoned, Doctor!'

I looked up from Juliana's dead face. First I saw Doctor Biddell frown, then I met Edie's wide and accusing gaze. She was staring straight at me.

'*Poisoned!*' she echoed, and there was something triumphant and vindicated in her voice, as if she believed she knew what I had done.

Forty-Three

I dismissed Edie for the remainder of the night while Doctor Biddell was still there, and told her that Dorcas and I would see to Juliana's lying-in.

'Go to bed, Edie. Thank you for your help but you are not needed now.'

It was a relief to me when she had gone.

'Might I have a word with you alone, Miss Maud?' said Doctor Biddell.

I nodded, and told Dorcas to stay with the body until I came back, for after death a body must never be left alone until it is buried. She was weeping copiously, though I knew she had had no fondness for Juliana. I was feeling light-headed and numb and still somewhat nauseous, my own eyes dry but sore.

I took up a lamp and the doctor followed me into the hall.

'I am sorry to leave you alone after such a terrible death,' he said, his jovial manner quite gone. The sympathy in his voice made me want to weep but I fought against it. 'The death of a relative is always a sad business for those closest, especially when you are so young.'

'I am used to mourning, Doctor, having lost both parents. Besides I shall have plenty to keep me busy. I must inform her solicitors, organise the funeral.'

To my surprise, Biddell shook his head. 'I fear we must postpone the funeral for a while.'

I was disconcerted; I felt my composure crumble. He seemed suddenly to possess a new authority. 'Why, Doctor?'

'I am unsure of the cause of your cousin's death, Miss Maud, and cannot sign the death certificate. I must refer this to the area coroner first. He will want a post-mortem to establish the cause of death before her body can be buried.'

'I don't give my permission for a post-mortem!' I cried, aghast. 'Juliana would not want her body mauled about by strangers! Let her be buried quietly, as is fitting.'

He looked at me sadly. 'I fear that if the coroner orders a post-mortem examination, it does not need the consent of the family, Miss Maud.'

'You mean it will go ahead even if I do not wish it?'

He nodded.

I stared at him. 'But you said her digestion had failed.'

'I believe I was mistaken. The symptoms your cousin presented were extreme. In view of what she claimed—' He did not finish but laid a hand on my arm, a gesture intended to be paternal and sympathetic. I drew away and took a deep breath.

'She was right when she said she had been poisoned,' I said, in a low, rapid voice. 'It was Quilter's Restorative Powder that killed her! I should tell you now that I believe it contains arsenic. It has killed half the village! And poor Juliana was taking it to the end though I tried to stop her!'

He looked at me sharply. 'What makes you think the powder contains arsenic, Miss Maud?'

I put it in Jonas Dorley's packet and he died.

'I suspect it is so, that is all,' I said weakly.

He shook his head, frowning. 'As I have said before to you, Miss Maud, I am certain it contains nothing untoward. Why should Quilter wish to poison his customers? It can be analysed, certainly, but I think it will be found to be a harmless and ineffectual concoction mixed up by Quilter to hoodwink the village!'

'Juliana believed she had been poisoned, Doctor, and she was right! I tell you, it was the powder that killed her!'

He hesitated, then said carefully, 'You have forced me to admit that your cousin's symptoms did, indeed, resemble those of arsenic poisoning – the blood, muscle cramp, convulsion and coma. However, I cannot be certain that arsenic was the cause of death without investigation. I shall return tomorrow, once I have heard from the coroner. We may have to remove her body then.'

I put my hands to my face in shock.

'Would you like something to calm you?' Biddell said gently. 'To help you sleep? I have laudanum in my bag.'

I had committed such wrongs to obtain more and now he was offering it to me freely when I had a plentiful supply in my bedroom! I shook my head. I longed for him to go, but it seemed he wanted to say something else to me, in these new ponderous tones of his.

'Forgive me but there is one other thing, Miss Maud, somewhat trying for you at such a time yet unavoidable given the circumstances of your cousin's death.'

I looked at his kind, genial face, drawn into lines of gravity by the night's events. 'Yes, Doctor Biddell?'

'I'm afraid that in the meantime the police will want to investigate. You may be troubled by a visit from them as early as tomorrow.'

A chill ran through my blood. 'The *police*? Why should they come here?'

'If your cousin was right and she has been poisoned as she claimed, then this is a case of murder, Miss Maud.'

The wind had died at last and dawn was breaking as Dorcas and I turned down the lamps in Juliana's room and lit fresh candles around her bed. I thought the green too garish for death, so Dorcas brought in the remaining plain ones from the storeroom.

I was well practised in the business of mourning.

Juliana's corpse must not be left alone, so I sat with it, and instructed Dorcas to draw the curtains and pull down the blinds throughout the house, to stop the clocks and turn the mirrors to the walls.

I watched Juliana as her face sank inwards to her skull and took on a pale sheen. She had become a husk of skin and bone, resting on linen and lace. Then Dorcas took over from me, her eyes red from weeping, and I left Juliana at last and went upstairs through the heavy gloom of the house to my own room.

I did not go to bed. How could I sleep?

I changed out of my night clothes and put on my old mourning dress. The black swallowed me up again as if I had never been a real person through the previous summer and winter – someone who had once worn dresses of delicate sprigged muslin and rich magenta velvet. My arms goose-pimpled beneath the clammy crape. I clutched my cold hands together and wondered if I should ever be warm again.

When I told Dorcas that the police would be coming and an inquest held, she cried out, 'Shall I be a witness, miss? What must I say?'

'I don't know, Dorcas,' I said wearily, 'except tell the truth. Nothing bad will happen to you, I do assure you.'

Edie prepared breakfast earlier than usual and brought it

to me in the dining room. She looked pinch-faced and pale. She did not offer her sympathy or regrets.

'You know, Edie, that we may be visited by the police very soon?'

Something sparked in her eyes. 'I expected it, miss, even before Dorcas told me.'

Unlike Dorcas, she asked no further questions, nor seemed in the least bit perturbed.

I tried to eat but could not. I carried my tray through to the kitchen and Edie was there alone. I laid it down on the table as silence hung heavily between us. She broke it suddenly, as if the words had been fighting to get out.

'I'm surprised to see *you* in mourning, Miss Maud.'

'What do you mean, Edie?' I was taken off guard by her confrontation.

'I thought you cared nothing for Miss Juliana Greenwood.'

I drew myself up. 'Then you were mistaken. How dare you say such a thing?'

Her lip curled. 'Because I am a servant, you mean, miss? I should be polite to someone who is now my mistress?'

My heart beat rapidly. 'No, because it is not true!'

I held on to the table. I must accuse her now, I thought. I must do it first.

'It was you who used the arsenic, not me! You put it in her food, didn't you? You feared your mother would return to Windward House very soon and that the work would kill her!'

She opened her cat's eyes very wide. 'You say this to cover for yourself, Miss Maud! I tried to warn you but it was no good. It didn't stop you. We know what you did, Dorcas and me. You wanted her money!'

I clutched the table harder. 'You are quite mistaken. How would I get hold of arsenic?'

'There was the Fowler's, half empty.'

'But I gave the box to *you*! And you were already poisoning half the population of Rending with the Restorative!'

Her mouth opened as I continued my attack.

'There was arsenic in Quilter's Restorative, wasn't there? That was what killed my cousin and so many others from the village! Juliana took it unaware, like them. You are a murderess, Edie Brundish, in cahoots with Samuel Quilter!'

'I am no murderess, unlike you, Miss Maud!' she hissed.

'You must have known what was in the powder!' I flashed back.

'Not I. Mr Quilter always kept that secret to himself. I am sure it contained no arsenic! Why should you think it?'

'Because so many died this winter. Sly, Jonas Dorley – there were others, too.'

'Sly was weak in body and brain, due to die anyway. Jonas coughed his heart up. He had consumption.'

So I had not killed Jonas Dorley. It was not my doing, after all.

I could not feel relief; I felt nothing.

I took a deep breath. 'Once the police have interviewed you, Edie, and all this is over, you are dismissed. You will understand why.'

Such hatred simmered in her face that I stepped back. 'Oh, I do, Miss Maud. I will go and gladly. I couldn't continue working for someone who has done what you've done.'

I pulled myself together. 'Come now, Edie. You have said things you do not mean. I am sure that you must be as tired as I am, and as overwrought.'

I left her, then. It was best to have the last word and be dignified about it.

After all, I was now mistress of Windward House.

Tiggins and Miss Potton came into Juliana's room soon after to pay their respects to the body.

Both were very shocked, Tiggins especially. He stood by the pale coverlet in his earthy overalls and wrung his hands.

He had known Miss Greenwood as a small child, he said. Always trying to get her stepfather to laugh at her little dances. She was a charmer, then, with her wheedling ways.

To my surprise he blinked a good deal over the body.

I asked him to go to Smallbone and Bagge and inform Mr

Smallbone of the sad news; also to say that I would rearrange a meeting with him.

Miss Potton was purse-lipped. 'I suppose, Miss Maud, I'll be receiving my instructions from you now.'

She did not look as if she would relish that.

'We shall carry on as usual, Miss Potton. That is the best thing.'

'But who is to do the cooking?'

'I shall advertise for a new cook,' I said, more positively than I felt. 'In the meantime, we must manage as best we can.'

Shortly after nine o'clock, Doctor Biddell arrived with two other doctors from Halesworth and they took Juliana's body away. The doctor told me they would start the post-mortem immediately and that the inquest would be formally opened around noon.

Then, just before ten, the police arrived.

Forty-Four

Two of them, in tall hats like chimney pots and long-tailed dark blue coats, one wiry with greying sideburns, the other much younger. I had been expecting them and answered the door myself, for I feared Dorcas might turn hysterical at the sight of two policemen, with handcuffs and truncheons swinging from their heavy leather belts.

They looked at me gravely as I stood blinking after the darkness inside the house. Then the older one stepped forward and took off his hat.

'Miss Maud Greenwood? I am sorry to trouble you at such a time, miss. Superintendent Stainless and Police Constable Catchpole. We're here to conduct some enquiries.'

I kept my voice under control. 'I understand, Superintendent. Please come in.'

I led them into the darkened parlour, which seemed very cramped with two tall men standing there. I drew the curtains back and as daylight flooded in, looked at them at a loss before realising that they were waiting for me to sit down.

So I sat down in the armchair that Juliana had always favoured; I avoided looking at her day bed where she had spent her last week. My hands were shaking and I clasped them in my lap so it should not show. Both policemen seated themselves then, the three of us around the empty grate.

I apologised for the chill, the unlit fire, said things had not been attended to as normal, what with my cousin's death. Superintendent Stainless shook his head kindly.

The younger one was awkward on a covered stool. He had fair sideburns and a ruddy beardless face. I remembered that no one in the police force was allowed to wear a beard. Small things come to one at such a time.

He brought a pencil and notebook out of his deep coat pocket, licked a thick forefinger solemnly and flicked to a clean page.

'How can I help you?' I looked at the superintendent, who rubbed his long chin.

'First, miss, are you here as a guest of the deceased, or do you live here permanently?'

I answered that my parents were dead and that Juliana, my cousin by marriage, had written to me in March the previous year while I was seeking work as a governess, and offered me a home.

'Were you glad to have a permanent roof over your head, Miss Greenwood?'

'Very glad.'

'Thank you. Now, if you could give us the names of those who work here, miss?'

Stainless had a mild, diffident manner and spoke with courtesy. I began to relax.

I listed the servants for him: Miss Potton, Mr Tiggins, Dorcas, Edie. I hesitated as I gave Edie's name and he looked at me closely.

'She is here in place of her mother, who was taken ill,' I said quickly. 'It has been a temporary arrangement, nothing more, and she is leaving shortly.'

'We will still interview her, particularly as she was a witness to the death, I gather. And her mother's name?'

'Mrs Brundish, of Marsh End.'

I could hear the young constable scratching away with his pencil.

Stainless placed his hands on his knees and leaned a little towards me. 'Miss Greenwood, I am sure you are aware of why we are here. The inquest will be opened this morning into the cause of your cousin's death but until the results of the post-mortem are known, we are treating her death as suspicious. I hope that will turn out not to be the case, but meanwhile we will need to interview everyone working in this household.'

I licked my dry lips. 'As well as Dorcas, Edie and I, my cousin's doctor, Doctor Biddell, was at my cousin's death bed. You will need to talk to him too.'

'We have already done so.'

'Oh?' I was startled.

'Perhaps you could give us your account of the night of your cousin's death, miss,' he said calmly.

I did so, again keeping it brief. I described her symptoms, our shock. I thought I did well. My voice was firm.

Stainless rubbed his chin again. 'Miss Greenwood,' he said mildly, 'Do you believe that your cousin's death was unnatural?'

'I cannot say,' I said at last. 'She had not been in good health.'

'So her doctor has reported.' He looked at me levelly. 'You know of no one in this house who might have had had a motive for poisoning her?'

My hands were still clasped and I felt the pulse in my wrist beat fast against my fingers. 'I don't think so, no.'

'Did she have other visitors yesterday evening before she died?'

'The vicar came in, the Reverend Wissett.'

The pencil continued scratching busily.

'What about during the day? Indeed, during the last week of her life?'

I shook my head.

'No one came to see her when she was so ill?'

'Oh – only her solicitor two days before. She asked for him.'

'Remind me of his name, Constable.'

The young man flicked back some pages. 'Mr Smallbone of Smallbone and Bagge, sir.'

'Thank you, Constable.' Stainless focussed on me again. 'So would you say Miss Juliana Greenwood had few friends, if no one visited when she was so unwell?'

I whispered, 'I think she had enemies.'

'Enemies, Miss Greenwood?'

'People in the village disliked her. The shopkeepers—'

'We will make enquiries. So there was no close friend?'

'Only – only Aveline Dimchurch. She has never stayed at Windward House while I have been here, but Juliana visited her at her home in Scarborough last summer.'

'And you, Miss Greenwood.'

'Me?' I said, puzzled.

'You were close to Miss Juliana Greenwood. You were more to her than a mere relation by marriage. Doctor Biddell tells me that you cared for her unstintingly during the last year of her life.'

'She had taken me in and I had no one else.'

'She must have been very grateful to you,' Stainless said softly. "Did she show you her gratitude in any way?'

'She gave me some dresses.'

'Nothing else?' His mild manner was deceptive. His questions could trap you. But he would find out soon enough if he had not done so already. It was best to tell the truth.

'As Juliana lay dying, she told me that she had left me everything in her will, apart from a small bequest for Aveline Dimchurch.'

'And it was the first time you heard that you were to inherit her estate?'

I hesitated. 'No – she told me shortly after I arrived here. Only – only later I thought she must have changed her mind.' I found I was stammering.

He bowed his head. 'Thank you, Miss Greenwood. You have been most helpful. Perhaps you would find Miss Potton for us now.'

Not a flicker had passed over his face. His manner remained courteous, even deferential.

However, he and his constable had been very busy that morning even before they came to Windward House. Later I found out that, as well as talking to Doctor Biddell, they had already been to see Mr Smallbone, Juliana's solicitor.

So it was a good thing I told the truth about her will.

But in doing so, I had betrayed myself.

They interviewed Miss Potton in the parlour and then Dorcas and Edie in turn in the kitchen. Dorcas came out very flushed in the face; Edie cool and contained. I heard them whispering in the kitchen together after.

The policemen interviewed Tiggins in the back garden and then they left, thanking me again most politely.

* * *

The inquest opened at noon at the Magpie Inn, the village public house, as was the custom, and thirteen local men – tradesmen and farmers – were sworn in as members of the jury. I heard from Tiggins, who attended, that it was very quickly adjourned by the coroner, after Doctor Biddell had related an account of what had taken place previous night, the night of Juliana's death.

It would reopen once the post-mortem results were known and the coroner had gathered all the paperwork he needed – statements from the police, Juliana's medical records and any other relevant paperwork. All of us at Windward House were warned that we would have to attend as witnesses.

It was a strange few days in that shrouded house, all of us going about silently in the half-darkness, with stiff faces. Juliana's death, which should have given us lightness and freedom, oppressed us. We were very aware of the emptiness of her room; we avoided entering it, now that Dorcas and I had stripped her bed.

I found myself listening for her bell, which would never ring again; the thump of her stick on my bedroom floor; her querulous cry.

The inquest loomed over all of us.

The police came again: Stainless, with his gentle, courteous manner and the awkward young constable. They asked me the same questions as before. They saw the others, too.

Those days hung in time, seemingly endless, while I yawned with boredom and apprehension. I didn't want to venture into the village, for I knew that with the opening of the inquest the tittle-tattle had started, so I sent Miss Potton instead for anything we needed urgently. Otherwise the deliveries came as usual to the kitchen door.

I became frightened to draw back the curtains and look outside at the daylight.

I thought that Sly might be there, come for me. I thought he would look back at me, his nose pressed flat and white against the glass, his tongue wagging soundlessly in his open mouth and his eyes – his dead eyes – staring at me and knowing . . . everything. I didn't want to go with him now; I was too afraid.

I told Edie that she need only stay for the mornings and not overnight, that Dorcas and I would manage well enough on our own. I repeated that once the inquest was over she was to leave.

She nodded silently. She was not dressed in mourning but in her usual flowered dress and pinny, and it looked out of place in that house of death.

Each night as I took off my crape and shut it from my sight in the wardrobe, I would feel a sudden freedom, only to be reminded of what had happened when I awoke in the morning.

* * *

The inquest reopened a few days later, this time in the village hall, for gossip had spread and people came from Halesworth and Southwold to fill the public seats. The local press were there also.

Tiggins took me in the carriage. It was a cold spring morning, overcast, the wild daffodils still tightly closed and shivering on the verges of the road. I felt sick with nerves and as vulnerable as the flowers we passed. The results of the post-mortem would be given today.

The jury were resworn. Doctor Biddell was called first, to give the post-mortem report. The medical terms made little sense to me, only what he said in his conclusion. He and the other doctors had performed some complicated test on Juliana's body and found that arsenic ingestion was the cause of her death.

A chill came over me, hearing it confirmed, and a horrified gasp arose from the spectators.

The coroner turned to the jury. He had a loud voice and commanding manner, and the hall stilled.

'Jurors, remember it is your job to find out the circumstances of Miss Juliana Greenwood's death, nothing more.'

Then we were called, one by one: me, Dorcas, Edie, the vicar, the solicitor Mr Smallbone and others. I was shaking so hard I thought I might fall over. I could see

Superintendent Stainless and Constable Catchpole waiting to take their turn.

They must be certain already that I have murdered her! I thought.

But the coroner merely asked me to give an account of the night Juliana died, as he did of Edie and Dorcas after me.

I went back to my seat in relief.

Edie gave her account confidently. Dorcas, bright red in the face, used a little high-pitched childish voice and was told to speak up; she was as nervous as I had been.

The inquest dragged on. The police gave their statements. I was the one who would benefit by Juliana's death, as Mr Smallbone had already said in his statement.

At last the coroner gave his verdict.

Unlawful killing.

Forty-Five

The inquest did not finish until six o'clock. On my return to Windward House I went up to my sitting room and shortly afterwards Dorcas brought me some food on a tray.

She was red-eyed and one of her cheeks flamed as if she had been slapped. I thought she and Edie must have had a quarrel before Edie left and was in no mood for such pettiness.

Dorcas set the tray down on the table and gripped her hands together. 'I am sorry, miss.'

I thought she meant that such a verdict had been reached by the jury. I nodded; I wanted her to go. 'Thank you, Dorcas. It is a shock, I admit.'

'Let me build up your fire, miss. You must keep warm.'

I was touched by her concern but there was something agitated in the way she said it. I thought only that she had been disturbed by the inquest.

I roused myself as she went to the door. 'Miss Potton and Edie will have gone home by now, I expect?'

She nodded.

'So it is the two of us alone here, Dorcas, until the police come visiting again. We must not let them interfere with our lives. They will discover what they have to, in good time.'

'Yes, miss.' She kept her eyes downcast and put her hand on the door handle, repeating, 'I am sorry.'

Then she had sidled out, was gone. A pause as the door shut again and the latch clicked into place, and then I heard her shoes thump away rapidly down the stairs. I was alone and thankful for it.

I picked at the food. At length I pushed it aside irritably and took the tray to the door, thinking to take it down to the kitchen and save Dorcas returning upstairs.

The door seemed stuck. I tried it with one hand while my other held the tray, but then I had to put the tray down on the table in order to leave both hands free. I pushed with my shoulder. To no avail. The door would not budge.

What was the matter? We had had no rain, so it could not be damp swelling the wood.

I pushed again, using all my strength this time. I didn't like the idea of being stuck in my room until Dorcas rescued me. The door remained solid, ungiving. I was shut in.

'Dorcas!' I shouted. 'Dorcas!'

It was a thick door. I doubted my voice would travel. Surely, sooner or later, she would return for the tray.

I crouched by the door and shouted at intervals but she

did not return. I could not tell how much time was passing, for of course we had stopped the clocks in the house after Juliana's death; but when I stood up at last, my legs were so stiff and cold I could only hobble back to the dying fire.

It had been cloudy all day and dusk was beginning to fill my room, so long a haven to me but now a prison. I stared at the bars across the window, at the four walls which crept towards me.

Rookyard, I thought. *Rookyard.*

I remembered how they had shut me in and locked the door. The mistress made the servants drag me there. She screamed that I was a liar to accuse her husband of such a filthy thing; and she had wrapped her arms around her pregnant belly.

I had cowered in a corner weeping, while the rooks beat their great black wings between the window bars and their beaks made scratches on the glass.

Or had that been one of my dreams?

I could hear the rooks now, swooping past outside in great black whorls against the darkening sky, filling the air with their noisy clacking as they flew to roost in the lime trees.

They will be watching me again.

I must keep the shadows away.

I lit a pair of candles and put them in the holders at

either end of the mantelpiece. Then I poked the fire and went to huddle in my chair.

I was beginning to feel decidedly unwell. I was shivering, though the evening was not cold; then a sweat broke out upon my brow, as if I had a fever. My bones ached and it hurt me to bring my hand up to my face to wipe the perspiration away.

Time passed; the candles burned lower. Outside, night fell and the windows turned black but I did not have the strength to draw the curtains over the bars.

I shook so my teeth chattered. I could not keep my jaws closed. My stomach churned. I thought, what if I should soil myself and no chamber pot?

I knew that Sly would come for me now, now that I was so weak and vulnerable, and I would not be able to resist him. Already something was moving in the corner.

It was about to show itself when I heard a noise outside the door, something stealthy, creeping.

'Dorcas?' I cried out, 'Dorcas, is that you?'

I heard her sniff.

I lurched towards the door, caught hold of the handle and leaned my weight upon it to support myself. The door did not give but I heard breathing, light and fast. I could smell Dorcas's smell – the familiar mixture of sweat and roasted meat fat and the harshness of coke from the range.

'Dorcas! The door is jammed! Let me out!'

She *was* there. I heard her say, 'I'm sorry, miss.'

'What do you mean? Fetch Tiggins to loosen it if you cannot!'

'I've locked it, miss, I am so sorry.'

'*What?*'

'Edie told me to, miss. She made me do it. She said it was for the best, since I was frightened to be here alone with you.'

'Whatever do you mean? Unlock the door this minute! Are you mad?'

'No, miss. It is you—'

Then I heard the shuffle of footsteps going away, the thud, thud, as she reached the stairs and ran down, away from me.

I cried and beat upon the door but she did not return.

I yearned for my drops.

I have never known such longing as I felt in that small, night-filled room. My agitation was extreme. I shuddered from head to foot. I thought I might die without them.

And my bottle was beneath my pillow in my bedroom next door, so near – yet I could not get to it.

I crouched, small as a mouse in the chair, and put my arms around my knees to still them. I think I wept a while before I dreamed of Rookyard and woke screaming.

Sometime in the slow silent hours of that night I felt the

chair lift beneath me and slide over the floorboards towards the dark shape that waited in the corner.

I gripped the arms. 'No!' I screamed.

I would fight against Sly, resist him with any strength I had left.

It was not Sly who came out of the corner.

I saw the small red eyes, the teeth bared in a leer, the spiny back, the lashing tail. It was the devil from the Doom. And now the doom was my own. I would take my place in the queue for hell, where I belonged.

The devil himself had come for me and there was no escaping.

It pranced across to me, grinning, as if it danced a jig. I smelled sulphur and ash. I shrank away as it clawed at my black skirts.

In horror and revulsion I tried to pull them back – 'You will spoil them!' I cried, 'I wear them for Papa!' – but the devil was strong, so strong, and my hands trembled, so that I lost my grip. I felt it tug again with supernatural strength.

It drew me, helpless, to the edge of the chair. I fell forward on to the floor and darkness consumed me.

When I opened my eyes again, there was a faint dawn light in the room. The fire was out and it was very cold. I saw yesterday's food, untouched on the tray. There was no one in the room but myself.

I was lying curled up on the floor before the ashy grate. Bewildered, I struggled to my feet, supporting myself on the chair. I was shaking from head to foot and my stomach felt empty and raw.

Somewhere in the house there were footsteps, heavy and masculine, and a man's voice.

I knew it was John.

He had come for me at last. He would unlock the door, put his warm, strong arms around me. I would rest my head against his shoulder and breathe in his sweet, young man's smell. He would carry me away from this prison. I need never return to Windward House.

The footsteps came up the stairs. It sounded like several pairs of feet. Had John brought Tiggins with him?

I frowned, puzzled. I heard voices. Someone said, 'She is in here, you say?' A mutter. Then, 'Have you the key?'

I could not make sense of it. I turned to face the door, still clutching the chair.

The key turned easily, the door opened without a creak. I saw the tall top hats, the dark blue uniforms, the thick leather belts. I stared at three policemen and they stared back at me, expressionless. There was no pity in their faces; they were simply doing their duty.

Then one stepped forward from behind them and I saw it was Superintendent Stainless. His voice was mild and polite as ever.

'Miss Maud Greenwood, I hold a warrant for your apprehension on the charge that you did wilfully murder Miss Juliana Greenwood on the night of 10th March.'

They put handcuffs around my wrists which bit into the bone. They had to support me down the stairs, for I could hardly walk.

As we passed Dorcas in the hall, her frightened face pasty, she dropped her eyes in shame. She had locked me in, given the police the key and led them upstairs to me. No doubt it was Edie who told her to do it and gullible, foolish Dorcas had obeyed the stronger girl without question.

There was some fire in me still, some protest. A fury took hold of me and I fought against the men who held my arms either side.

'It is not me you want!' I cried. 'It is Edie! Edie Brundish!'

Forty-Six

John

I wait for Ben to turn up in our usual meeting place, a public house on the King's Road, near my studio in Tite Street. I order a pint and one for Ben, too.

I have not had time to read that day's paper so I open the *Morning Post* under the gaslight.

And that is where I first see it, somewhere near the back, since the event has occurred outside London.

Wealthy Spinster Murdered by Own Cousin

Yesterday a young woman, Miss Maud Greenwood, 18, was tried before the magistrates at Halesworth Town Hall and accused of poisoning her own cousin, Miss Juliana Greenwood, of Windward House, Rending, Suffolk, on the night of 10th March.

The victim of this heinous crime was a lady of

considerable wealth and standing in the local community. Recently she had financed the restoration of an ancient Doom painting in the village church. She had taken the accused in out of the goodness of her heart and given her a roof over her head. With innocent generosity she had also left the girl well provided for in her will.

The conclusion of the post-mortem, during which the Reinsch process was used, was that the victim had died through ingestion of arsenic leading to kidney failure. Miss Juliana Greenwood had been taking Quilter's Restorative Powders made up by Mr Samuel Quilter, an apothecary in Rending, but upon analysis it was found that the powders contained nothing but a harmless mixture of potato, flour, magnesia and sulphur. However, during the police investigation a box of Fuller's Solution was found in the storeroom at Windward House, and it seems likely that this provided the accused with the means to murder. No other member of the household had a motive for murdering Miss Juliana Greenwood, save the accused, who stood to inherit upon her cousin's death.

Money, then, was the motive for this most unnatural act. How can any of us rest easy in our beds if we think a member of our own family may turn to murder in the dark?

> Miss Maud Greenwood is presently in custody at Ipswich gaol. Enough evidence of her guilt has been found for the magistrates to commit her for trial at the Lent session of the Suffolk Assizes at Ipswich Crown Court. She has pleaded Not Guilty to the charge of murder.

I read the piece with utter incredulity.

It takes several moments for me to register its full horror. I am no longer aware of the hum of conversation around me; the smell of beer and sweat; the bodies pressing about the bar, blurred by wreaths of smoke; the painted women waiting hopefully, as they always do. I sink back on the leather seat and my mind races.

I must save her. There has been a terrible mistake.

I think of Maud's frail wrists imprisoned by handcuffs as she sits between two burly policemen on the train to Ipswich gaol. I think of her confined in a cold, damp cell, unable to sleep or eat, as she awaits her trial. I think of her frightened, lonely. Someone so refined, so delicate, will wither and die before she even faces the hangman's noose.

And then I cannot prevent the thought of that thick, coarse rope biting into the soft young skin of her neck and tightening mercilessly around her windpipe.

'You look a trifle fatigued tonight, old fellow. Bad day?'

I have not even noticed Ben arrive. He sits down beside me, leans back, gulps a mouthful of his beer and lights a cigar. He takes his time, giving me the space to pull myself together.

'What is it?' he says gently, as the fragrant smoke curls up.

And so I tell him. I tell him everything. It is a great relief to tell of my love and agony during the time at Rending.

And now this.

He takes the newspaper from me and reads the report slowly, while every minute I grow heavier with despair. Then he leans forward and looks at me intently out of his bright black eyes.

'Might you be wrong? Might it be possible that your Maud is indeed a murderess?'

'Never! She is the most gentle of souls. If you met her, Ben, you would feel as I do.'

'Perhaps,' he says, with a wry smile, 'for I see you are altogether smitten.'

I run my fingers through my hair. 'What is to be done? She will not be allowed to speak in her own defence. How can she be saved?'

'Can she raise the money for a defence barrister?'

I shake my head, then stare at him. 'I will pay! I have the money now – the American sales and more commissions coming in. It must be the very best defence, Ben!'

His face grows grave. 'Even if you have the best defence barrister in the land, it may not make any difference. My dear old chap, you must face it. Unfortunately, the motive is clear and will be so to the jury. Maud's cousin's will.'

'There must be something you can do! Help her, for God's sake!'

'Are you instructing me to act for her?' he says quietly.

I nod vehemently. 'I want you to save her, Ben!'

'That is a tall order but I will do what I can.'

'I will pay even if it ruins me!'

'I should like you to paint my wife. That is all the payment I want from you, old friend. I would not want money to pass between us. The barrister will charge highly, I fear.'

'So you will take it on?'

He regards me thoughtfully. 'There is a clerk with whom I am on good terms. I have instructed a certain barrister in his chambers on several occasions and he may be prepared to act for Maud. Let me sound out the clerk first.'

I grip his hand. 'Please do so! At the earliest opportunity!'

His face is sombre. 'Don't get your hopes up. It doesn't look promising for Maud. Not promising at all.'

We agree to meet several days later at the same public house. I have not been able to concentrate on work; I can scarcely hold my paintbrush. At home Mother frets about my poor appetite, knowing nothing but believing she knows everything.

Now, the tankard trembles with agitation in my hand and I still it with the other.

'What news, Ben?'

'Mr Munroe will take on the case and, as his solicitor, I shall be instructing him.'

'That is wonderful!'

'Early days, dear chap, early days. There is much preparation to be done before the trial. A little detective work.'

I look at him doubtfully. Detectives are a new-fangled notion, a tiny section of the police force whose work is held suspect and unnecessary by the public. 'What kind of detective work?'

'We shall look for clues, John! They will lead us to the truth.'

'Clews?' I say, bewildered, and I think of Theseus and his clew, the ball of thread that led him safely back into the light from the Minotaur's maze.

'Clues!' Ben's black eyes snap with excitement. 'A little groundwork. I have been researching previous arsenic poisoning cases. They have given me some ideas. But I need your help.'

'Tell me! I will do my utmost.'

'List the servants at Windward House for me, John. Give

me character sketches.'

I try to remember. As I mention Mrs Brundish's name, something stirs in my memory. Edie's face, suddenly ugly, as she hisses, 'I could murder that woman!' Edie had meant Juliana.

It was a throwaway remark, that was all. All the same, I am suddenly perturbed and fall silent.

'Don't hide anything from me, John,' says Ben, as if he guesses.

I have to tell him. 'It signified nothing. She was anxious about her mother's health.'

He looks thoughtful. 'If you think your mother may die from overwork, that is a strong motive for killing her employer!'

He leans towards me, all his intelligence concentrated on me.

'Next I want to know everything that Maud may have told you about her relationship with Juliana. And what was Maud's relationship with the staff at Windward House?'

So I do my best. Maud said little about the servants at Windward. I say nothing about our quarrel over Edie, nor of Edie's feelings for me, for they do not seem relevant. As for Juliana, it seemed to me that Maud was genuinely pleased when her health recovered from time to time.

Ben frowns. 'So Juliana Greenwood had periods when she appeared to be in good health?'

'Yes. One week she would be unwell, the next seem to recover. Or so it appeared from what Maud told me.'

'What do you think brought about these changes?'

I shake my head. 'A different prescription from Doctor Biddell, perhaps, or Maud's own ministrations. Juliana suffered with her digestion, though I am not certain there was anything truly wrong with her. However, Maud looked after her tirelessly. She even rose in the night when Juliana needed her. She tried to please her every whim. She and the maid, Dorcas, were forever moving her upstairs and back down again. She was the most demanding woman.'

I cannot help the dislike in my voice.

'Good, good, John. This all helps me get a picture of how it was.'

Ben claps his hands together. Energy vibrates from him. He is enjoying the challenge. Maud herself means nothing to him.

'I should like to visit Windward House, John.'

'Why should you want to go there? It will be shut up, I'm sure.'

'A detective should always visit the scene of the crime. You will come with me, won't you?'

Forty-Seven

My last visit to Rending had filled me with anguish. But this is the least I can do for Maud.

So I write at once to Mrs Brundish, asking her to let us into Windward House around noon in two days' time. I know she will receive my letter the following day, if not before, such is the dependability of the Royal Mail. And I know she will still have kept her key.

So in two days, as planned, Ben and I take the Great Eastern train to Suffolk.

Tiggins meets us at Marsham station in the trap. When I thank him he grunts something at me. He appears buried in his own misery. He is still living above the stables at Windward House, the sole member of the staff remaining there, and he works in the garden unpaid.

'Don't let 'em hang her!' he growls out, as we stop before the front door.

I murmur something and then the door is opened and Mrs Brundish is there. The rest from work has done her good, for she looks much better and has put on some weight.

But she, too, is clearly upset about Maud's arrest and forthcoming trial.

'Mr Goldstone is here to try and help Miss Maud,' I say.

She gazes at Ben dubiously and I admit his attire does look somewhat out of place in the country, his black solicitor's coat a little too fitted, his sleek black hair a little too long, his briefcase too new and shiny.

'There's not an ounce of wickedness in that girl, Mr Goldstone,' Mrs Brundish says, shaking her head, 'and I would stake my life on it.'

Ben looks at her with interest. 'You were not here when Miss Juliana Greenwood died, is that correct?'

'Yes, sir. I'd been taken poorly whilst working. My daughter Edie came in my place temporary like.' She sees the expression on Ben's face. 'Edie's a good girl, nicely brought up,' she says sharply. 'She tried to help out, that's all.'

We are standing in the small chill parlour where I drank a nervous cup of tea during my first interview with Juliana so long ago. The whole house smells sour, the windows long closed tight against the spring air. No fires have been lit here for weeks and there are no candles burning. The furniture is shrouded in dust sheets, adding to the ghostly atmosphere.

'I am sure Miss Greenwood must have been very grateful to Edie,' Ben says gently.

'It's my belief it was one of them powders that killed Miss Juliana,' says Mrs Brundish, primping her lips. 'There was all sorts of poisons in that store. Easy for Quilter to make a mistake. He used to make up the powders himself all secretive and his eyesight wasn't good, Edie says.'

'Might I see the room where Miss Greenwood died?' Ben says politely, and so she takes us through the hall to a room at the back of the house.

It is dim in there, for the curtains are drawn, but she pulls them back for us and looks around with a shiver. There are no dust sheets here but the furniture looms darkly and the dark green wallpaper, printed over with peacock feathers, makes the room gloomy even with the light from the windows.

'First time I've been in here since she died. Nothing's been touched, Mr Goldstone, it's all as it was that night. The police told us to leave it like this.'

'She also used a bedroom upstairs?'

'Sometimes she did, yes. It was more convenient for Miss Maud in the night. But Miss Juliana made such a fuss about moving upstairs! She liked this room the best.'

'Thank you, Mrs Brundish. Would you leave us for a little while? Then I should like to see the rest of the house, if I may.'

Ben's manners have won her over. She nods without demur and closes the door quietly behind her.

'What are you hoping to find?' I say. 'There's Juliana's desk, her papers. Are you thinking of going through them all?'

Ben is pacing round the room in the gloom and does not answer. The bed, of course, is stripped. He stares up at the walls, examines the medicine table with its array of bottles, picks up one bottle and sniffs it, then another. They will all have been analysed already.

I begin to feel irritated by his showy behaviour and wonder impatiently if he is trying to impress me. There is a curious smell, too faint for me to place. It is oddly eerie in that room of death and I long to leave it.

Then Ben draws back the curtain of the half tester above the bed head that lies flat against the wall.

'Good God! No wonder she wanted to cover it!'

I go over and we both stare in fascination. A large piece of the wallpaper is missing, torn down in strips, leaving scars in the smooth green paper. Ben prods the gaps and dust falls down on to the bed.

I protest. 'Don't make it worse!'

He prowls around the bed, his eyes gleaming. He picks up a candle stub and turns it in his fingers. There are candles everywhere, I notice now, white and green, mostly burned down. They would have been lit for Juliana's lying in.

Ben goes over to the desk and opens it. It is crammed

with papers. I sigh; it will take him an age to examine them all.

'I will go and thank Mrs Brundish while you busy yourself with those. It was good of her to come up here for us today.'

'I'll not be a minute,' he says absently, and indeed he is not, for to my surprise I hear his footsteps coming down the passage after me as I reach the kitchen.

We examine Juliana's other bedroom upstairs; nothing remarkable in it except for yet another medicine table. Mrs Brundish shows us Maud's bedroom next door and her sitting room, and the sight of them, bare and pathetic in their ordinariness, sends a dreadful pang through me. I look around for some mark of her but there is none. Ben opens a drawer or two in her bedroom, and the clothes chest, but they are empty, already rifled by the police.

As we leave, Mrs Brundish places a hand on my arm. I look into her face and it is full of fear.

'Do not concern yourself, Mrs Brundish,' I say, in a low voice. 'Edie is not a suspect.'

'But she will have to give evidence, won't she? That young man will try to trip her up.' She nods at Ben, who is already halfway down the drive, his briefcase tucked under his arm.

'It will not be him, but a barrister. Besides, we know Edie is innocent.'

However, as I walk with Ben up the road to Doctor

Biddell's house through a slight but persistent drizzle, I begin to wonder.

Edie was cooking at Windward House that last week when Juliana was taken ill. It would have been easy for her to slip something into Juliana's food.

We are fortunate that Doctor Biddell is at home and not attending a patient, but I think Ben would have waited all afternoon and into the night for his return, if necessary.

I have not met Biddell before. I find him an avuncular, decent man, much shocked by the death of his patient.

He looks at his notes and lists the various remedies he prescribed for Juliana.

'She was a highly excitable woman, of a nervous disposition, easily fatigued, and her digestion suffered accordingly. I confess I thought it was little more than that, and that the advent of a young relative in her house would do much to lift her spirits.'

'Would you say that her health improved after Miss Maud's arrival?' asks Ben.

'At times it most certainly did and I may say that Miss Maud nursed her unstintingly.'

Ben questions him endlessly. At last Biddell says wearily, 'Mr Goldstone, I can see you are a capital fellow and only doing what your profession requires, but I have answered all this to the police – again and again!'

'I apologise, Doctor. One last question: in your opinion, do you believe that Miss Maud had it in her nature to murder her cousin?'

He is thoughtful for what seems to me a long time.

Then he says, 'Miss Maud always appeared to be most concerned for Miss Juliana's health. She asked my opinion on many occasions.' He sighs. 'But there is the question of the will. Who is to say that any seemingly gentle soul may not be tempted by money and the promise of lifelong security? And women have such frail natures, have they not? Their morals are not the same as ours.'

On our return train journey to London through the rain Ben and I are both silent.

A heaviness descends on me. What has this day brought us? Has it helped Maud in any way?

I look at Ben and can see nothing in his face that gives me hope. He stares out of the window, watching the flat wet fields flash by beyond the streaming smoke with the same interest he brings to everything – as if he is not dwelling on the day as I am.

'Ben,' I say urgently, 'tell me your thoughts.'

'I cannot, John' he says, 'not now. Give me time.'

But we have so little of that.

Forty-Eight

Ben visits Maud in Ipswich gaol two days later.

I do not go with him, as it is best that Maud does not know that I am paying her legal fees; I don't want her to feel beholden to me in any way. I don't think she will question Ben's visit. I assume she knows little about legal practice and will think it part of the proceedings.

When Ben returns I ask him endlessly about her appearance, about her health and spirits, until he holds his hands up in mock despair.

'All I can tell you is that she did not look well. If you must know, she seemed very confused about the events of that last week at Windward House. She said they were like a dream to her now, she could not say what had happened, exactly. It was not a helpful visit, John, and I wish I could tell you otherwise. I know you feel for her but she is a strange little person, difficult to fathom.'

'But you do believe she is innocent?'

Ben looks at me and his long, clever face is inscrutable for once. 'You have asked me to act for her, John, and so I will. Whether she is innocent or guilty is immaterial.'

On the day of Maud's trial I arrive at the Shire Hall well after the indictment has been read and vetted by the grand jury of merchants and professional men. They have decided there is enough evidence for the trial to go forward. I don't wish Maud to see me and be distracted.

I slip into a back seat in the public gallery.

The twelve men of the petty jury have been sworn in, all ordinary members of the public. They will deliver the final verdict. The clerk of the court reads the charge against Maud. I can see her in the dock, tiny and white-faced, but very upright, dressed in a heavy mourning black that seems to weigh her down, her fingers clenched on the wood in front of her. I can also see Ben with a sheaf of papers in his hand, sitting beside the defence barrister, Mr Munroe.

I hardly recognise either of them in their wigs. Mr Munroe, whom I have met briefly, is a lean-faced Scotsman, hard but fair, with sharp grey eyes, his red hair hidden by the white wool.

The prosecuting barrister presents the case against Maud. I long for him to do it badly, to stutter, to make mistakes, but of course he does not. He is smooth and concise as he goes over the facts.

Then he calls in the witnesses one by one, starting with

Superintendent Stainless, who describes the police investigation. Then he is dismissed and the solicitor, Mr Smallbone, is called up to confirm the details of Juliana's will.

'To your knowledge was the accused aware that she would benefit on her cousin's death?'

'I assume the thought must have crossed her mind. She was Miss Juliana's sole living relative and the inheritance had skipped a generation already. Instead of it going to Miss Maud's father, Miss Juliana had inherited everything on her stepfather's death.'

Why had it not gone to Maud's father? Had there been a quarrel?

Mr Smallbone hesitates. 'It was thought by his older brother that he would squander the inheritance. He believed he had a tendency to drink. I was too junior to act as the family solicitor at that time. It is what I was told by Miss Juliana.'

Mr Munroe stands up. 'My Lord, I protest! That is hearsay evidence.'

But the damage has been done. Maud comes from an unstable background.

Now the doctor takes the stand. The prosecutor asks him the same questions that Ben put to him last week. Biddell describes Juliana's death agony and the results of the post-mortem somewhat luridly and the jury look in horror at Maud. Then he praises the way she nursed Juliana and I feel better.

'A bottle of laudanum was found by the police amongst her belongings. Have you any knowledge of this, Doctor Biddell?'

He shakes his head. 'She must have bought it across the counter. When I suggested after her cousin's death that I give her laudanum to help her sleep, she refused it.'

Dorcas is called to give evidence. She avoids looking at Maud and twists her large red hands together as she answers the prosecutor's questions. He asks her about the events of the night of Juliana's death first, then questions her further.

'It was you who led the police to the accused, was it not, Miss Copping?'

'Yes, sir.' A whisper.

'Why did you lock her in her room overnight?'

'I was alone in the house with her. Edie Brundish told me to because I was frightened.'

'Do you always do what Miss Brundish tells you?'

'She is older than me, sir.' Laughter among the jury, which is quelled by a frown from the judge.

'Why were you frightened?'

'Miss Maud had turned very strange. Edie and me, we was both frightened of her by then.'

'So you locked the accused in her room on the night following the inquest?'

'Yes, sir.'

'Were you and Edith Brundish frightened of her because you believed she might have poisoned Miss Juliana Greenwood?'

'My Lord, that is a leading question!' This from Mr Munroe.

'Let me rephrase it, My Lord. Why were you frightened of the accused, Miss Copping?'

'She wandered about at nights, scaring the wits out of us. We wondered if she was mad.'

A murmur runs through the jury.

'In your opinion, Miss Copping, was there any reason for this odd behaviour of Miss Maud's?'

'She was plotting the murder, I expect. She accused Edie of poisoning Miss Juliana afterwards!' Dorcas sounds indignant. 'She wanted Edie to take the blame.' Her voice trails away. 'And I thought Miss Maud such a pleasant person when she first come to Windward.'

Edie is called next and takes the oath clearly. She looks very young and innocent, her hair down, her face smooth and untroubled. She wears a simple print dress. Somehow her bright glossy presence diminishes Maud, who shrinks back in the dock, clutching the wood in front of her for support.

Edie affirms her name and address and answers that she came to Windward House to cook whilst her mother was poorly and was there the night Juliana died.

'Had you met the accused before you came to Windward House?'

'Yes, sir. She often came into Quilter's, the apothecary where I worked, to collect Doctor Biddell's prescriptions for Miss Juliana Greenwood. She also took Mr Quilter's Restorative Powders for her. Sometimes she—' Edie hesitates.

'Yes? Speak up.'

'Sometimes she helped me write the labels.'

'Did you pay her for this?'

Again, Edie hesitates. 'It was in exchange for laudanum, sir. Oh, I know it was wrong and I am very sorry for what I did. She tricked me, sir, said she could not sleep without it and had no money to buy it! I was sorry for her, sir.'

I see the jury shake their heads. This will not help Maud. Of course the prosecutor will know all this already – his solicitor will have done the research – but it is a shock to me.

The prosecutor asks Edie about the period leading up to Juliana's death. Had she noticed anything different about Miss Maud's behaviour?

She nods vigorously.

'Yes, sir. I found her going through Miss Juliana's medicine bottles one day when Miss Juliana was out. She was doing it in a secretive way and seemed upset when I came in. I began to get a bit suspicious, sir, especially when I found her with the box of Fuller's.'

A murmur runs through the jury.

'Describe that episode for us if you will, Miss Brundish.'

And so she does.

'Where was the Fuller's Solution usually kept?'

'In the hut where the gardener's boy slept. She said she had been looking for it on account of the rats in the cellar.'

'What happened to the box?'

'I put it on a shelf in the storeroom.'

'Should you not have taken it back outside or used it to poison the rats?'

'Yes, but while it was in the storeroom I thought it would serve as a trap.'

'A trap? Explain yourself, Miss Brundish.'

'I thought I might catch Miss Maud coming in for it, so I slept there and not with Dorcas in the kitchen.'

'And what happened?'

Edie pauses. The jury is hanging on her every word.

'I woke up one night. Miss Maud had come in. She made to reach up for it before she realised I was there. I caught her in the act.'

Then she adds, and it is damning: 'Why should she need a box of Fuller's in the middle of the night, sir?'

'But did she know it was there?'

'Oh, yes, sir, she knew very well. It was Miss Maud herself who told me to put it there.'

* * *

I see Ben bow his head and my heart sinks.

Oh, God, she cannot hang! She is too young. Her life is not half lived. And I love her!

Then as the prosecutor is about to ask more, there is a commotion. Something is being passed to Ben, a piece of paper.

He stares at it and everyone stares at him, at his expression of extreme gravity. The prosecuting barrister hesitates. The judge looks up and frowns. A curious atmosphere of both dread and anticipation falls over the courtroom.

In the silence Ben shows the paper to Mr Munroe. He reads it, jumps up with a raised hand. At this interruption the prosecuting barrister looks at a loss, his question stopped in his mouth before he has even uttered the words.

Mr Monroe clears his throat and addresses the judge.

'My Lord, I have just been passed some extraordinary information relevant to the case. May I inform the court? It will change everything.'

And so it does.

The following day I open the *Morning Post*.

I know what I heard yesterday and what the report will say, but am in a fever to see it with my own eyes, in sharp black print. Now the whole world will know the truth.

Yesterday, at the Lent sitting of the Suffolk Assizes held at Ipswich Crown Court, the trial of Miss Maud Greenwood for the murder by arsenic poisoning of her late cousin, Miss Juliana Greenwood, to which the accused had pleaded Not Guilty, was brought to a dramatic halt by new evidence.

The results of an analysis of the green wallpaper in the victim's bedroom, together with the green candles she had habitually lit, now revealed that they contained arsenic – both in the wallpaper paste and in the make-up of the candles. The late Miss Greenwood had been inhaling the paste for some years. This would have caused a slow poisoning over time while she slept in that room.

The conviction was accordingly quashed. Miss Maud Greenwood is therefore absolved of all blame.

When asked what she would do now, she could say nothing.

1870
Forty-Nine

Two years later I am leading some sort of life in London, being commissioned for portraits, painting landscapes and even selling some of them. My bills are paid; I am not in debt; I have money to spare in the bank. You might say I am doing nicely. I have enough to support myself and Mother in a modest fashion. Ben is still my closest friend.

But at the end of the day when I come out of the extreme concentration of working, my thoughts always turn to Maud.

I have not found anyone else.

I believe Mother quite despairs of my ever marrying. She doesn't know the whole story, of course. How I loved Maud and let her down, yet in the end saved her, thanks to Ben.

Have I saved her?

I don't know. I have no idea what has become of Maud. After the pain of our last parting when it was evident she retained no feelings for me, I've not contacted her. I assume she is the grand lady of Windward House now, and married. She would be a fine catch, with Juliana's wealth and her own beauty.

I hear nothing at all, until one day I receive a mysterious package.

I return late from my studio and Mother holds it out to me with a quizzical look.

'It is postmarked Rending.' She sighs. 'That murder. Can we never leave it behind?'

'It was no murder,' I say shortly. 'The conviction was quashed,' and I take the package from her. I do not recognise the hand that has written the address.

When I open the package in the privacy of my own room, I see Maud's face staring up at me. It is the drawing I left for her the day I departed Rending two years ago, with the message I wrote on the back. The paper is dirty and creased.

I looked at it in bemusement. My heart beats hard and quick.

Enclosed with it is a letter. I look at the signature first before I begin reading.

My hopes are dashed. Not from Maud, and why should I expect it? It is from Mrs Brundish. It is a long letter and must have been an effort for her.

I sit down at my desk and with some puzzlement begin to read.

Dear John

I hope this finds you in good health and doing well with your artistic work.

I hardly know where to begin, I am in such confusion of thought and feeling, but I must do so. I owe it to you, we both do, Edie and I, for all that she was a silly, foolish girl at the time and meddled in what she should not. She does not know that I am writing to you and would be mortified, I am sure.

Edie is engaged to the boy that was apprenticed to Mr Quilter. She has moved to my sister's in Southwold to be closer to him, and they work together there in the big apothecary.

Edie was very young when you knew her and I hope that excuses her behaviour. I found this drawing beneath her mattress when I was cleaning out her room. I fear it may never have been seen by Miss Maud.

I have returned to work at Windward House. After the court case was over, Miss Maud asked if I would come back. I was much surprised at Miss Maud's asking, for I knew that Edie had not been good to her.

Edie is properly contrite these days for what she did, and for ruining your work in the church. It was to warn Miss Maud, she told me, to stop her. She *was still suspicious of Miss Maud at the time. Why she thought Miss Maud would poison her own cousin, I do not know. It was only the last figure she drew, she says, the one that looks like Miss Maud. The others she does not know about.*

I regret to inform you that no further work on the Doom has been done since you were here.

The past is over, though not yet repaired. I see that all is not well with Miss Maud. She roams about the house and seldom smiles. After what she has suffered, it is not surprising, I suppose.

I am returning the enclosed to you, in the hope that you will do what you think best with it.

Yours very sincerely

Margaret Brundish

Maud

The people in the village are still afraid of me.

When I walk down the street they turn their faces away and scurry on. Though the shopkeepers are glad to do business and be paid on time nowadays, they would rather send their trembling delivery boys to deliver a murderess's order than have me pick it up in person.

I drag myself to church on Sundays, for I must, though it

takes a deal of courage. I hold my head high. A hush falls over the congregation as I enter and I ignore the stares as I walk up to the front pew. I do not look at the unfinished Doom in the corner.

Even Wissett the vicar on his occasional visits to Windward House does not meet my eye, as if he is not quite sure—

Of what?

Of whether I poisoned Juliana.

The suspicion is there, and it is not only his. I will always be tainted despite my acquittal in the courtroom.

I don't receive invitations from the local gentry to dine. No one leaves their calling card. I am rich but no suitor wants my money.

Society shuns me. Just in case.

In case the verdict was wrong.

The nightmare images have stopped tormenting me. They stopped a long time ago, a little while after I was in custody. It was the laudanum that made me see things that were not there; I know that now. It is easy for the weak to take more and more, hoping for comfort and relief, and so become addicted.

I am clear-headed these days; it is only my memories of that time that blur like reflections on water.

I wanted to punish Jonas by giving him stomach cramps for

a little while. I am deeply ashamed now that I did such a thing. When he died I did not know what to do. I thought I had murdered him and feared I would be found out.

I drew his figure on the Doom to confuse and terrify – so that the village would think his death was the work of the devil. When Sly died I added his; then two more, to add to the fear and agitation. Those stick figures might have been anyone: there were several winter deaths in the village.

And then the drawing of me appeared. I guessed a little while later that it must have been done by Edie.

I did not need her warning; I knew already that she was watching what I did. We both suspected the other during those last terrible days.

I admit there was a time when I wished Juliana dead. Yet I had so wanted to love her and be loved in return.

It was not to be.

But there was someone I truly loved and could not trust enough to tell, for I had suffered so much already at the hands of men.

Tiggins still remains at Windward House and is deaf to any gossip.

Dear Mr Tiggins – he takes me for little drives in the carriage, over to Southwold for a change of scene or to the wilds of Dunwich, where I can walk alone, free from spying eyes. I inspect the plants in the garden with him and have asked him to direct men to tear down Sly's old hovel. I peck at the meals that loyal Mrs Brundish prepares for me.

They are the reason I have stayed at Windward House; their kindness makes up for much.

Otherwise I have employed a new housekeeper and live-in maids from London, for no one from the village dares work here.

I have promised Wissett that I will get the drawings cleaned from the Doom, but I have done nothing yet. No one could do it better than John.

He must have read about the trial in the newspapers. He will not want to conduct business with someone who was accused of murder.

The days are long and soon the spring will turn into summer and they will be longer still. Already the days are warm with cruel promise and birds sing among the wild cherry blossom with no care for an aching heart.

I look in the mirror and see myself pale and unfocussed, for all that my thoughts are so clear nowadays. My eyes are empty; my mouth unsmiling. I thought I saw a line in the smooth skin of my forehead today. I am growing old, my delight in life all sapped, though I have not yet had my twenty-first birthday.

I am turning into Juliana.

In time I shall become a dried-out husk, issuing orders to resentful servants. I shall become vile and bad-tempered, hated by the village. I imagine myself old and stooped, listening for an echo of laughter that will never come in this house, for it holds no happy ghosts.

I wander into her old room and stare at the torn wallpaper, the green wallpaper that saved me. I drift on through the house and don't know what I search for. I stare out at the gravel paths where once Sly walked and walks no longer. I have become a ghost myself, haunting Windward House. At night I dream of the long hot summer with John and how I lost my chance of happiness.

And when summer comes, that pain will return again and it is too late for weeping.

I shall sell Windward House.

I made the decision this first day of April. There is nothing to keep me here.

I shall move and start a new life somewhere else, somewhere far away where no one knows me – a city perhaps, where I can be yet another face in the crowd. I shall buy a modest house and have more than enough to live on, after all. But my life will be empty. I shall know no one and no one will know me and that is the way it must be.

I must tell Mrs Brundish and Mr Tiggins of my decision today before I change my mind. When the sale has gone through, I will make sure the new incumbent of Windward keeps them on.

* * *

I put on my bonnet and mantle.

The sun is shining outside and I shall go for a last walk through the forest to the marshes and the seashore. I know there is no devil there now, no Sly waiting to follow me. There are only the clouds sliding away far above the sea and the billowing air and the crunch of shingle underfoot, over which I once walked with John, hand in hand.

The new maids from the city fuss about me. 'On your own, miss? Is it safe?'

'Perfectly safe,' I assure them, 'and I don't wish for company, thank you.'

I set off down the drive.

The daffodils have opened their trumpets at last. The lawn is beginning to grow green after its winter brown. But I can take no interest in nature's turning. I hurry on, dwelling on the sale of Windward, my head bent low.

Then something makes me look up.

There is someone standing outside the gates.

I know him at once, of course I do. The tousled hair, the wide-eyed, eager, innocent gaze, that I remember so well, the blunt, paint-stained fingers gripping a splendid new hat.

My soul's partner. My other half. My *salvation*.

It is John, and he sees me and the colour comes up in his face and he drops his hat in the mud as if it is of no account at all and holds out both hands.

And I hesitate a long moment.

I hardly dare believe it is him. Is he just another figment of my imagination?

But, no. He is standing there behind the gates, solid and real, and his hands are stretched towards me.

And then I hold out my hands, too, and run – *run* – towards him.

Acknowledgements

My thanks to Richard Barraclough and Amanda Malpass for trying patiently to answer my questions regarding the law and art restoration respectively. Any mistakes are entirely my own.

Thank you also to Radmila May and to Gill Vickery.

The Doom painting in the story is loosely based on one in St Peter's, Wenhaston, Suffolk.